"Dark fun, with mourning, tragedy, and loss, but permeated with wicked humour and enough glimmers of queer hope and love to sustain me. Recommended"'
Joe Koch,
author of *Invaginies*

"Preaching to the Perverted is masterful storytelling, a marvel of authorial style, pacing, and plot. At times shocking and other times shockingly funny, Bennett's great gift is his expert use of voice—he is at once wry and antiquated, modern and mythic. These stories comment uniquely and individually on the LGBT experience, but taken together they're nearly overwhelming. A brilliant addition to any library of the weird."
Polly Schattel,
author of *The Occultists*

"Some cracking horror stories (and humour too)... at least one story may well have you punching the air in delight. Bennett is doing a fine job of making all of us a bit less bitter and afraid, and I can think of no greater compliment to give than that. What a marvellous collection."
John Llewellyn Probert,
author of *House of Mortal Cinema*

"Bennett's stories flit effortlessly, flirting with the delicate, the extreme, and wanton whimsy. The bold and confident prose crafts a seamless collection that is indefatigable in its purpose and merciless in its approach. Beautiful. Brutal. Brilliant."
Dave Jeffery,
award-winning author of the *Necropolis Rising* series

Typesetting: Ryan Vance

Cover: Ryan Vance

PREACHING
to the
PERVERTED

James Bennett

One must conclude that God
created most men simply with a
view to crowding Hell.

−De Sade

*This collection is dedicated
to the survivors.*

Content Warning

THE AUTHOR HAS taken pains to avoid the gratuitous. Nevertheless, this collection is a work of dark fiction and as such features scenes of drug addiction, assault, domestic violence and sexual abuse, homophobia, gore, suicide and self-harm, murder, profanity and explicit sexual material. Reader discretion is advised.

Contents

PREACH

THIS COLLECTION IS drawn from my lived experience as
a gay man. There are coming out tales. Tales of sex and
revenge. Damnation. Loneliness. Love. And yes, a tale
about hate crimes too (namely *Queer Norm*, which I'm
afraid I couldn't manage to place, but which I include
here). All of these elements haunt the stories in one way
or another. As does joy, because all queer expression is
joyful, simply by the fact we get to do so.

This is catharsis. And reconciliation. But it isn't
autobiography, at least not in the purest sense. Rather,
Preaching to the Perverted comprises a sequence where
experience meets the imagination, that being my abiding
love of dark and fantastical fiction. Such stories have
thrilled and inspired me for most of my life. Once upon
a time, a boy discovered fairy tales. Later on, a teenager
discovered Clive Barker, Poppy Z. Brite and Anne Rice,
and nothing was ever the same. These were my beacons
in the dark who, among others, led me to write in the
first place.

The tales herein are arranged accordingly, ranging from the days in the closet to a future one hopes will never come to pass. The intended grace note of *End Times in Paris* should serve to show that I see all as romance. In the meanwhile, these thirteen stories emerge blinking in an era where such tales can readily be told.

It wasn't always thus, gentle reader. Like many of us, I grew up in the shadow of AIDS, Section 28 (the UK version of 'Don't Say Gay') and widespread social exclusion. Oh, you didn't see queer-themed fiction in bookstores back then, not unless they were wrapped in plastic, on the top shelf and in a niche at the rear (so to speak). There were no queer superheroes on screen to cheer for. Even as a young man, it would've been (and was) a perilous thing to admit that one was gay. To be queer was to be considered a pervert. Like many, that was the world in which I found myself and in which I learnt to survive.

Thanks to stories, I did. And thanks to stories, I thrived. Enough to see the world change. Enough to see the advent of equal marriage and broader social inclusion. Enough to understand that hate is a poison and that the bigot *wants* you embittered and afraid. Enough to see that the *true* perversion lies in those who dehumanise their fellow humans simply for being born different.

And yes, enough to write some stories of my own. *Preaching to the Perverted* began as a deeply personal project. After some mainstream success (and, yes, some failure too), I decided that the time was nigh to tackle these ghosts head on. If only to know that I'd done it, I sat down and tentatively tapped out the opening lines of *Husk,* which I view as the seed of this collection. No way did I expect to see one of these tales get published. Perhaps to write them was a challenge to an exclusionary industry, a primal scream or a litmus test. But I can pass on my surprise when all but one of them found their way into print. (*Frankenstein Uncut* was written exclusively for this collection, a nod to one of my favourite novels with the deepest thanks to Mary Shelley.)

Five of these stories landed in the illustrious pages of The Dark magazine. *Husk* was published in two anthologies, one of which topped the Amazon charts on both sides of the Atlantic. *Changeling* came third in the British Fantasy Society's annual short story competition. *Ídolo* was nominated for a Brave New Weird award. *Morta,* the first in my table of contents, went on to win a British Fantasy Award. The anthology in which the story appeared, *The Book of Queer Saints,* also earned a well-deserved place on the shortlist.

The others? Well, they appeared to catch a wave in popular Horror at the time and received some pretty good reviews, not to mention great feedback from readers. In this, I am eternally grateful. But the project became more than the reviving of an author's midpoint career. In fact, it proved me wrong. And I was delighted to *be* wrong. I got to see in real terms how much things had changed since the Dark Days. In turn, that changes you.

Make no mistake. Those were dark days. And these

tales reflect that.

In the end, I hope that *Preaching to the Perverted* stands to show that it does get better. That there's more to life than surviving. That there's a space for such stories to be told.

As for preaching, well, it's likely that those with narrower minds would sooner cut off their hands than pick up this book, but one lives in hope. Listen, being who you are is no choice. Hate, however, is. Hate is the perversion. And these stories speak to those people just the same: Grow up. Educate yourself. As many of us so often are, I'm preaching to those who refuse to listen. Until my lungs give out, I shall continue to do so. And maybe, just maybe, these words will remain.

For the rest of you, my wonderful readers and friends worldwide, I hope you enjoy this collection.

And I hope you thrive.

Sevilla, 2024

MORTA

EVER SINCE THE day I ate Frank, I knew I wasn't like the other boys. This was in Cinder, Idaho, about two years ago. And I didn't exactly eat Frank, to be fair. It isn't like it matters now anyway; no one ever found him and no one is going to find him either. At the time of Frank's disappearance, nobody gave me a second glance. I looked like any other teenage boy going through their junior year at the Cinder County High School. And through the long dark tunnel of adolescence, which is why I was sitting on the bleachers that August afternoon after Math, watching the football practice and, more specifically, Tiger Perez.

I sat there, my podgy, pale self with the scruffy hair and spectacles, watching the boy of my dreams. Tiger, the quarterback, moved like his namesake, a rippling, bubble-butted, second-generation Puerto Rican in helmet, shoulder pads and oh-so-tight white pants. Every time he caught the ball, my heart flip-flopped in my chest a little.

Frank Kovalevsky materialised from the fading sunlight to remind me that Tiger Perez didn't know I existed.

"What you mooning over him for?" Frank asked, round faced and sneering. "Is it because he's an *alien* like you?"

By the sound of him, Frank thought this was hilarious. He'd obviously got the word from somewhere, his folks probably, but he knew better than to use something truly offensive. Teachers frowned on that these days. It was true Mother had told me we weren't from around here, and the dreams I'd been having supported that. One thing's for sure—wherever we're from, it's a lot farther away than Puerto Rico. It explains my name anyway, Morta, which sounds anything but local to Cinder, Idaho. Or anywhere for that matter.

"My worm. We gave you a strong name. A *Brood* name," Mother told me one night long ago, closing her book at my bedside and leaving me to sink into dreams of purple skies, blasted hills and the high, wild shrieking on the wind. The stories and the past she had given me. "A name for an imago. A herald."

Oh, I was special to Mother. And to Frank, it seemed, the latter for less obvious reasons.

"You look weird," his seventeen-year-old mouth offered out of nowhere. "Your hair is all grey and your eyes are funny. It's no wonder the other kids hate you."

I cringed, expecting further insults or even a fight, right here where Tiger would see us. Under this, a grim thrill that at least it might get his attention.

Instead, in that distant, fateful moment, Frank Kovalevsky offered me his hand.

"But I like you. You're cute. Lemme buy you an ice cream downtown."

I looked up at him and I could see from the fire in his cheeks that he meant it. Half bewildered, half hopeful, I reached out and took the hand in question. I didn't even know what I was doing. Was I betraying Tiger by doing so? Such stupid teenage fears...

By the time we reached the entrance to the stadium, Frank was screaming. A minute ago, he'd been whining that my grip was too tight. Sticky. When he tried to wrench it away, I looked down and saw that his hand was melting into mine – and not in the romantic sense. My crotchets were out, excited by contact, I guess. Shit. I was *secreting* again. It'd been happening more and more that last semester, but nothing like this. As Frank wrestled and yelled, the noise from the football field covering his anguish, I placed my other hand over his mouth. It was all I could do. Frank's hand was a liquefied mess, hanging in pink and red rags. Blisters. Shards of bone. Blood and acid peppering the grass. The substance of him absorbed by my own.

Mother had warned me about this. "You're drawing to the end of your larvae phase," she said. "All grown up now."

Frank wasn't going to stop screaming. If I'd tried to free him once digestion had begun, I'd only do damage to myself. There was nothing else to do but drag him into the shadows of the bleachers and devour him whole.

*

MOTHER WAS THE first to come out here. She was proud of it, often telling me, her captive audience, how she'd lain her eggs under the skin of the world and pushed through the membrane that kept it apart. The effort had seen her emerge in the Craters of the Moon National Preserve on the Snake River Plain, central Idaho, a vast volcanic park a few miles to the north of us. But Mother's arrival had nothing to do with outer space or Jurassic activity. Clutching her surviving egg (hello!), she crawled and fluttered her way into Cinder, twenty-one years ago. Father never made it. Burned up in the translation, she said, though the way her eyes flashed made me wonder whether she maybe hadn't consumed him. Post-natal cannibalism wasn't uncommon among the Brood, I'd learned. If you looked into her eyes, you'd find the same shade of violet as mine. If you really looked, you'd notice each one is divided into these tiny hexagons, thousands of ommatidia—compound eyes, Mother calls them—but you wouldn't see any of her secrets.

"Never speak to the Watchers," she warned me last year, gripping my arm over the breakfast table in our darkened kitchen. It was the first day of my senior year and I guess she thought I was old enough. Plus all the fuss over Frank Kovalevsky had since died down. "A missing person," the police chief said on the news with an air of sad finality. Even the posters on the telegraph poles were fading. Fading like Frank in my system…

"Damn scientists. You know they're watching the house, right? Always watching. And they'll only get spunkier the older you get, Morta. Another season and you'll be ready. The Hour of Emergence will come. And then glory, glory, sweet glory," she sang it, buzzing. Then frowned. "It's your purpose, my worm. So watch out!"

This answered why the blinds were always drawn, even in summer in the middle of the day. I mean, it's true we don't like the light much anyway—weren't my spectacles made of a special material to keep out the worst of the rays?—but there was another reason too, a darker one. It was why we only spoke to the neighbours if necessity forced our hand (Oh, we'd gone without cups of sugar just fine). Perhaps it answered why the cars with the smoked glass windows sometimes pulled up on Gannett Lane, their engines rumbling, but never stopping. No one ever getting out.

"Watch the Watchers," I said. I thought I was so smart at the time. "But how will I know if—"

"You'll know." My arm was hurting; Mother didn't stop squeezing when she got her panties in a bunch. "The Exterminators have a smell. All in the cult do. And you don't want one of those fuckers to get their mitts on you, trust me."

"Mom!"

"Hush now. Give thanks to the Nest and eat. You'll be late for class."

With this, Mother shrilled out a brief prayer. She kept it low; It'd burst next door's eardrums if they overheard.

Then she regurgitated over the flesh on the table, the raw, bubbling lump that hailed from a source I knew better than to ask about, and that was the end of the conversation.

I went off to school, to my senior year and my last, with Frank Kovalevsky—the essence of him, that is— howling faintly in my mind.

Our prey doesn't die right away, you see. Mother taught me that too. The flesh dissolves, but the spirit lingers, granting energy. Strength.

In a way, Frank didn't die at all.

It's kind of a comfort to hear him in there.

I'M... EVOLVING. THE fairy tales Mother told me have turned into dreams. The glint of purple skies off a carapace, the flutter of wings and the shrieking on the wind (the swarm song, Mother tells me) often wake me at night in the upstairs bedroom, covered in sweat and a kind of mucus, acidic and white. It isn't noxious to me. It's still pretty gross. Wet dreams. I read about them in a book. Nocturnal emissions don't soak you from head to foot though. They don't stink of batteries and rot.

Believe me, I'd much rather dream about Tiger Perez.

I'm nineteen now. A third instar, Mother says, if not quite a man. Frank is a distant echo. I'm the Herald of the Brood. But to Tiger Perez, I may as well be dead.

Tiger never made it to university. Some kind of misunderstanding with a cheerleader, as I understand it, that saw him kicked off the football team. And no team, well, no scholarship. It wasn't like he was acing Math. Tiger got a job pumping gas in downtown Cinder and sure, it sucks balls, but it was good news for me.

It's good news because I'm not going to university either. Mother told me she didn't think it was smart, what with incubation and all. "No one wants to see that in the canteen," she said. "They'll try to stop you, Morta. They'll bring fire and Lord knows what else."

This ominous prophecy faded into insignificance next to the fact that I could spend all afternoon at the Cinder Public Library. The Cinder Public Library has big clean windows and sits on Main, right opposite the station where Tiger pumps gas, checks oil and kicks tyres.

"Always the same book," Mrs. Blum said over the counter one day. I was returning *Changing Bodies: The Easy-As-Pie Puberty Book For Boys* (which hadn't been helpful at all), but it was the *Birdwatching For Beginners* book that she was talking about. "I don't think you're gonna see a woodpecker or a red-tail on the intersection, honey. Might wanna get up to the preserve for that."

I blushed. What the hell did she know? I could tell her things about Craters that would make her squeal and piss herself. Instead, I mumbled something about a roosting owl in the gables of the store over the street. It explained the binoculars hung around my neck. Traffic often got in the way and sometimes Tiger was at the register or in the garage and I couldn't see him. It was worth it for the times I could. He'd lost none of his draw in his dirty overalls, his sin-black hair slicked back under a baseball cap. Sure, I couldn't see his ass as well as I used to in his football pants, but when he leant over a hood to clean it—*phew!* And his sleeves were rolled up to show his forearms, the fuzz of hair and pop of veins on his golden brown skin, suggesting how they might feel wrapped around me, how they might feel against my lips…

"Heck, it's your life. If I were you, I wouldn't wanna spend it in this dump."

With that, Mrs. Blum returned me to the pond of oblivion and turned to another customer. Grey-haired, bespectacled, half-drowned in my clothes, I shuffled over to the tables by the windows, relieved to find my usual seat empty. I could already see Tiger across the street, grinning his diamond grin at another satisfied customer (why wouldn't they be?) and accepting a dollar bill tip. There was always the fear that he'd look up and see me, a thrill in the pit of my stomach, even though I was far away and stood behind glass, like a bug pinned to a display case.

Today, there was a different thrill. Before I sat down I heard books falling, slapping on linoleum. When I turned in that direction, I saw a man looking at me through a gap in the shelves. His hat was tipped down over his face and for some reason he was wearing shades, even in the gloom of the library.

It was only a split second. Had he pushed the books aside to get a better look at me? Mother told me I'd *smell* it when I saw one, and the prickling of my skin confirmed the fact. As did the faint stink of batteries and rot, a thin sheet of gunk bleeding from my skin. Crotchets, a multitude of tiny barbs, emerged on the palms of my hands and scratched at the cover of *Birdwatching For Beginners.* The book hissed, the slip-on polythene bubbling.

Only a split second. Then the man spun on his heel and vamoosed. All he left was an echo of heels as he took off, swallowed by the depths of the library.

A *Watcher.* An Exterminator.

I didn't stay to watch Tiger that day.

MY DREAMS WERE getting intense. Even in daylight, the memory of purple lingered. The swarm song was growing louder and so it should, Mother said. "They're waiting, Morta," she told me. "Behind the sky. Waiting for the Emergence." In my mind, the shattered plain of Craters didn't compare to the landscape I wandered in sleep.

Perhaps the dreams were why I kept seeing the cars, their smoked glass windows rolled up, their engines running in the neighbourhood. Twice, I saw them downtown. In fact, I was heading downtown when the Watcher appeared, stepping out from an alley between a hair salon and a shutdown bookstore.

"Pardon me, young man. May I have a minute of your time?"

He sounded friendly enough. He looked like all of the others. Dark hat. Dark glasses. Dark suit. And the smell. The smell that was really *my* smell. Sulphur and sewage. Instinct. Alarm.

"Sorry. I'm late," I said, stupidly. Sure, late for the Cinder library and peeper-creeping on Tiger Perez.

"It'll only take a *moment.*"

The word was more of a grunt. The man lunged towards me. Too late, I saw the flash of metal in his hand, heard the jangle of handcuffs ripped from his pocket. On the street, a car pulled up, black as death, its rear door popping open. The Watchers, the cult, meant to abduct me. It didn't take a genius to see that.

"Get offa me!"

I'm no fighter. Usually I prefer to sit in the shadows, happy to be forgotten about. It's safer that way. The attention on me now was like a lamp and despite the man's greeting, unkind. I lashed out, a clumsy swing as he made a grab for me, a handful of sweater in his grip. He stumbled, shimmying towards me, and this time my hand connected—a perfectly aimed slap to the face.

A few things happened at once. One, the man dropped his handcuffs, steel tinkling on the sidewalk. Two, the car pulled off, its door slamming, screeching out onto Main. Thirdly, the Watcher, the member of the Cult of Unseen Stars, started screaming. And why not? My crotchets were hooked in his face. His cheek was already waxen, giving way to runnels of blood, dissolving flesh and tissue. His scream was lower than Frank Kovalevsky's had been. Less shocked, I guess. Later, I put it down to the fact that the man knew exactly who I was, what I was capable of. He knew who Mother was too, according to her. Where she'd come from and what she meant to do.

Her son's glorious purpose. Her worm.

The Watcher was screaming and I had to put a stop to that. Traffic on Main wasn't so dense. Thankfully, there were few pedestrians, the town drunk and some old dude. In seconds, however, someone was going to come running. So I clamped my other hand around the man's throat. It was all I could think of to do.

He flailed at me. Blindly, because one of his eyes had gone the way of milkshake, a ball of white bubbles. Relief spread through my guts. The Watcher's cries sank into a gargle. Then silence. He slumped, his head lolling on his chest as his Adam's Apple deliquesced, the mess running over my hand, my sleeve. *Ew.* Teeth clenched with the effort, I dragged the man (I'm pretty strong too. Did I tell you that?) into the alley from which he'd sprung, tossing him down in a clatter of garbage cans, a fan of trash.

I couldn't exactly leave him there. Absorption took a good ten minutes, but at least he wasn't making any noise.

The rats looked on, dumbfounded.

THANK THE NEST that I'd wiped my mouth by the time I stepped out of the alleyway. My hair must've looked like Einstein's, a wild grey mop. All the same, the stars smiled down, or maybe they didn't, because Tiger Perez was standing right there on the sidewalk.

"Hey! It's Morta, ain't it?" That's what he said, my flame, my light, the one I was drawn to like a moth even though it burnt me so. "Morta from school?"

Now it was my turn to melt. I shifted from foot to foot. Stuck a hand in my pocket, my fingers closing with a squelch. My binoculars threatened to pull me into the dirt, as heavy as the One Ring in that movie I'd watched with Mother.

In a voice that came from dimensions away, I said, "Sure."

Tiger was on his way home from work. He worked at the gas station down the street, he said. Roses shone in his cheeks, his eyelashes batting, and he confessed he'd dropped out of school. Like a goon, I nodded along to all of these things, trying to convey the absolute truth that all of it came as news to me.

When he looked at me again, it was furtive. Was I losing my mind?

"That's why you never saw me no more on the football field. Guess it must've taken a while to realise that. Sorry."

"I never... I didn't..."

"It's cool." Tiger took a step towards me. I thought I was going to die, my heart was beating so fast. "I appreciate the support."

"You..." It was like my throat had collapsed. Karma is a bitch. "You play good."

Tiger laughed. "Right."

There was a pause. The street, the library, the world had all gone, swept away in a storm of nerves. Tiger Perez was all there was, grinning at me on the sidewalk.

"I should probably—" Escape. Run. Cut a hole in the sky and scram. Anything.

"Say, are you hungry?" he said. "'Cos I know this great burger joint. It ain't far. Come on, amigo. You can keep me company."

The last thing on my mind was food.

I stood there, my belly full, my skin damp under my clothes. My mind full of screams. Loud ones.

The last thing I was gonna do was say no.

I AM IN love with Tiger Perez. Oh, it's dumb, I know. Ever since our date (well, it wasn't really a date, but yanno), Cinder, Idaho, has become a different place. Not to bring the schmaltz, but the sound of the wind through the trees almost drowns out the rustling behind the sky, the membrane that keeps this world from beyond. And I've stopped visiting the library. I've stopped because I message Tiger instead and we go to the movies or the park. It's summer and we sit on the grass. Drink Coke. Talk about what a shitshow school was.

Sometimes Tiger starts to talk about football and girls. I always change the subject and he drops it. Guess he can tell I'm not like the other boys. He's lonely, I think. An only child like me. His Papa works over at the Wilson Packing Factory and saved up everything to put Tiger through school, so times aren't *estupendo* for Tiger. His future is far from as glorious as mine.

Still, he's my flame. There's this feeling in my stomach, a new thrill. We sit under the drowning trees and I'm going to make him love me back.

Last Friday, he told me, "You got funny eyes, you know that?"

He tried to take off my glasses, but I wouldn't let him. The last thing I wanted was a migraine.

"Yeah."

That's when he touched my face. Only lightly. And oh-so-brief.

"Don't worry about it," he said. "They're kind of... special."

He was the quarterback of Cinder County High. I guess appearances can be deceiving.

I want to hold his hand, but I can't.

AUTUMN. THE BEST time of year. The long evenings were made for me, the shadows stretching over the lawns like arrows to a future I couldn't see. The Emergence. Glory. My eyes hurt less in the dwindling noon light. The screams in my mind were dwindling too. With Frank Kovalevsky it'd been a new thing; the Watcher's torment wasn't such a buzz.

Yeah, I was glad to hear him fade, sucked into my system like the leaves into next door's yard vacuum. No bones. No problem. It was like Time had drawn the blinds on the world, not just in the house on Gannett Street. The pervasive smell of rot was everywhere—in the grass, the bark, the wilting flowers—and it felt like a cocoon of comfort, the cause of which was hard to place. Mother said that the earth itself was a fruit. As it ripened, at the peak of its sweetness before the first brown spots of decay, the swarm would muster and come.

At my call.

"But before all that," Mother said, her eyes gleaming in the kitchen. "Comes incubation." It'd been a long hot day and she was tired from the housework and the spinning; she'd peeled back her hairband, her wig and a bunch of borrowed flesh to let her antennae weave free. "Soon, Morta. Soon."

I never told her about the fight with the Watcher. I told myself it was because I didn't want to worry her. The truth was I was scared she'd ground me, her defences going up like bulletproof wings. If that happened, I wouldn't be able to sneak off to see Tiger anymore. Tiger, at this point, had turned into an exquisite torture, and I was sad, sure. I'm not like him (or any boy), and even if he were to kiss me, I can't guarantee he wouldn't get, well, *stuck*.

There was a sweetness to the sadness too. An ache. It made my balls hum. My cock felt bruised when it swelled against the front of my jeans. It was like every five minutes! I couldn't stop thinking about him on top of me, brown and slick, my hands on his butt like I'd won bags of gold. At night, I'd grit my teeth as I jerked off so Mother wouldn't hear me in the next room. I was dying, I guess. It was a kind of death. The sheets were caked every morning. Acid burned holes in the mattress.

"Adolescence," I said, shrugging at Mother's frown as she once again crouched before the washing machine.

"Metamorphosis," she snapped back.

Embarrassing.

*

THAT THURSDAY AFTERNOON in late September, I wished I'd told Mother about the Watcher. I was coming home from the park when I heard the scream. Too low, too gruff to be hers. The stink of batteries, a sulfuric tang, joined the aroma of dead leaves, the ghost of rain. My crotchets were out and the twin lumps under my hair—a new addition—were throbbing by the time I reached the front door. It stood wide open, and in the middle of the day, an event so rare it sent sparks up my spine. Between that and the cars parked on Gannett Street, hoods askew, engines running, I knew that things were far from peachy.

I crashed down the hall and into the living room, tearing thick strands of silk out of my way. I was only half-surprised to find the Watchers in the house. Three of them, two men and a woman. One of the men had Mother in a headlock. The woman (*agent,* some memory that wasn't my own whispered) was on her knees, the coffee table upended. *Time* magazine lay open, splayed in this place where time was running out. The bitch was trying to cuff Mother's ankles with what looked like a bicycle lock (but wasn't).

The other man was dancing in the doorway with his back to me, an object in his hand that I took for a gun at first, then realised was a Taser. Darts on thin copper wires speared Mother's breast, her belly. She was spasming and hissing, foam on her lips, a distended, impossible leer. Scraps of blouse and appropriated flesh flew this way and that from her struggles. Her wings had unfurled with the volts jolting through her, veined, iridescent and purple. Their span had smashed pictures from the walls, dislodged ornaments and toppled the lampshade. The air in the room was a pall of electricity, gunk and dust.

When her eyes met mine, I heard her voice ring in my head.

Morta!

I was the Herald, but she was my own. To witness her pain was a slap, snapping me out of my daze. Oh, I was *lightning* then. The man with the Taser was shrieking—a soprano now—as I grabbed his neck with both hands, his skin sizzling. Pale goo ate through his collar and muscle in no time, the bastard falling face first to the floor, his limbs jerking and steaming. Caught off guard by my presence (it was clear that nothing here had gone as planned), the other man tightened his grip on Mother, shaking her slender, transfiguring body like a threat.

"Don't come any closer, bug."

Half of Mother's face sloughed away, her round left eye regarding me with the glitter of a million hexagons. The flash of a purple sky.

No, Mother. Don't.

Mother was the imago. I, the worm. Shit, she'd crossed worlds to bring me here, to Cinder, Idaho. Nowhere. Who knows the sacrifices she'd made? She wasn't about to stop now. With a squelch of parting flesh, her maw grew wider, viscera and fluid slopping on the rug. Long and slick, her proboscis whipped out, flailing like liquorice lace over her shoulder and shooting up her assailant's nose. Uncoiled, it was down the man's throat in seconds, the meat of him drawn to its glistening length.

And his *essence* too, what humans like to call a 'soul' but we regard as substance. *Strength.* He was still screaming (in my mind, at least) as his chest caved in, his ribs cracking under her immense suction, the otherworldly fury of the Brood. I blinked and his neck was looking like a wrung bath towel. His eyes came popping out of his skull. One of them landed on the couch, wet and bloody. The iris was wide, observing his own undoing. Mother drained him like a pouch of Kool-Aid, his skin wrinkling, dry.

In the madness, I'd forgotten about the woman, the agent. I was powerless when it came to time. Even so I was lurching forward, meaning to grab the gun in her hand. Well, it *looked* like a gun. The muzzle was strange, an opaque bulb that pulsed twice and exploded with light, the walls of the living room shuddering. The shadows cringed and me along with them, shielding my face and hitting the deck, the coffee table legs snapping under me. *Ouch.* My head burned in the radiance. A high-pitched whining skewered my ears. I heard Mother scream, a brief, shattering song. Then bits of her skull were landing on me, her brains decorating the walls, the floor. The lampshade. Whatever heat the Watcher had unleashed, it had proved too much for—

Mother...?

When the shadows pooled back in, the agent was on

her knees, cussing and fumbling with the weapon. Mother lay in a heap beside her, her wings dull and unmoving. Her tongue slack, without a head.

Mother!

"Please." This from the remaining Watcher. The Exterminator. An agent of the Cult of Unseen Stars. She couldn't seem to get the weapon to work. She forgot all about it as I rose from the ruins. The blood. "You don't understand," she yelled. Garbled. "The Brood. You're gonna..." The Watcher was gasping, beginning to hyperventilate. "It's *our* world," she sobbed. "You'd do the same."

I took a step toward her. Her jaw hung wide. Purple reflections shone in her eyes.

Before she could scream, I beat her to it.

My first notes. The song of the swarm.

The Watcher was like glass before me. I shattered every window in the house.

THE DREAM WAS over. Or rather, the dream had turned into something else. An expectation. A ticking clock. For a day I waited, but nobody came. If anyone on Gannett Street had noticed the cars or heard all the ruckus, they'd either run away or they knew better than to interfere. I suspected the latter. Mother had put some kind of trance on the neighbours, I think, spraying spores along with her roses. Or gazing at them over the fence until they found they couldn't look away.

No one dialled 911. No more cars showed up, black or otherwise. I was left with the death in the house.

Damn it, I wanted to go see Tiger so badly. He was my anchor now Mother was gone.

"I love you," I told the darkened house.

To the bodies in the living room, I said, "I wish things could've been different." I said this before I bent to consume them. Mother wouldn't have wanted to go waste. She was the sweetest of all.

Shit, I wish *I* could've been different, but a glorious purpose was a glorious purpose. It left no room for regret.

And there was… something else going on. Another kind of pull. In my mind, in the whirlwind of screams from the Watchers, shocked, disbelieving and in pain, I kept seeing Craters, up there in the preserve. The volcanic hills and the black plains that for all their bleakness were nothing like the landscape under the skies of home. Not long now. I could feel it in my bones. The throb of my antennae. The stench of every secretion. The flaking of my skin and the slowing of my system. Not long and I'd make my way up there, sing the song that Mother had taught me. Tear at the skin of the world, the membrane between us and triumph.

The fluttering was louder now, a constant, furious gyre scratching at the walls of reality. Praise the Nest. The swarm was ready. The Hour of Emergence was at hand.

"I wish you'd come," I said to the webs that covered everything, the strands that stretched from wall to wall in the hallway, the bedroom, the kitchen. Mother had been busy. Mother had prepared everything.

Know what's sad? Despite my body and my head and my purpose, my heart was beating for Tiger Perez. Tiger in his tight football pants. Tiger with the diamond grin. Tiger under the drowning trees. Was his skin as smooth as the silk between my hands as I wove it back and forth? I thought so. Its stickiness was a reminder that to touch Tiger would be to risk everything. But as I wrapped the stuff around me, again and again and again, I began to look at things in a different way.

I'm not like the other boys. I felt so sleepy as my grey and withered body sank into the warmth of the cocoon, the pupa that Mother had told me about, slipping into incubation and unknown dreams. It was a kind of death, sure, but not forever. At the same time, something bright and sharp was twisting inside. A seed. A worm. A week, a month, no more than that, and the purple would claim me completely. The chrysalis would crack and the new me Emerge. An imago, according to Mother. Emerge and take flight. Go to the plains and herald a new age.

I'm coming out.

Cinder, Idaho, hadn't gone anywhere. Tiger was downtown, I guess. Probably pumping gas. Maybe he'd ask around, find out where I lived. Come to the house looking.

Will he still think I'm special? I wondered.

It was my last waking thought.

Will he find me beautiful?

HUSK

I'M A FACE in the rain. A sketch of shadows under streetlight. Mostly I'm a memory, a ghost of myself. Adam was my name. It's confusing, but every time I even the score for us, I grow stronger. Isn't that why I'm here, standing outside the restaurant, born of tears and blood? I'm the shadow Adam. Your husk.

The wind, a swirl of dead leaves, gives me shape. The rain silhouettes my shoulders. Fumes from a passing car lend the hint of a jacket, a turned-up collar. My hair is wet, the half-remembered colour of rust. A fluttering crisp packet picks out my face – a face you'd recognise if you looked out of the window. You'd see me, standing here on Blank Street, Nowhere. Know me like you know your own reflection.

I'm what you left behind.

When you look out, you see only rain. The city in your eyes is a washed-out limbo. Buildings that don't care about you, that don't know you like I do. You're laughing and drinking, amused by something the man sat opposite you says. Miles? I caught his name as I followed you from the station, you a torch in the dusk. I can see what you see in him. Those dark looks you're such a fool for. His rich brown skin. The voice you could bathe in. The hands that'll grip you as you fuck... It's your birthday. Why wouldn't you flirt? You don't know about Brick yet. Or the killings to come.

We're the same, two sides of a mirror. One silver. One black. But I can't say it's *my* birthday. I began in the garden shed, in the mosaic on the floor. In the rage and the fear you cast aside.

Ghosts don't have birthdays. But the living sometimes have ghosts.

Oh, Adam. What happened to us? We used to be so close.

WHERE DID IT start? This seed?

"I see how you look at me, fag."

Ah yes. You were on your way home from school. Aged sixteen, circa two years ago. Brick said that as he stepped out from behind the big tree. I remember the smell of the grass on the playing field. The janitor mowing it, the slaughter of bugs in the air. Brick blocked your path. You saw his fist by his side, trembling. The fist of his *face,* screwed up in disgust. His smirk at the cruelty to come.

"Don't flatter yourself." You knew he meant the changing rooms after football practice, Adam. You knew what he was getting at, same as you knew he was wrong. When the boys in class were showering, you tended to look at your feet.

You tried to laugh it off. Brick wasn't laughing though. In fact, he looked hurt by your rebuff. There was this… atmosphere, I remember it well. It made no fucking sense whatsoever. There wasn't time to examine it, because then Brick was punching you. You fell to the ground. Blood in your mouth. Your ribs on fire as he kicked you. It went on and on. Was it a relief when he ripped your face from the earth, spat on you? Shock carried you like the wind, borne with laughter in your ears. Across town. To your house.

In the garden shed – there was no way that Dad could see you like that – you sat and licked your wounds.

Tears and blood fell to the floorboards, bright in the dust.

A beginning.

GHOSTS ARE MEMORIES. How weird is that? Mine, of course, are only recent. They began last Thursday at the 'party' in your apartment. You had to make a song and dance about it, didn't you? You stood there in your tee-shirt. Nevermind. Was Dad about to kick off again? Hit you like when you were ten? Hit us, I should say. Only you remember the feel of it, his knuckles… That day you spent in the shed thinking on your sins. Like you did after Brick beat you up. The tears and the blood. The shame. It's an abstract. A recollection torn from me like tears and blood. Like skin and bones were torn from me when you decided to up and leave.

"I'm sorry," you told Mum and Dad. You'd promised yourself you weren't going to apologise. "This is who I am."

Shouting ensued.

"No son of mine is a poof", Dad said.

Mum cried. She held her pocket Bible in trembling hands. "How could you do this to us?"

I'm sorry, you wanted to say. *I'm sorry for not being who you think I am. But every day, every hour, I was fading, you see. Rubbed out by your expectations. What you think of me. What you want for me. What you want for yourselves. Soon I would've disappeared completely...*

They cried. They mourned you to your face. No one asked you if you were in love. If you were alone. If anyone had hurt you. So you showed them your scars. Another thing you'd sworn not to do. Oh, how you betrayed us, Adam. My little Judas. All eighteen years of us standing in the living room on Any Street, Anywhere, showing them the marks you'd made with the razorblade.

Don't you understand? you said. Shouted. *I hated myself. I wanted to die.*

They didn't understand. They left, the door slamming. Like the door of the garden shed. Or a coffin. The funeral was over before they'd even put you in it.

But a part of you *did* die last Thursday.

And I came back.

*

I SEE HOW you look at me.

They don't call him Brick these days. *He* doesn't call himself that. The Arsehole Formerly Known as Brick got a job in the local shoe shop. No one likes grownups with nicknames, so he's plain old Bill now. Boomers don't take us seriously as it is and Brick was a bully's name. A hero on the football field. In the Court of the Changing Rooms. That kind of shit doesn't fly in the real world. Bill found that out last Friday night. He was polishing the shoes in the window display. Then he locked up shop for the manager and got on his bicycle.

In a swirl of dirt and leaves, I followed him. The first time he looked back, his pug of a face squinting in the gloom, I saw the misgiving in his eyes. The dark comes on quick in winter. So did I, hissing through the trees beside the cycle path. He sensed something then. He pedalled a little faster, through the cut towards the railway bridge. Keeping up wasn't a problem; I'm empty enough to ride on the wind. In some way I was attached to him. I could see his trophies gathering dust on a shelf, a reminder of past glories. It pulled me on like a rope, passing through whatever lies behind the world and pushes against the emptiness. The next time Brick – let's call him that for old time's sake – glanced over his shoulder, he saw me. Saw *something,* at least. Swooping under the streetlights, invisible, I saw him look up. His eyes were full of sodium, circles of fear. I gusted towards him, viciously. He had to cover his face. He let go of the handlebars to bat at the swirling grit.

You hit us, I said out of the darkness.

His bike pranged. It crashed into the wall of the bridge. Flesh met tarmac with a satisfying thump. There was nothing to him but meat. Brick groaned, but he didn't sprawl there long. He had bigger concerns. A troubling of the branches above. A flicker of the streetlights. A voice that belonged to no one. One he might've recognised, if he'd had time.

When we got home and took off our shirt, your shoe had left an imprint on our back.

"Please," Brick said. He thrust out a hand, flailing at the murk. No one can fend off a shadow. "It was years ago. We were in school..."

Sweet that he remembered.

It isn't over. It never is.

Brick was crying. He covered his face. There wasn't much there to see. Only the bridge. The trees and the night. A spindle of dirt. I pushed against the wind. Against his face. A damp patch spread across the front of his trousers. Thank God I couldn't smell it.

In the distance, the rattle of a train.

"He was looking at me in the changing room!"

That isn't true. It's what you tell yourself.

Adam was too scared to look. I know that. I was there. How the tiles, the noise would press down on us. Every snap of a towel a bullet in our ears. Adam thought that if he looked a siren would go off above his head, flashing and wailing.

And everyone would *know*.

"Get the fuck away from me!"

Brick was climbing to his feet. Fear will do that to a person. He was brawny once. Much like that day on the playing field, Adam still wouldn't have stood a chance. But Adam didn't have the wind on his side. It was a simple thing to blast the bastard over the wall. I'd timed it just right. The six o'clock train slammed into Brick's tumbling body at a hundred miles per hour. He burst apart like a melon. His spine went one way carrying his head. His legs another.

When I found him beside the track, he looked uglier than usual.

Still, he tried to crawl away in the undergrowth.

He didn't get very far.

SOON AFTER THAT day on the playing field we started to use the razor. One night we got up and went to the garden shed. Dad was right. We were a waste of space. We'd come to suspect we were different, anyway. When the lads in class talked about girls, boasting about a hundred dirty things, Adam, well… we found we had nothing to offer. We knew we were supposed to be turned on by it. The other boys were. We could tell by the way they shifted themselves, plucked at their trousers. Chuckled and coughed. It became clear that they were the ones turning us on. Making us hard. Burning our cheeks.

Desire has a smell, I think. So does fear. We must've stunk of it. That's where the idea of the siren started, invisible and waiting. We started pushing it down. Burying it. Us. We started to change the subject. Then, when Brick laughed at us – *virgin!* – we avoided the guy talk completely. We went to the library. Hid in books. It's the story of a thousand boys like us, Adam. It's corny as fuck. But none of their stories are like ours.

We thought we could get it out of us. We thought if we linked the thought to pain that it would fix us. God was useless. There was nothing in His book but blame. We gritted our teeth. We sat in the dark. Drew steel across our skin. We wept, holding ourselves when no one else would.

Make it stop. Take it away.

It isn't always God who listens.

Blood and tears speckled the floorboards. Enough over time to make a mosaic.

All that hate. It had to go somewhere.

I'M STOOD HERE on this rainy street, remembering. Why not? I'm a memory, after all. Well, a little more perhaps, seeing as I get to even the score. It's something to do with fear, I think. And the blood, which gave me substance. I'm half-shadow and half-air, but litter flutters to a stop when it hits me. Puddles ripple when I pass by. The more I remember, the more the world allows for my presence, it seems. It makes sense that blood would build a bridge from the emptiness. The blood is the life. I read that somewhere. Saw it in some dumb film. Blood is where

I came from, that's for sure. Leaking in drops. Fed on tears. Blended with dust on the shed floor. With rags and dried paint. The husks of dead insects. A nightmare brewed behind doors.

I got bored of watching you in the restaurant. All your laughter, the way you stroke your throat as you talk to Miles or whoever. It's such a come on and he knows it. His eyes never leave your face. He thinks it's happening, first date or no. When he pays the bill and you exit, his arm hangs around your shoulder. I whirl through the rain and the headlights of cars to follow you. That's what shadows do.

At the door of your apartment – you're such a cliché – I watch you from the stairwell as Miles leans in to kiss you. He touches your hair. Looks into your eyes. If you weren't so distracted, you'd notice me there, a not-quite-solid shape. A puckering of angles and corners. Of course you're not paying attention. Jealousy, cold and bright, stabs through me. How fucked up is that? Part of me envies you. Part wants to rip the guy away from you, hear his bones crack against the hallway wall. What happened to *my* say in things? Six months ago you'd have gone to the shed for even thinking like this. We were together. *Together.*

It was all that counsellor's fault. Rachel Marsh.

When did it begin, the pain? She asked us.

Adam, you're kissing him back. He's taller than you. His weight presses you against the door. The edge of the frame is between your buttocks like a promise of what's to come. And I'm thinking about the counsellor, Marsh. Whether I should pay her a visit as well. The throbbing in my head makes it hard to focus. When there's heightened emotion like this it becomes uncomfortable. It makes perfect sense, seeing as I am you. Or *was.* I can feel you growing hard. The same way you can feel Miles. You shiver at his size through his jeans, another unspoken promise.

"Miles..." you say. "I'm not -"

That's when the lightbulb shatters, dousing the hallway in darkness. I don't want to see.

"What the hell?" Miles says. His jacket is up, shielding you from the flying glass. I guess that you like that.

Still...

"Miles, I'm not ready for this."

Miles takes a breath. You expect snark. Resentment. Maybe he'll call you a timewaster like that other guy did. Instead, he smiles and strokes your cheek.

"They hurt you too, huh?"

You're no longer thinking. You turn to unlock the door and you drag him inside.

I'm a whirlwind. I'm a fury. I'm out of here. The hallway window shatters, not that there's anyone around to hear it. And I take to the night.

I am *not* going to watch you fuck.

ANGER IS A magnet, drawing me to the source. You better believe I was pissed off. And the truth is the both of us know where the pain began. When you were six years old. When you saw him punch Mum for the first time. Years later, you thought of it yourself, the razor between our fingers in the shed, slick and red. We wondered, our sixteen-year-old self (selves), whether we should take it to in the room upstairs. We stood there, watching him sleep, his throat bared. It was only our fist closing on the blade that forced us to step away. To forget the whole thing. It doesn't matter now. Whether we imagined it or not. It's in us. It's a thing. And it gives me a foothold in the emptiness.

I roll with the wind. That's how I find myself flying along the freeway of all places. Lights leave an orange smear above. The shutter speed of passing bridges. *Click. Click. Click.* Dad is driving home.

He's the boss at the factory these days, grey haired, fat bellied. Respected. He gets the job done. He's changed his shirt. He made sure to pack a fresh one in his briefcase that morning. He took a shower in the hotel. It's the only way to be sure there's no trace of perfume on him. Mum would notice, he thinks. She doesn't know about the girls downtown. At least she tells herself that. Dad believes he's doing what any man would. That it's part of who he is. It's funny when you think about it. He sees his needs as reasonable when he's cheating on his wife.

You're the pervert, remember.

Dad is listening to Elton John ('Tiny Dancer', I think), crooning along without a shred of irony. *Elton!* It doesn't help my mood. On the one hand, I lack the bond you have. You took that shit with you, Adam. Your *daddy issues.* On the other, I'm grossed out by looking into his soul. Seeing all his dirty little secrets.

That's where Brick comes in handy. Or the mess I made of him. I have the juice to fuck with the car radio. The music washes out in static. There's the whine between stations. Then Dad is listening to his own voice. His Bible bashing over the airwaves.

"It's against nature. God. You represent the death of the human race."

He said this to you, glaring over the pages of the Book in his lap. You'd gone to see him with beers on Saturday, tried to talk to him about it. *I can't help who I am* et cetera. He didn't even ask you to sit down. Blamed you for all of the evils in the world. The destruction of everyone, everything. He called you a plague. His only son. These people… they never think about the pain they cause. That it never goes away.

I won't go away.

"Jesus!"

Dad – *your* Dad – might well invoke the name of his Lord and Saviour. I am filling up the car. I am shadow uncoiling, a black serpent in the cramped space. Just like I uncoiled in the shed. He thinks I'm smoke, I guess. First thing he does is slam on the brakes. Then, one hand on the wheel, he tries to roll down the driver's side window. But I'm holding it fast. He gives a wail as darkness engulfs the car. The streetlights, the motorway eclipsed.

The radio squeals. Half music. Half bigotry.

Homophobia. The greatest hits.

There's a second, a moment of regret. He thinks about you, Adam. Honestly he does. *Sorry.* The wheels screech on tarmac – he's struggling to get control – and the car slews to one side. I don't think I can hold him like this for much longer. I'm only shadow and wind. So I let myself go. I'm a whirlwind of blood and glass (I kept the shards from the hallway window), exploding in the car.

Dad screams. I'm in his cheeks. His eyes.

We are a flower of flame as the car slams through the railings of the freeway.

ACCEPTANCE IS A terrible thing.

"Learn to love who you are," Rachel Marsh said, sat in her plush green armchair in the office.

Marsh was the kind of woman that people admire. She looked crisp in her nice grey suit. Marsh emanated patience. It was an aura around her. She wore just enough make up, but that's up to her. There was a photo of her with another woman on the desk. They looked happy, but we were never going to be friends. We went there full of shadows. It wasn't a good starting point for pleasantries.

We were on the couch.

"I hate myself and I want to die."

OK. We didn't actually say that. Kurt Cobain said it best. I'm sure he wouldn't mind us borrowing it, considering. Hey, maybe I could ask him. But then I'm in the emptiness and Kurt...well, Kurt is really *gone.*

"Hate is a poison, Adam," Marsh told us. "It seeps

into every corner of your life, spoiling everything. Most of all you."

Soon after that you locked up the shed. The one in your mind as well. You threw away the razorblades. They'd become blunt. It was hard to see which bits were blood and which rust. You hadn't used them in quite a while. Into the trash they went, wrapped in newspaper and a faint, frightening hope.

Soon enough, we found ourselves in bars. Under neon. In strange beds. We were *trying.* Under every sweep of laser, with every discarded condom, you were growing brighter.

And I was fading, Adam. You didn't care. You left me behind. Dust. A pile of rags. A mosaic of blood and tears. A husk. That was me.

But Marsh was right all the same.

Yeah, she was right about that.

Poison.

SOMEWHERE. SOME TOWN. Miles is walking home from your apartment. It's dawn. We're in that dull grey hour that seeps into everything. The suburbs smell of dog shit and dew. Miles left you sleeping. He has to go to work. The truth is he's pleased with himself. You can see it in his step. Miles really likes you. That just won't do.

The streetlights are blinking as he reaches the underpass. *Blink. Blink. Blink.* One by one they go out. Through the pools of shadow I drift. Low to the ground.

Clothed in litter. If it weren't for the traffic, Miles would hear me, the tinkle of glass in the wind. Oh, I'm more than that now. More than blood. Than *hate.* The car crash was fuel too, you see. Your Dad's scream has sharpened me. But I wait until Miles is halfway through the underpass, passing graffiti that wishes him dead, and then I make my move.

Shadows engulf the underpass. *I* engulf the underpass. At first, Miles doesn't notice it. Concrete makes everything grey. The tunnel stinks of piss and death. If Miles runs, he could probably break through the web of shadows. I'm not strong enough to hold him. I have to move fast. Still, there's a certain satisfaction in watching it dawn on him, the same way it dawned on Brick and Dad. His eyes grow wide. A curtain falls over the tunnel. There is no light at the end.

Smoke? he wonders. Sweat glitters on his brow. He doesn't know what to do. When he turns back he sees me. Me and my shadow. Blood and dirt floods the underpass. Rags weave in the wind. An odd spot of paint. The chips of glass that pass for my eyes. The fire of my smile.

"Adam..?"

He knows I'm not Adam.

He isn't yours, I tell him. *He's mine.*

Miles is trying to speak. There's a sound in there somewhere. It's no surprise that he can't get it out.

I burst into flames. I carry the car crash with me now. I'm feeling much stronger. *Brighter.* If I push, I could fill up the underpass. The shadows have him cornered. If I push, flames will rip through the tunnel. It is all over for Miles.

Grief will bring you back to me, Adam. All the fear. All the hate.

This time, you'll never leave.

If I *push* -

"Stop this."

And I see you. Adam. The real you. You're standing in your jeans. An open shirt. You pulled your trainers on without socks. Fuck, you were in a hurry, weren't you? The emptiness of the bed next to you had you running for the door. You didn't know what you were going to say to him. You don't know now.

Oh, Adam.

Miles screams, a shatter of echoes. He tells you to run. To get away. But we're not listening to him.

You left me, I say. *You left me behind.*

Fuck, I'm angry. I'm a fucking funnel of fire. I'm a shoeprint on your back. I'm a razorblade in the dark. I'm a pocket Bible in trembling hands. I'm rags and dust and blood and glass. I'm your shadow. Your husk. And you should be afraid of me.

But you only smile.

"No," you say. "I didn't."

Before I can stop you, you step forward. You step forward with your arms spread.

You embrace me.

Us.

*

THE SUN HAS slipped behind the clouds when we walk out of the underpass. Miles is shaking. He winces when I take his hand. We're a little hot from our tantrum, you see. All the same we know that Miles likes us. Really likes us. Enough to overlook the darkness inside. The blood we've spilled. The shit we never wanted. The poison.

We smile at him. He smiles back, uncertain.

He understands. We know he does.

It isn't over. It never is.

CHANGELİNG

Are you a witch or are you a fairy?
Or are you the wife of Michael Cleary?
Old Irish nursery rhyme

IF ONLY THE boy had kept his secret, but Fiona had secrets of her own. The one that returned her to the windswept moor this September had come down to her on her mother's side, her Great Aunt Boland having compiled the family folklore in Tipperary, Ireland, many years ago. That's how she'd come to learn about the Crick Stone. It was why she'd come here at the spring equinox, six months ago. Oh, they'd been full of hope then, Simon and her! It was also how she knew, despite her everyday vocation in the village pharmacy, that the stone was said to work best at certain times of the year and shortly after moonrise.

'*You'll want to put your coat on backwards*,' Old Boland had written, her crabbed Gaelic hand on the faded brown pages, '*and a pair of iron scissors to cut the cord*.'

Fiona had done so, itchy and uncomfortable under the moon, the scissors bright in her hand as the Horned One, the Undergod, had drawn Rory through the stone and bidden her cut, to sever seventeen years of motherhood, skinned knees, failed exams and lately, the fact of his awful confession. How her palm had stung when she'd slapped him... *It's unchristian. Unnatural,* she'd told him, the boy washed out by her tears. *Against all that's right and good.* Yes, Fiona couldn't forget her reasons.

But she'd cut herself too. The Undergod hadn't told her about that.

"Oh, Simon." She wasn't sure that her husband could hear her over the station wagon bouncing up the track so she leant in close to his shoulder. "How could it have gone so wrong?"

"We weren't to know," he said and swore. It was directed at the track, she thought, the flitting of moths and the scratching of brambles rather than her. Then he seemed to remember compassion, taking her hand as he'd taken the hands of so many who came to the vicarage for tea and sympathy. "What choice did we have? It was either this or... you know..."

Fiona shuddered at what he didn't say. She was a Robbins now, wed to Simon these twenty years past and she wished that the Boland in her blood had never had cause to stir. She couldn't bring herself to dwell on it, the act they'd both thought of that night in bed after Rory had told them his... news. Lord knew that Fiona had access to a wide array of pills in the pharmacy. It would be a simple thing to slip some into his food. Something tasteless, painless… Simon had decided it was more trouble than it was worth. How would they explain it? For a term or two they might say that Rory hadn't come home from uni ('Probably met a girl' they'd say, and laugh), but year after year? And conversion therapy, which Simon knew about through the clergy, was too expensive for a priest on parish wages. Plus Rory would never have agreed to it. Still, her husband was no Abraham and it was folklore, not God, who'd intervened.

Fiona had told him about the Crick Stone. About the *exchange.*

A MONTH. THAT'S how long Fiona had been happy with the trade. The morning after returning from the moors that first time, she'd resolved to put the matter out of her mind. It had simply never happened as far as she was concerned. And Simon had promised never to speak of it. Rory got up late as always. He got crumbs on his shirt at breakfast as always. She brushed them off and kissed him before he left for college as always.

"Love you, Mum," he told her, as he always did.

"Rory…" She checked him at the door of their Salisbury home before he ran off to catch the bus. "Do you remember our chat the other night? You know. About… *boys.*"

She still couldn't bring herself to say it. The G-word. The thought alone made her want to cry.

I'm not telling you this for your benefit, he'd said. *I'm telling you for mine.*

Rory – her bright, handsome Rory – grinned in the doorway. With a mother's eye, she could see he had no idea what she was talking about. Warmth spread in her breast as she realised that the trade, the exchange, had worked. It was gone, the sickness. The tendencies. Whatever one wanted to call it.

The *queerness.*

Fiona shivered in the doorway and forced a smile.

"Good lad. Off you go then."

It was only later as she cleaned the house that she found the flowers in his bed.

Gorse, she thought, judging by the petals. Then she noticed the dampness of the sheets, the dark patch where the changeling had lain, and hissed as the thorns pricked her fingers.

"We should've known better," she told Simon, jouncing with the car up the night-bound track. "The locals call it the 'Devil's Eye', for Pete's sake."

The locals called the stone that on account of its rough circular shape and the hole through its middle, bored by centuries of moorland wind. Fiona wouldn't forget that any more than she'd forget that the stone was a door. Tonight, they'd come to knock on it a second time.

"So it's our fault, is it?" Simon said. "What about my reputation? Were you prepared to see Rory gallivanting about the village, hand in hand with some... some *freak* he brought home from uni? Heaven forbid! Lillian Reed was bound to find out anyway. We're lucky it wasn't the whole bloody village. What would your friends at the WI think? They didn't speak to the grocer for a week when he raised his prices after Brexit!"

Simon killed the engine, the headlights dimming. Moths escaped in ways that the two of them had never been able to. And he was right. What *would* the ladies say if they knew she'd cast aside her Christian values in favour of such a pagan practice? If she was here now, at night on the moors? If they knew what she and Simon were up to, the truth of their dark exchange? It was hard to picture, but she didn't think the vicarage dinner parties would remain such a calendar highlight. Her cheeks burned at the thought of the pointing fingers at the village fete. They might even find, given time, that the pews dried up on a Sunday morning, the flock discouraged by the *queerness* in their midst...

"Well, we don't have Lillian to worry about anymore," she told Simon, her voice cold. "Do we?"

In her mind, she pictured a single wedge sandal lying on the back lawn of Bright Water Lane. She shuddered.

Offering her a tight smile, Simon patted her leg.

As her husband fumbled for the torch in the glove compartment, Fiona heard a moan from the bed of the vehicle, the seats down and her son lying there. Or what passed for her son. Turning, she could see Rory's hair under the blanket, his dark curls another gift from Great

Aunt Boland. But any resemblance ended there. The rest of him was a lump under the covers and had nothing to do with her Rory. The Lump – how she'd come to think of the thing – was still out of it. The Rohypnol hadn't been hard to procure. She'd had to use ten times more of it than she had when she and Simon had bundled her son to this place six months ago, laid him out under the bright March moon.

Oh, Undergod, hear us! Hear a mother's plea!

There was no way to stifle the guilt she felt for slipping the stuff into Rory's tea, nor to rebuff the claw in her guts as she watched him sleeping. *It.* Even though Rory – the *real* Rory – was gone now, passed into the Underland, it was an echo from how she'd watched him sleeping as a boy, lulled into dreamland by stories of fairies long before she'd learned the truth of them. Rory was a handsome lad and she missed him. Six months ago, Rory Robbins had changed. *They* had changed him. And not for the better.

"Come on," Simon said, pocketing the torch and climbing from the vehicle. "He's as heavy as a log." He said this and didn't see her wince in the car light at his poor choice of words. "Luckily, I brought the wheelbarrow."

Fiona pushed down reverie and remembered hope. These were her last blessed minutes with the Lump, the clod of twigs and mud that she'd exchanged for her son. It had been a mistake, a terrible one. Surely, the Horned One would understand.

They'd come to ask him to give Rory back.

*

FIONA WORKED PART time and Simon was often out on church business, comforting this old widow or that, arguing with the council about the steeple fund, printing leaflets for lost pets. That was how Lillian Reed caught her alone that Tuesday morning in early April. The chairwoman of the village council, head of the local WI and the doyenne of any fete, gala or charity raffle going, the woman was a beige bumble bee in her pant suit and wedge sandals as she buzzed up the garden path. There was no point in hiding. Unfortunately, Lillian was also the Robbins' neighbour. She'd gone to school with Simon long before Fiona had met him and certainly long before she'd married him, which Lillian often liked to remind her about, asserting the fact that Fiona would always be the invader in her eyes. That she saw it as her job, Saint Lillian Reed, to chase the snakes out of the village.

That day she'd come to complain about her roses.

"I can't fathom it," she said, her obligatory cup of tea rattling in the living room. "All winter I tended the roses in the hedgerow. I've fertilised regularly. Pruned to the best of my knowledge. The floribundas only bloomed last week and now -"

With a squeak, Lillian placed a withered black flower on the coffee table between them. As they watched, it crumbled into ash.

The hedgerow she mentioned was the bordering one.

"No, Simon isn't using any weedkiller," Fiona told her, meeting her eyes, the accusation there. "It must be some kind of bug. A fungal blight."

"Funny you should say that," Lillian said, her tone no less pointed. "In the pub yesterday, Farmer Bell mentioned a calf born with two heads. And Mrs. Evans said that all her neighbours on Little King Street found sour milk on their doorsteps only this morning. Seems like an ill wind is blowing through the village."

The woman crossed herself. For Fiona's benefit, she thought.

"I'm sure there's nothing of the sort, Lillian."

"By the way, where were you and the vicar off to the other week? I couldn't sleep – I have terrible reflux, you know – and looked out of the window at midnight. Your station wagon was gone. Didn't return until the following afternoon. Odd for a weeknight, I thought."

"Did you? Well, never mind. We took Rory to visit an aunt. She's sick."

"Hmm. Speaking of odd... he's a one, your Rory, isn't he? Got that look about him."

"What look?"

Lillian put down her tea and spread her hands. The gesture was feigned, Fiona knew. She'd obviously come here with more on her considerable chest than dead roses.

"He's rather friendly with your gardener, isn't he? Why, the other day the two stood chatting by the shed for an hour. I only noticed because I was waiting for a delivery from Amazon. I looked out and there they were."

Lillian gave Fiona a look.

"Rory's a friendly boy," Fiona said. Deep inside of her, she cringed.

"I'll say. They were standing like conspirators, whispering. At one point I thought they were going to..." Lillian gave a laugh, the tinkle of dropped porcelain. The jab of a knitting needle. "Still. Boys like that. It's nice that they have friends."

Resisting the bait, Fiona didn't ask, 'Boys like what?' Instead, she ushered Lillian to the door. Then she swept up the ash and the thorns and threw them into the fireplace. Half a Valium later and she was feeling calmer about her escape. Things were different now. She didn't think that Rory would be speaking to Tom the gardener in future. And Lillian wouldn't find anything more to gossip about.

Everything had changed.

To be on the safe side, Fiona fired the gardener the following week, the day before he was due to come and look at the hedgerow. Fiona hadn't been willing to discuss the matter and put the phone down as Tom babbled something about unpaid wages.

Everything was fine, but she noticed things. She noticed how the women's smiles had grown tighter at the WI meetings and how they stopped talking whenever she entered the tearoom. On Bright Water Lane, no less than seven neighbours reported missing pets, cats and dogs, and even a cockatoo. Simon was forever handing out leaflets. In the house, Fiona noticed things too. Jewellery she could never seem to find. Mirrors turned to face the wall. Food in the fridge that went off long before its use-by-date. Freshly washed laundry on the line that had tiny muddy pawprints across it and doors that banged without the hint of a draught. There was an abundance of weeds that she couldn't identity in the back garden, the colours too green, too purple. Perhaps she'd fired Tom too hastily... When she turned on the TV, it was always tuned between stations. And always playing the same song, a pipe piece or something, strange, high and shrill.

Until the end of June, everything was fine on Bright Water Lane. Rory slept late as he always did. He went off to college as always. Told her he loved her as always.

Then, one morning near the end of term, she looked up at breakfast and saw the twig sprouting from Rory's head. She might've taken it for a cowlick, sticking up from his neatly combed hair, if it hadn't been for the leaf on the end of it.

"What is it, Mum?" he said around a mouthful of Fruit Loops. "What are you staring at?"

"Sit perfectly still," she told him and, not daring to breathe, went to retrieve her scissors.

She hesitated, a smile frozen on her face. She'd used the same pair to cut the cord on the moor. What if she broke the spell?

Snip.

Rory didn't seem to notice. Mouth full, he kissed her and ran off to catch the bus, leaving her to watch the bright purple sprig curl up and wither to ash on the tablecloth.

Now, UP ON the moors, the moon climbed through the bramble and gorse. Following the dancing spot of the flashlight, Fiona and Simon had pulled their jackets on backwards and rumbled over the sward. Rumbled because they'd shifted Rory – the Lump – into Simon's old wheelbarrow. The boy was too heavy to lift otherwise and they weren't about to wake him. Lord knew what it would do. He slumped there like a guy on Bonfire Night; it pained her to know that she wouldn't think twice about throwing him onto a pyre. In her hands she clutched her iron scissors. Under her arm, Aunt Boland's book.

One couldn't uncut a cord, she knew. There was nothing on the faded brown pages about giving a changeling back.

Both her and Simon had decided that while they'd never be able to accept Rory's... *tendencies*... and stern discussions would have to take place, with firm rules and a code of silence (and maybe, if they could siphon a little off the steeple fund, they'd look into therapy again), nothing could be worse than life with the Lump.

With a mother's eye, she knew that the Lump was only going to bring more trouble.

Before the Crick Stone, the rough round ring in the darkness, Simon brought the wheelbarrow to rest. Rory's arms hung out of it, the roots and leaves that sprouted from his fingers trailing along the ground. Some of them had become tangled in the wheel, she saw. Simon handed the torch to Fiona and under the silver shield of the moon, she opened the book and read the summoning, scrawled in crabbed and credulous Gaelic.

"Oh, Undergod, Lord of the Wild, hear a mother's plea. I beg you come, step through the veil of mist and starlight that divides our worlds. Come from the Underland, from Old Cockaigne, and grant us an audience, oh lord."

It was as Great Aunt Boland had written. It had worked before. But then she'd had a living boy to offer and not a greedy lump of wood.

For a while, the wind sighed over the moors. A crow cawed, reminding her of a woman's scream.

By THE END of August, Fiona was visiting the supermarket four times a week. Her Rory liked to eat. At meal times, she'd done her best to overlook the fact that he liked to eat anything. Raw or cooked. Packaged or no. On a few occasions, she'd had to wrest a plate or a spoon from him so he didn't swallow them too. All the while Simon hid behind his latest copy of Gospel Standard and pretended that none of it was happening.

One day, when she found a little red collar with a bell in his bedroom, 'Luna' embossed on a disc attached to it, she'd confronted the boy. In return, he'd belched at her, his mouth oddly distended. And she was always hoovering, it seemed. There was dirt everywhere. Clumps of mud and grass in the cupboards. Ash on the kitchen counter. Thorns inside his pillow case.

All of these things, Fiona pushed to the back of her mind. When neighbours came knocking to ask if she'd seen this or that dog, she smiled and shook her head. She helped to arrange the jumble sale with Lillian Reed and she sat in the church in her Sunday best, listening to Simon warn of the devil. She squeezed Rory's hand who sat beside her while she prayed and ignored how her fingers came away wet. She kissed him on the cheek as he went to play soccer (or whatever he got up to in the village) and wiped the mud off her lips with a faint, bemused smile.

He was her Rory, her boy. And there never had to be mention of other boys or *tendencies* or *queerness* or any of that nasty, unchristian business ever again.

But on that Friday when she came home early from the pharmacy, she couldn't ignore Tom's gardening van. It was parked on Bright Water Lane.

"Rory?" she'd called, stepping into the house. "Are you home?"

Fiona had agreed to babysit for Mr. and Mrs. Birdwhistle across the road. The school was putting on a Shakespeare play at the village hall and wild horses wouldn't have kept the couple away from seeing little Jane do her turn as Helena. Fiona had obliged by saying she'd look after their new-born for an hour or two, so the mite didn't squall the rafters down and ruin the show for everyone else. It was well after lunchtime and Rory hadn't said he was going out. Still, the van in the street had startled her. Had Simon rehired the gardener? Surely he'd have said something. There was no response to her warble in the hall.

She could hear the noise, however. The *rustling*. The sound reminded her of trees in the park at night, thrashing in a storm, and the hairs on the back of her neck stood on end.

Fiona found him in the back garden. Rory. Or what passed for Rory. Because her mind could only cope with so much, she took in the surrounding litter of objects first. A can of beer discarded on the grass. A mobile phone. A scrap of material – fluorescent orange – that took her a moment to place as a pair of underpants. With widening eyes, Fiona looked up at the rustling horror before her. Whatever it was, it took up half the lawn. Ice jagged through her, a blade of speculation. Had Tom paid a visit, come to see Rory? Had they engaged in some kind of… she couldn't bring herself to think of it… some kind of *act* and then had Tom perhaps discovered, as she was discovering now, that Rory wasn't Rory at all. Instead, Rory was this… this ball of weaving roots and shivering leaves, a great round bulge of vegetable matter and her caught standing in its shadow.

Fiona couldn't help herself. Dropping her handbag and edging closer, she searched the monstrosity for any sign of Tom. Any at all. And then, lips trembling, for Rory. For -

Her son.

"Good God!"

It was all she could manage. Fiona sank to the turf at the sight of him. *It.* The Lump. It was as if a giant turnip had sprouted from the garden, all green and purple and grey. Whatever it was, this thing of tubers, leaves and bark, it was wearing Rory's face. The boy leered, his lips wider than the flowerbed and dripping with streams of water and mud.

The Lump seemed blind to her shock – blissfully so. Frozen, Fiona watched as it gave a resounding belch and a root came up to pluck a sock from its maw, chewed, wet and mired, and flung the article into the hedgerow. She blinked when the scream came trailing through the air, shattering the bright afternoon.

It was Lillian Reed, her face a mask of horror over the garden fence.

UP ON THE moors, the Undergod spoke.

"You said this was what you wanted," he said, all antlers and hooves under the moon. "We asked if you were certain."

Fiona and Simon sank to their knees before the Crick Stone, the Devil's Eye. The crows laughed, joyous.

"How were we to know? We didn't understand," Fiona sobbed. "Please."

"Thrice, we asked you." The Undergod spoke in the voice of the wind, his shadow falling over them. "Are you certain, we asked. Should we bear him to the Underland and forever away from these shores? Thrice, you said yes."

"But -"

"Are you certain, we asked, that Rory Robbins should become ours and thus subject to the Tithe, as all our subjects are."

"The Tithe?"

"Aye. The Tithe. The one we pay to Hell come every seventh year. All must draw the lots. Those chosen are sent to the gate."

"Wait. What?" Fiona looked up, wincing at the Undergod's nakedness, his hooves, his fur. His horse-like willy that reached to his knees. "You never told us that."

"It's in the small print of your book, Fiona-'o-Bright-Water-Lane." The Undergod sounded anything but sympathetic. "You made the trade regardless. Your son is now bound to the Underland and all of the Underland's laws."

"Damn you!" Her husband put a hand on her arm, but Fiona shook him off. "Damn your trickery! This... this *lump* you've given us *isn't my son.*"

"No soul is replaceable, woman. Each is unique. It was love you traded, was it not? Love in return for -"

"You bastard. You *fucker!*" Fiona was on her feet at once, slashing with her scissors at the night. "Do you know what the fucking thing's done?"

*

EVENTS ON BRIGHT Water Lane had unfolded like a flower – a grotesque one, with purple petals. In Fiona's head there was a strange piping song. Had the TV been on when she came in? As Lillian Reed screamed, her hands to her powdered cheeks, the Lump gave another shudder. Had it grown a degree, its bulk swelling?

Fiona might've rushed to her neighbour, tried to push Lillian away and told her to run. There was no time. The Lump was definitely growing, she saw, its turnip-like skin bulging and splitting, her son's face stretched across it like a sketch on an overblown balloon. Blossoms swirled, pink and crazed. The changeling belched, loud enough to rattle the bird feeder, and Fiona watched, frozen, as roots crept out from its swollen girth, weaving across the garden.

Lillian screamed again – a note she'd never quite hit in church – and then the Lump was plucking her up off the ground. Shouting and kicking, she was wrenched without ceremony over the fence. *Bet you think he's a 'one' now,* Fiona thought, uncharitably. One of Lillian's sandals went flying and landed on the turf, a wedge that couldn't stop anything.

"Take your hands off me! You dreadful boy! You filth! I'm the chairwoman of the WI, I'll have you know, and I'll write a formal letter of -"

There came a shriek and an unfortunate crunch. The Lump, the mound of earth, leaves and roots that the Undergod had given them, swallowed Lillian whole.

*

Up on the moor, before the Crick Stone, Fiona Robbins slashed at shadow. Her aim was clumsy and she dropped the scissors, the iron blades thumping into gorse. But the Undergod stood unmoved.

"It was your choice," he told her. "Yours alone."

Sobbing, Fiona fell to her knees, a diadem of moonlight and muck going up from the puddle around the stone. Simon, ever the Good Samaritan, half crouched to help her, cowed by the Horned One's shadow. Behind them, the Lump groaned in the wheelbarrow. Soon, the drugs would wear off and it would start demanding food again. Vaguely, Fiona wondered where the nearest supermarket was. It wouldn't be wise to wait too long with a hungry Lump in the station wagon and only her and Simon on offer.

She was about to commence another round of bargaining – take the house on Bright Water Lane, she'd say, or one of her childhood memories, or the wedding ring she wore – when Simon was tugging the sleeve of her jacket and she looked, as he looked, into the eye of the stone.

"Goodness," he said.

Through the stone, a forest spread out, Fiona saw. It might well be moonrise in Cornwall on this side of the stone; the land beyond didn't much care. Sunlight speared in green and gold through the whispering canopy. A river flowed glittering like honey and blossoms and bees danced on the air, carrying the scent of distant summers and an innocence that Fiona had forgotten or perhaps never known. And there she saw Rory. *Her* Rory. Young, he was, his head a mess of Boland curls. A boy-shaped smile beamed on his face.

Rory wasn't alone. He walked arm-in-arm with another boy. One who looked about the same age, she thought, a bit taller, though any similarity ended there. The stranger had hair the colour of winter and small, curling horns that poked from his brow. Eyes locked, laughing, Rory and the goat-boy ambled along the bright riverbank, clothed in the swirling leaves.

Fiona clutched her breast to see them. Something inside her shifted and cracked, a tiny sound in the darkness, but the Undergod seemed to hear it clear enough.

"The cord is cut," he told her. "As you wished."

She looked up at him then, her eyes wet.

"He looks happy," she said. Though it stung her, she managed a smile.

"What would you expect in the Land of Plenty?" the Undergod said. "Rory Robbins has his fill of nectar, berries and cream, along with everlasting youth. Look! He's fallen for an elf-knight of the Hidden Court. There are none who'll judge him there." He offered this without blame; Fiona cringed all the same. "For seven years, your son will know joy. After that time, he must take his chances with the lots as we all must. Should he be chosen, he shall bid farewell to the Underland and enter the Kingdom of Hell."

Fiona could no longer look. She'd seen what she'd seen with a mother's eye. Inside, her heart was a dead rose, crumbling into ash.

"What have I done?" she whispered. The wind came up to carry off her tears.

"Why do you weep, Fiona-'o-Bright-Water-Lane?" the Undergod asked. "Although I cannot undo our exchange, seven years isn't too long a wait. You have as good a chance as anyone. If luck is with you, then Rory will come home to you again."

Fiona stared at him. "I don't understand. You said -"

"Oh, I know what I said." The Undergod laughed and gazed over the moor, frowning at the mired station wagon, the Lump in the wheelbarrow, the two of them, husband and wife. "It's your world that's Hell, woman."

Then there was only the night and the stone. The moor and the long days to come.

FRANKENSTEIN
UNCUT

The many men, so beautiful!
And they all dead did lie:
And a thousand thousand slimy things
Lived on; and so did I.
Coleridge,
'The Rime of the Ancient Mariner'

INGOLSTADT, GERMANY, 1816

IT WAS ON a dreary night of November that I beheld the phallus of my dreams. With an anxiety I could barely contain, I had waited until well after sundown to slip along Jesuitenstrasse to the Kreuztor Gate, bound for the charnel house that stood squat in its ancient shadow. Rain pattered in dismal rhythm with my footsteps, but none so quick as my heart, I keenly aware of the illicit business that I was about and thrilled by the near culmination of my work. With three knocks as prior arranged, the leather-hooded watchman unlocked the stout barred door, regarding the pale, shivering student on the step with a world-weary grunt. As young and green as I was, it seemed mine was not the first crepuscular visit from the university, my fellows seeking the discarded organs and bones of the city – some old, some fresh – without the risk of discovery of theft from the established laboratories. How my poor father, neither one for the supernatural nor the gruesome, would have shaken his head to observe me there, lank haired and red-eyed from my experiments, and most likely have urged me to rest and a physician come morn. He could not know that his eldest son, I, Victor Frankenstein, embarked on the great and unexplored ocean of truth, longing with a fervent desire to penetrate the very secrets of nature.

Such had occupied my thoughts and hours since arriving in Ingolstadt two years ago, by day an avid spectre in the library, lecture theatre and dissection room, by night sequestered in my workshop, in truth little more than a cell at the top of my house. My labours in those grim confines had brought me to the mausoleum this eve and the brightness of the lantern with which the watchman led me inside was naught compared to that of the exhilaration in my breast. Like the shadows that shirked the flickering flame, soon death itself would retreat in flight!

Between the coffins he led me, keeping several paces ahead and his face turned in gruff decorum, each wooden lid prised open for my methodical inspection. In the dim light, the cuff of my shirt clapped to my nose to ease the stench, I surveyed the naked dead. Limbs, torso, head, these I had already procured from sodden graves and unmarked carts around the city, each time selecting a different location lest my efforts drew unwelcome eyes. Tonight, I had come for that most vital of instruments, the crowning jewel of my desire, and I would choose one with the same degree of utmost care, both scientific and lubricious. The phallus in question must match the one closest to memory and want, glimpsed but once in the Thonon baths yet remaining the thrust of my ambition.

Pallid and still, the men lay before me, prepared for their final audition. As ever, I relied on medical detachment to proceed, forcing myself to refrain from thought of moral turpitude and the visible rot that accompanied such an endeavour, threatening disgust and subsequent disgorgement. Here, I spied a sun-browed and sinewed labourer, his *mons pubis* reminiscent of a bush in the Bois de la Bâtie, his member a walnut in the briar. There, a gaunt cadaver held the air of a priest, his prepuce shorn in the Jewish fashion. Allowing for *livor mortis*, the natural settling of the blood and thus affording me only a conjectural gauge of erection (which, I had learnt, could vary alarmingly), I struggled to find either fitting for my creation. Indeed, the phallus I had once sighted through the thermal steams of Thonon had been of impressive length and girth, pinkish and dangling before me with a gentile purse of skin budded over a round and corpulent glans. How strange to think in such dispassionate terms of Henry Clavel's manhood! My veins fair thudded with the remembrance of my unclothed friend and grasped it then as the root of my longing, the very seed of my radical enterprise. Brooking no distraction, I shuffled on between the caskets, peering with mounting despair at the poor, flaccid fruit on offer, each one shrivelled by the gelid hand of death.

By the seventh coffin, I faltered, and after a moment to assure myself of the adequate value with a measuring rod from my satchel, I levelled my grin on the watchman, exultant in the gloom. "This one," said I, breathless and perspiring in the dust. "This shall suffice."

The man vented frustration, a filthy hock of a hand held out for the agreed gold mark, a payment that would doubtless supplant all judgement.

None in that sombre chamber had any cause for haste while patience remained the surgeon's friend. I deemed that compensation must wait. My triumph gleamed in the blade of my paring knife as I leant into the coffin, as eager as Eve to pluck the forbidden apple.

This night would see the end of my toils.

ONE MUST WONDER how a man of my standing, born to an idyll on Genevese shores and raised like an idol by my parents, could have come to such a lewd and perilous pursuit. There was a time when all my concerns were occupied by play in the grounds of the Belrive mansion, flitting with the clouds across the gardens and the meadows beyond, my childhood companions in tow. Fortune had bestowed me with the most beauteous of friends and ere any storm broke over the mountains of Jura, no shadow of loss or longing darkened my heart. How could it be when one heard daily the trill of the red-crested pochard and the sweet laughter of Elizabeth Lavenza, my marvellous 'more than sister'? Golden and gay, she was, given to the aerial creations of the poets and the wondrous scenes that surrounded our home.

It was my mother's wish, the gentle Caroline née Beaufort, that one day I should wed my adopted cousin and continue the Frankenstein line. Of Elizabeth, poor Elizabeth, I can relate no ill, though she had ever seemed so ethereal to me, more Alpine spirit than flesh, and the gleam of her eyes reminiscent of glass that covered her in some fairy tale glade, rendering fancy distant and moot. Even from a tender age, my affections were reserved for Henry Clavel, the son of a merchant and firm family friend. Tall, lean and dashing Henry who always strode first through the long grass or waded headlong into the lake, dreaming himself some hero of old and begging we play our parts. Dark haired and practical, Henry was my Apollo and my Galahad, and a warmth coiled in my breast at the thought of him long before my veins thrummed with the adolescent urges. In truth, I loved them both, and deeply. Both endured my occasional outbursts, for I was a creature of will and violent passion, and Elizabeth and Henry the balm to cool me. In the black shade of all that came after, I think it paramount to remember, perhaps only for some to think less ill of me, the wild aspiration that was long germinating inside, later birthing death and horror.

It was with Henry that I discovered the ancient tome in the inn, one day huddled under wayside beams on a return jaunt from the city, sheltering from the brisk Swiss weather. Together, we leafed through the strange words and the scrawled diagrams of one Cornelius Agrippa, Henry soon frowning and I delighted at the wonderful theories at hand, clues to an invisible world. How startled we were when a sheaf of sketches fell from the cover, displaying gentlemen and ladies in lifelike deshabille, all silk corset and stole, or sporting a top hat and nothing more. At once, my quick eye was drawn from the archaic text to the rigid poles of flesh before me, proud and rearing from dark pelvic thatch, one-eyed serpents of mystery. Was it destiny, hanging in the stars, which guided a finger to my lips and then to trace a wet line up the length of one considerable member? When I met Henry's incredulous eye, I coughed and feigned to brush dust from the sheet, claiming that the portraits might be of some worth. "Victor, you shall not show these to your father. And your mother would perish of shock!" my companion had informed me sternly, then stamped away, red-cheeked, to unite with the throng waiting for supper. But a deeper alchemy was sparked in me that day, hot in the alembic of my soul. When the snows ceased and the road cleared, both Agrippa and the sketches joined me in our carriage, hidden under my coat.

*

By the time I turned fifteen, I was more than well-acquainted with the old necromancer, and Paracelsus and Magnus besides, having procured most of their works in the interim and pored over their treasures with glee. The sketches, for their part, had become all but engraved on my mind, lifted from the browning paper and fuelling my vibrant imagination every night under the bedclothes, my throbbing puberty in hand. Every vision, every incubus, wore the face of Henry Clavel, his proud and valorous lineaments as near grown to manhood as mine – not to mention his physique! There were other books, the Bible chief of all, that poured condemnation on such proclivities. Hushed as it was in polite society, the sin of Sodom was a matter of opprobrium, promising scandal and brimstone. Nevertheless, it was not shame but wonderment that moved me. The magicians pierced the secrets of heaven and earth, the veiled face of Nature, yet desire seemed to me the greater force, the tide that moved all the creatures of God and spurred us from the primordial clay to build our glittering cities, discover America, the steam engine and suchlike. What was it, I asked of the dark, that lit the fire of life in Man and inspired one to greatness? What miracles might one perform if one could harness that power in one's hand, direct the furious heat of it? Flesh made for the essential matter, my damp sheets reminded me, along with my shuddering breath. What of the need that compelled it?

I was thinking this, and of Clavel, on the day that the storm rolled up from the mountains of Jura. Violent it was, and terrible, the bursts of thunder shaking the mansion and all the quarters of the sky. Fraught with curiosity, I observed the progress of the tempest from the hall doorway with Henry, the both of us crying aloud at each flash and rumble, the clouds black high above. All of a sudden, I beheld a jag of white fire strike an old and beautiful oak a mere twenty yards from where we stood – one as gnarled and veined as any sketched phallus – and once the dazzling light dispersed, naught remained of the tree but a blasted stump, smouldering in the grounds. Electricity, of course, was a science not unknown to me and while Henry, excited by the catastrophe, expounded on all he had read of galvanism, my mood sank into despair. How antiquated my alchemists seemed then, but it was the random act of heavenly destruction that aggrieved me the most. Had love struck me in the same fashion, igniting my youthful veins with such raging and unfulfilled longing? If only God would hearken to my prayer and send another bolt into my friend, elucidating on the step beside me and blind to the passions I hid. Foolish in my gloom, I drew closer to him and sought out his hand, closing his fingers in mine. Perhaps the current could pass from me, conducted by his strong and handsome bones. Perhaps it could fuse us into a new shape, one bound in soul as well as the bright potential of flesh.

Instead, as though shocked, Henry wrenched his grip from mine. "Victor," said he. Then he granted me a reproachful look before turning on his heel and withdrawing in silence into the house.

How strangely are we constructed, and by such slight fortune bound to our affections and tastes. My heart ached to acknowledge the truth of it.

It was plain I was alone in my need.

TONIGHT, IN INGOLSTADT, high in my garret, I turned my mind once more to the matter of my creation. Through the hatch in the roof, the moon beamed down on my midnight labours. His bulk lay before me on the gurney, broad and insensate, his composite parts complete with the phallus I had plucked from the Kreuztor charnel house. His physique was ably stitched together, greased and waiting for breath. It had been no mean feat to attach the associate nerve endings to the dorsal veins, spermatic cord and the femoral canal, the testes as pale and swollen as ripe Japanese plums. On the sacral couch, his generous portion hung, slack yet filled with the promise of life and a thousand envisioned carnal delights. Though I had since learnt the art of restoring animation, the preparation of a frame for its reception, with all its intricate web of muscle, fibre and bone, had proved a task of inconceivable difficulty. Who can conceive the horrific lengths to which I had gone, dabbling among the unhallowed graves of the city and the many tortured animals that had led to the sparking of the lifeless clay? I still tremble with the memory and yet the greater effort was due to the aim of my exacting eye; my ambition, loathsome as it was, must conclude with the nearest model to my dreams that my strained mind could conjure, or fail utterly.

Well I might reflect on the pain that had brought me to this hour of triumph, the culmination of my work. Four years had passed since the day of the blasted oak and two since I had decamped from Belrive, the incident at Thonon in my wake. Aged seventeen, and not long before I embarked on my journey to Ingolstadt, my dear mother was taken ill, stricken with the scarlet fever. Alas, that fair doyenne of the mansion had passed away peacefully one night and grief came to haunt our corridors and halls, Elizabeth a shadow of herself and Henry forever with hat in hand, both beyond my comfort. I need not describe the bitterness that comes when those we hold dear are torn from us by the evil hand of death, plunging them into the void that presents itself and the one that follows their vanishment. Indeed, the demise of my mother induced two momentous occasions that rendered clear the desperate path before me. The first, when my father discovered my ancient tomes and dismissed the lot as 'trash', though went on to declare that my curious nature and sharp intellect would be better served in formal education and thus determined to dispatch his eldest son to university. The second when my closest friend, Henry Clavel, arranged for a brief respite before my departure, an opportunity to relax and for a while forget sorrow, and so we had ridden together for the baths at Thonon. With these events in mind, my fist shaking at the scythe that hangs over us all and my hopes of romance shattered, I rattled forth in the carriage for the city.

Those dark days were always with me, yet I had been idle in neither my heartbreak nor my studies, and remained engaged with the most feverish passion in the pursuit of discovery. In my mind conspired the teachings of old, of the alchemists and their long lost hypotheses, newly joined with the latest advances in science, both chemical and anatomical. Indeed, the phenomena that most beguiled my attention was the structure of the masculine frame, the principle that imbued one with life and the requisite dynamic desire. I would challenge the gods themselves and force Nature to grant me my wish!

My days were spent under the instruction of my professors, the squat and repulsive M. Krempe who held no truck with occult speculation and long exploded systems, and the aged M. Waldman, a wiser, gentler tutor who advised me that only a fool would deny themselves the breadth and depth of philosophical knowledge, his grey head nodding in cautious regard at my youthful chimeras, my claims of miracles, an elixir of life. By night, however, I ventured in Ingolstadt the same as any student on his first jaunt away from the familial home. I drank in taverns across the Old Town and some along the Danube. Long before my eye considered graveyards, charnel houses and unmarked carts, I wished to learn the skills of human congress to a degree of expertise, and to quell the lingering ache in my breast, for I sorely missed Elizabeth, my father and most of all Henry Clavel.

Stumbling I would go to this or that hovel with a host of willing fellow students. On occasion, I would accompany a charming barkeep or a silver-tongued merchant on his way by diligence to Berlin or Budapest and naught left in his dust to speak of it. On mold-speckled bunk and threadbare rug, I licked my finger and traced the length of a phallus for the first time and slipped another into an oiled anus, to probe and suck and eventually allow the entry of that cherished member into my own deeper parts. After many a breathless, hazy climax, I came to discover that I preferred this particular fashion, to be the one penetrated, and hard, yet in no supposed submissive state. Rather, my predilection echoed my approach to my studies, that being to remain in firm control of the reins, either riding atop the paramour to hand or gasping out commands as I sweated under him.

Such darlings were always dark haired, lean and tall, given to the practical rather than the passionate. Yet none of them, not for all the gold in Europe, could compare to my Prometheus, my sweet friend Henry Clavel left three hundred miles and more behind me in Switzerland and his remembrance of me irrevocably marred. In despair, experienced yet hollow-hearted, I abandoned these wanton engagements soon enough and set my mind anew to my books, my experiments and a grander endeavour, one which I have previously described.

Oh, Henry! If only he were standing beside me as I shivered in my tenebrous workshop and gazed upon the achievement of my toils. My creation lay before me, whole and ready for the energising force to shake him from death's cruel slumber. Tall, I had shaped him, and girthsome, equal in stature to my lurid visions. I had selected his features as handsome, the various parts of his countenance shorn from the corpse of a stout farmhand, the servant of a Duke, a young beggar in a Bavarian inn – no one that any would miss. His limbs were all in proportion, his teeth like pearls, his hair a lustrous black. Lips touched by the kiss of decay might soon part to offer up their own. Once invigorated with the universal fire, roused and throbbing with life, my creation, my creature, would take me in his arms and pierce me with a passion unlike any I had known and cure the constant longing inside me. Such had been my scheme. I had desired it with an ardour that far exceeded moderation.

I shall not impart the precise details of the process, for reasons of caution and care that shall soon become clear. Suffice it to say that when lightning leapt from coil to coil and the rafters shook with the fist of the firmament, the creature's eyes at last flew wide, blinking in the murk. It was there in that yellowed gaze that I beheld the thorn in my endeavour, spearing my soul to its core. Breathless horror filled my heart. For all my efforts, my months of sewing and shaping a suitable likeness, the monster before me resembled little of Henry Clavel.

Unable to endure the sight of my vanished dream, I fled from the room.

*

AFTER A WHILE of great agitation, pacing the floor of my bedchamber, exhaustion finally claimed me. Regular meals, rest, I had long forgone and all of it seemed for naught. I undressed and collapsed onto my bed. My spirit, disturbed, dragged me into the wildest dreams. I thought that I accompanied Henry, returned to the morn when we rode for Thonon yet no trace of concern on his face, his smile as gay as any I had seen. "Victor," he said from the saddle and reached out a hand to me, drawing my own mount close to his. "Galvanism refers to an electrical current, especially as produced by chemical action or a vital force which bestows life upon organic matter." I did not question this, revelling in his proximity and our happy embrace. But as I imprinted the first kiss upon his lips, they took on the bluish shade of death and his features sank inward like rotten fruit. Grave-worms crawled on his tongue and mine, startling me from sleep, my limbs iced with sweat and my teeth chattering. Nevertheless, I found myself aroused, my manhood fit to burst under the blankets and only waning a degree when the moonlight fell in through the shutters and happened to illuminate the wretch – the miserable creature whom I had created.

With one pale, outsized hand, he held up the curtain of the bed and the yellow lamps of his eyes, if eyes they may be called, peered down on me in dumb bewilderment. He uttered some inarticulate sounds while a slow grin spread across his face, pleased to discover his maker. Fright saw me scuffle to the headboard as the creature reached out, either to detain or throttle me, my shock threatening a swoon.

And oh! In the half-light of that long November night, the shadows wove a blessed illusion, concealing pallor, stitch and scar, the cadaverous skin that cloaked him. There in that moment it was as though my dearest Henry Clavel stood naked by the bedside, formed from sinews that I had positioned myself, propelled by a plundered heart and veins into which I had poured my fluids. Between smooth and muscular thighs swung the phallus of my dreams, procured but yesternight in the Kreuztor charnel house.

Oh, Henry! Oh, God in heaven! What had I done?

Later, I told myself it was the sheer instinct for survival that made me reach out and draw the creature's hand to my lips, one stout finger slipping between them. That fear alone inspired me to utter a series of soft mewling sounds and lure my creation onto the bed, his manmade bulk eclipsing me. That I, Victor Frankenstein, was no more than a cornered mouse and must find some way to soothe the savage beast if only with the frail music of my body. How the creature grunted and moaned when I turned my attention to the length between his legs, my tongue flicking over his prodigious scrotum, the tremendous girth of his swelling shaft and up to the gleaming eye of his glans. Thus, ingesting the rigid member that I myself had chosen, I laced the harness around my bringer of doom and bound him in the web of my passion. His strength was considerable, as I had wrought it, and his weight sufficient to reduce the bed to mere ribbons of wood, reminding me that he could snap my neck with as much effort as he might a hen's, and so I made my bid for escape. One must think it a necessary evil as I dragged myself to the bedchamber wall and lifting my nightgown, I parted my legs, my hands pressed to my rump to reveal the bud of me. "Come, enter," said I, my first command to my lumbering Adam and though I realised he lacked the intellect and learning to grasp the rudiments of European language, my gesture proved instruction enough. Feet around his bullish neck, I closed my eyes and endured the agony. How I squealed and clawed as the creature worked his way inside of me, bucking and thrusting in a manner I feared would dislodge my spine while an ecstasy hitherto unknown spun my mind to the yawning heavens. How the beams of the house shook.

Hours passed. In time, sunlight clapped the earth and it was most unkind. Beside me, the creature slumbered, his expression one of the deepest satisfaction. Yet no mortal could support the horror of his countenance, an ugly mockery of love such as Dante himself could not have conceived. It was not merely due to the creature's doltishness, the broad, cloddish lump of him. Whatever brain I had implanted, it could never hold the vainglorious fancies of my dearest Henry, nor his practicality and friendship. Nay, there was no gainsaying the bite of the worm, nor the black stars of lividity and the bittersweet reek. Aghast, with bile in my throat, I slid from under the trunk of his arm and wrestled my trembling limbs into my scattered clothes. With no thought of returning to that place, I crept from the room and hastened downstairs, out into the morning rain.

*

FROM THE UNIVERSITY, I wandered, a stumbling ghost. Through aching eyes, I peered up at the church of Ingolstadt, its white steeple and clock, which indicated the hour past dawn. The streets were all but empty yet offered no asylum. Porters stared at me as I passed, thinking me some dishevelled drunk likely woken in a midden heap. With quick steps, my gaze oft straying over my shoulder lest the creature came lurching after me, I turned corner after corner, drenched and dismayed beneath a comfortless sky. For some time, I continued thus, sore from my evening labours and keen to exercise the gloom that weighed upon my mind. Death had found its mirror in life; desire in despair. The latter was all that urged me onward without any clear conception of a destination. The fire of my experiment, my need, had guttered and gone out. Had I truly thought to extract the essence of my lust and serve up a simulated feast? All I hungered for then was home, for the sweet smile of Elizabeth and the green meadows of Belrive to offer me forgiveness and peace, such as any wretch deserved.

The purest coincidence proved my salvation. At length, I found myself opposite the inn at which various coaches stopped. The sight of the Swiss diligence arrested me, having carried me years ago to the city and all my dreams and damnation. How M. Krempe would have laughed to see the outcome of my alchemy, as exploded as any old theory. How M. Waldman would have shaken his grizzled head. As for my father… but it was better not to think of him then. Imagine my surprise when the carriage door swung wide and I perceived none other than Henry Clavel, my gaping mouth mirrored by his as he spied me standing in the street. "My dear Victor," he exclaimed. "How wonderful to see you. And how fortuitous that I should meet you here at the very moment of my arrival!"

Naught could equal my delight at seeing Clerval. Before I could prevent myself, I dashed forth and clasped his hand, yet in a flash the memory of the Thonon baths came winging back to me, on winds both hot and cruel. How we had eased ourselves into the steaming waters on that distant, diresome day, my eyes wide and my heart pumping at the sight of my unclothed friend. His physique, tall and lean, had overwhelmed all of my senses, his fine phallus impressed on my mind as if he were the potter and I the wet clay. How I had swallowed my fears and swum to him, pressing my own frail body against his and reaching for the organ of my dreams. Bold to the last, I had fondled him under the surface until he had grown somewhat tumescent, then he had cursed and pushed me away. "Victor," he said and the echo of a threat was borne on the ripples. Then Henry had heaved himself out of the pool, thrown on a robe and stormed away from me. We had barely spoken again before I decamped days later for Ingolstadt. I had told myself he could not bear to say farewell, but in my heart, I knew otherwise. In grief for my mother and my shame over my friend, I had braved the long mountain road that swept me away from him and chosen a darker route instead – one that had led me to the brink of the abyss.

There before the inn, I let my hand fall. My cheeks burned like the fires of Hell and I turned my gaze to my shoes, the puddles in which I stood. Then came my second surprise of the day when Henry reached down and renewed his grip on mine, drawing me close to his chest. Like I, said he, he had embarked on a voyage of discovery to the land of knowledge and had resolved to 'drink heartily of Greek'.

This music in my ears struck a false note when a shadow caught the corner of my eye. Glancing that way, I thought I spied a shape in the alley beside the inn, tall, broad and watchful. Reminded of my labours the night before, I wrestled with an unbidden urge to run and find the marvel that I had created, beg for mercy at his feet. My senses reeled, my mind crazed, and for a moment I envisioned how we might flee the city entirely, my creature and I, far away from the eyes of the world. Aye, a new species bound to our doom in an icy wilderness, warmed only in each other's arms...

Henry stroked my cheek, drawing me back to the present. I blinked and marked no phantom by the inn, merely the leavings of dread in my weary mind. I looked up at Henry and smiled.

"And I fear I have been unfair to you, dear Victor," he breathed and guided me into the inn.

İN HADES, HE
LİFTED UP HİS EYES

OBITUARY. At special behest, we mark this October 9th, 1832, the passing of one Abraham Farley, eighteen years of age, of late a hired hand in The Prospect of Pye, Smithfield. Farley was laid to rest in Blackshaw Cemetery and will be mourned by his mother and sister in York. "Come to me, all ye who are weary and burdened, and I shall give you rest" Matthew 11:28-30.

'Tis a curse to go to your grave as a young man and yet still breathe and weep. A lad shouldn't feel the worms slithering over his skin and the beetles nipping at his ears. A spider, outraged in the dark at the invasion and crawling over a fluttering eye – the eye of a lad such as I. Amongst the fruit, the salt beef and the jug my fellows gave me, here I rest in a narrow hell, my spine aching, with no pillow for my head. On my chest there lies no cross or flowers; instead, two pistols primed with powder, which cost a pretty penny from a soldier down at the Knightsbridge barracks, and still more to secure his silence. A twitch and my brow might knock on wood, bring the night watch running. My nails bite into my palms, my teeth a rictus to rival a corpse, keeping me still as the insects riddle and crawl, delighted by the blood-warm feast.

In a shallow grave, in the cemetery of Blackshaw Road, I lie awake in the coffin.

Oh, the taste of dirt and the waiting... Come, Hunter, I am your dead! Come at midnight like you always do, with the half-moon high, with your lackeys, your sack and your wooden spade, creeping past the watchmen with your lanthorn shielded. Come, come, I am your lad, your sweet Abe, who you took under your wing down Smithfield way and then like a man takes a woman, in shadows, secrets and sin. In grunts as you yanked down my breeches and took me roughly over the hop sacks all those weeks ago.

You said I was your golden boy. I was never as golden as Harry.

Aye, I was a green thing then, soft in the head like my mother used to say, with an ear for your pretty lies. I was tall and sinewed enough to gain employment in your tavern, but that wasn't why you hired me. You had me up and down the stairs, hefting your crates, your inebriated patrons and soon enough you, sweating in the gloom with your hand over my mouth lest the drunkards upstairs should hear us.

And later hefting bodies too, fresh and pale from the grave, bound for a handful of willing anatomists from Lambeth to Bethnal Green. Riding St George in the cellars or digging up cadavers would see the both of us swing and no mistake. They did for Burke up in Edinburgh, the notorious 'resurrectionist' hung in the square, his accomplice and the doctor to whom they sold escaping the arm of the law. But your own labours furnish you with guineas and guineas are your true love, are they not? Though you wailed to find me in the kitchen, silent, pale on the floor, the both of us know the devilment that squirms in your heart, Jebediah Hunter.

And so I wait, your Abe, your Lazarus, for the hour of my unearthing.

THE DAYS OF our labours and passions, how well I remember them now. In the smoky bowels of the Prospect of Pye, it wasn't much trouble to slip them the poison; often your quarry was blootered enough. The air in your establishment curdled with pipesmoke, lanterns and sour gin breath, with the laughter of merchants, soldiers and whores. All I heard was the slap of hand on bosom and scented thigh while I made your foul acquaintance, running trays to this and that table, lugging barrels and swabbing floors. Outside the stink of London, the belch of factories and Thames fog pressing against the window panes, the wind blowing in the odd traveller like how it blew in Harry.

Before all that, you'd watch me with eyes dulled by laudanum and long drudgery. On occasion you'd lick your chops, as if you were a dog staring at scraps. When you trusted me well enough, when we'd made sufficient congress for me to understand that to snitch was to risk my hide – not that anyone would take my word over yours – you showed me the powders you procured from Madam Canning, the druggist down in Holborn. From under her counter to yours, you said with a tap of your nose, pocked as a raspberry and just as red. You slapped my buttocks then, as I recall, hard enough to imply a warning. Such was my introduction into the business, the *true* business of Pie Corner, which took place around midnight on the odd eve and had naught to do with the drink.

How I wish I could say it was conscience that brought me to this pass, waiting here in my grave. It grieves me to confess a different calling. Truth be told, at first I didn't mind all the murdering. Having run away from home and living in the gutters for a month and more, I was quite content in your employ, suffering your pawing and your lips around old Captain Standish in the tavern cellars. It'd make a stuffed bird laugh to know where a hot meal and a bed can take you, turning one over to sins both venial and mortal. My eye turned from God the first time you lay a hand on me, Hunter. My heart with Colonel Hogwood.

The Colonel was disgraced, we all knew that. We never found out why, but the gossip pointed to desertion. In his hat and faded redcoat, the former tipped to shade his whiskers, the latter hidden under his cape, the old man liked to hold court in the barroom and regale anyone who'd heed him with tales of war. His pipe would swing this way and that, punctuating his prattle with coughs, wheezes and clouds of smoke, the battle in his chest serving as suitable background noise. In each tale he played the hero, rescuing French ladies from burning buildings, duelling with Napoleon himself. Hogwood was as much a glutton for an audience as he was for pork and gin, his cheeks ablaze whenever an unsuspecting sailor or slattern pulled up a seat or I plonked down another dish in front of him.

What the patrons never saw, when the evening stretched into the wee hours, was what a mean old bastard the Colonel was. When the tavern emptied, leaving only the swizzled dregs, how his cheeks would take on a deeper shade and he'd cuss and call out for more. Always more. More.

"Here, boy," old puff-guts would cry, drunk and abandoned in his corner, his shirt speckled with gravy. "You shabbaroon. You scullion. Stop pretendin' to wipe those tables and bring me some Mother's Milk. Hearken, or Mr Hunter shall hear of it. I'll lend him the use of my cane!"

This had proved no idle threat. The odd cuff around the ear, a boot to the behind I could stand, but the Colonel had sat, smiled and watched Jeb thrash me on more than one occasion, under threat o' his refusing to pay.

Why, King William and the saints forgive me, it was nigh on a pleasure to oblige him on that rainy night February last, giving him a fine stew laced with the old Inheritance Powder. Like expectant mourners, I stood trembling beside you, Hunter, and the jolly cook Mr Thorpe, as Hogwood – much like the beast he was named for – guzzled down his midnight supper, belched and soon turned redder than usual, clutching at his cravat. He thumped the table as if he could command the very air. At last, with a retch, he disgorged his meal back onto the table and all down his coat, a tide of carrots, spuds and gristle steaming like the pots on the hearth. Then he slumped face first into his bowl, the inglorious end of all his tales and ills.

I'd given a yelp, unable to check myself, and placed a hand over my mouth.

"Mind me now, Abe," Hunter had said. "You'll be wanting to steel your stomach for the work."

How was he to know how joyous I was? I wiped the sweat from my brow at my triumph. And the thrill of the tasks ahead.

"Do they pay you by the pound down in Lambeth?" The cook, Mr Thorpe, enquired. "Could buy a horse and carriage with this lot."

Both of the men had laughed.

*

Such was the business of Pie Corner and the vocation in which I found myself. "Feed 'em up, get 'em out," as Hunter was wont to say. And when the pickings were slim, as they ofttimes were, him, the cook and some rascal from the East End would go a-digging in the graveyards thereabouts, first scouring the obits in the Packet, then looking on the morrow night for corpses. The anatomists, Hunter explained, were a dainty lot and preferred to avoid maggots in their surgeries, let alone some skull splitting open like a rotten fruit or an unforeseen spill of intestines on a nice tiled floor.

"The sounder a body, the better." Hunter would say that too. And the cook once, jolly as he was, told a tale of how he'd danced with a corpse down in Bow Cemetery, the hem of her cerements sweeping the grass, her breasts pressed fast against him. "Fair as Mrs Jordan, she was," said he, and cackled. "But there were only heat in the one o' us that night."

That had earned him a slap from Hunter, although the bigger man had laughed and tipped me a wink. There's no knowing the truth of it. But I knew the truth about the snatching, because I happened to go with them once or twice. Only to keep watch, mind, lug the sack and shovel, or to test my strength against the odd stone slab or mortsafe. In the wake of Mr Burke, the cages to protect the graves were becoming more commonplace, and what with the increased patrols they most certainly fuelled the men's apprehension along with the canny shift to the poison.

Never did I hear Hunter justify his work – no tipped hat to God, no sighs for the exhumed and no shrugs for the doctors who gladly took his trade – until Harry came calling to the Prospect a month or so ago. Shorter, younger than I, I looked up at his skinny form on the threshold and fancied him filthier than I'd ever been, his feet bare and his clothes in rags. Under his chimney-brush hair, I could make out these flecks of gold, his eyes bright as he appraised me, I stood bent over my mop. As if drawing courage from a lad close to his age, I marked a spark of defiance in him and the boy cleared his throat, straightened and petitioned the barroom entire.

Quoth Harry, "'And in Hades, he lifted up his eyes,'" (Having had my nose pressed proper to the Good Book up north, I recognised the verse.) "'being in torments, and see-eth Abraham afar off, and the beggar Lazarus in his bosom. And the rich man cried and said, 'Father, have mercy on me, and send Lazarus, that he may dip the tip of his finger in' -"

Those were the first words I heard from you, Harry Pickett, my failing, my friend. Before you were done, Hunter was there, all barrel-chested and barking, a paw on the nape of your neck.

"Close the damn door, you quim!" he cried. "Or have you praps got the Asiatic? Might have by the looks of ye. Well, what's it to be, boy? A bath, a bowl or the gatehouse of St Bart's?"

Hunter said all this, naming the nearby church where he'd dug up one or two corpses, and both his hands were upon you then, grubby and sin stained as they were. Had he spied the same gold as I? Aye. It was shining in his eyes. To riotous applause and laughter, he dragged you squirming across the floor towards the door of his cellars.

Oh, you must've thought yourself in some kind of hell. Like me, I'll wager that the growl of your belly deafened you to the shriek of it, the merriment, the damned all around.

The door closed, your own coffin lid. And that's how you tangled with our fortunes.

YOUR FIRST, IF I may call her that, was the Dame Gertrude Baumann. Baumann was about as much a dame as I was a prince, and that's to put it mildly. A German woman, buxom and broad, and in truth, a longtime whore – albeit a poor one at that. Rumour had it that she went unpaid more oft than not, in her tatty skirts, her bonnet with the wilting feather and more holes in her stockings than the larder. How she liked to flounce about the gentlemen when in her cups and later sulk in corners, patting fresh powder over her sores, spurned, penniless and drunk. The Dame had a penchant for wine, wine of any sort, and it was a glass of musky Catawba that Hunter served her up one August night, courtesy of yours truly.

A glass, that was, laced with the old Inheritance Powder.

"No one's going to miss her," our jolly cook said. "Not from Smithfield to Saxony. God as my witness, we're but puttin' her out o' 'er misery."

Oh, I should've read in that a portent. What a buffoon I was! I should've known it, Harry, when I'd heard you bleating most nights, curled up on the bunk next to mine, your shoulders shaking up a storm. You seemed so much tenderer than I, less given to the business of survival. Perhaps you missed your mother as I missed mine. Perhaps she'd cussed you less and held you more, I cannot say. But had I thought less about my own ensnarement, the shifting of bodies and such, I might've realised then you weren't fit for the task, nor so at ease with closing your eyes and thinking of England as Hunter had his way...

One night, I think I gave you comfort, stroking your fine gold hair. Scrubbed then, as all of us were scrubbed, the brush leaving marks on your skin. If we kissed in the dark, I forget it. Praps I only like to dream it, assuaging my own part in things, the guilt that led me to my grave, patient, filthy under the earth. If I dreamt it, I forget the taste of your tears, the silk of you in the dark. Sentiment was of no use in the Prospect and I could not wrest your fate from thee.

The Dame Baumann had given this odd little sound, like a bird was trying to burst from her throat. Then the glass fell from her brass-beringed hand, smashing on the floor. With a sigh of motheaten skirts, she'd slumped sideways in her chair. One tit popped free of her corset and regarded Hunter, Mr Thorpe, Harry and I like a puckered, wounded eye.

"The lady fair looks comely in repose," the cook noted, his hands on his belly as if to quell his appetite. "And at last she's shut up."

"Well, she's still warm, Mr Thorpe," Hunter snapped. There was a threat in his gaze. "We have to get her down Lambeth by cart on the hour. Unless you have other plans?"

Thorpe laughed, but there weren't much to it. Hunter snapped his fingers to set me to the business of the ropes and it was then that I spied Harry, sheet-white and shaking his head at the miserable sight, the Dame Baumann undone. The barroom was empty, the patrons gone to the river to guzzle gin, fondle and filch, mafficking in the heat. Never did I see a lad look so cold as I did on that night.

In a mutter like bones, Harry said, "'Thou shalt not kill'. Exodus, twenty thirteen."

How Hunter looked up at that! Hell flashed in his eyes – yet under it a doubt, I thought, some vestige born of childhood prayers and scripture, perhaps. It softened his bark into a croak as he turned his glare on you.

"What's this, my saucy boy?" he said, and Harry fell into his shadow. "The woman was food for the worms regardless, hellbound since her youth, I'll warrant. You think to upbraid *me*, the man who put a roof o'er your head and a meal before you every eve? How do you think I pay for it?" The big man sucked in a breath, struggling to calm himself. Oh, how his hands shook! "Spare us your sermon, lad. We ain't got time for a thrashin' now. Assist Abe here with the ropes and shut your bleedin' mouth."

The ropes never felt so slippery in my hands; it was as if they resembled the knots in my stomach or flailed like the limbs they were intended to bind, prevent them from knocking about in the cart and drawing unwanted attention. My last act of grace, Harry, was to fire you my own look, and a sharp nod of my head, calling you back from the brink of your error. Secrets were a vital part of the business, friend. A lack of discretion in the Prospect was not to be advised.

Had you but heeded me. Instead, you ran for the door.

Mr Thorpe was upon you first, grabbing you by the scruff of your neck as you fumbled with the lock, desperate for the freedom of London and the company of rats. With a roar, our jolly cook flung you into the room, tables rattling, plates and flagons crashing to the floor. I winced at the crunch of bone, his fist smacking into your skull. Blood and teeth sprayed across the floorboards, painting the ale-stained wood. A boot lifted into your ribs and how you gasped, sobbing among the spilled gravy, the dog piss and chicken bones. Then you squirmed like you had at the start, Harry, trying to crawl under a table and away, away from the puffing Thorpe.

Quick as lightning, Hunter was there, a length of rope in his hand, set to give you the flogging of your life.

"Please, master. Stop," I cried, checking myself from leaping towards him. "The lad meant no offense. Ain't that so, Harry?" And here I pitched my entreaty at the boy who was trying to wriggle under the table, his eyes bright pennies over his shoulder, drinking in his pursuit. "Tell 'im, Harry. Tell Mr Hunter that you'll be good. Let's get the Dame to the doctor."

Heart thumping, I glanced up at the woman in question, attempting to draw all eyes in the room back to the business at hand. Dame Baumann stared back at me with no care for my dismay, no cares whatsoever in the world.

And no one in the Prospect was listening to me.

With one hairy hock of a hand, Hunter grabbed Harry's ankle and dragged him out from under the table. The lad squealed, the lanterns glinting off his hair, an angel wrestling in the gloom, but the proprietor held him fast. Then the ruckus was cut short when Hunter wrapped a length of rope around his neck. It weren't no thrashing he had in mind.

I wanted to scream, to call down the heavens. A part of me wanted to tackle Hunter and Thorpe head on, but I knew that would've been folly. I'd only have added my doom to your own. Nor could I look away as you clawed at the rope, your throat strained, your face turning red. Your spluttering assailed the rafters, faint among the wreathing smoke, until that too was done.

Oh, it was your eyes that I remember most, Harry, the way in which they bulged from your skull, meeting mine own where I stood in the room, observing what righteousness had bought you. You looked at me in a mask of shock, as if I had betrayed you. And as if I were lost.

Farewell, I'd whispered in my mind. *May God forgive me.*

By then, I'd learnt enough to know that God never gives back the dead.

SIN IS NO good for sleep. I learnt that quick enough too – and Harry, poor Harry, you haunted my dreams when I managed it. Golden, pale, you'd raise a finger and point out the stain on my heart. I'd awake sweating and gasping on my bunk, and weep to look over at yours, empty as the organ in question.

While Hunter and Thorpe spoke no more of it, and I never discovered what they did with your corpse (it's unlikely they could've sold it, what with the marks around your neck), I made it my business to find out where the brute kept his guineas, in a chest shut down in the cellars. In the days that followed your murder, I laid all of my plans. It was Hunter himself who paid for this coffin – a fitting purchase if ever there was one – and the rascals I dealt with down Hackney way who dug me this shallow grave. It was they who furnished my person with food and the flintlock pistols, and swore to unearth me should vengeance fail. The poison I procured from Madam Canning, some fine white powder from the tropics, she said, that'd send a man into the deepest sleep and render him as good as dead, at least for a day or two.

Drinking rum for courage, one September night I drank it all down. As wings of darkness claimed me, I fancied I heard you wail, Hunter, when you found me on the kitchen floor. You sold me to that doctor in Lambeth, yet my urchin cohorts followed you, appraised of the surgeries where we plied our trade. It's astonishing what coin can do and there was enough of yours in their pockets to see them spirit me away and leave me to rouse here in Blackshaw Cemetery, in the turned ground of the potter's field, under a sham wooden cross.

Thank God they kept faith with our bargain. Madam Canning told me they had reason to see you undone, either some old score to settle or an itch for the Prospect of Pye. Praps they wanted their paws on the business of snatching itself. It isn't a market open to all, with all its risk of hanging and despite London's plentiful corpses...

The last item on my list was the obituary. No pauper like myself, a runaway and tavern lad, would've ever gained a mention in the *Packet,* not for all the guineas in England. Yet times are changin', ain't they, Mr Hunter? I hoped that when you scoured those pages you'd spy my name there and wonder. Were you going mad?

Hope alone sustains me. Well, that, and beef and water. I keep my reed for air and the pistols, loaded in my grip. The worms wriggle, nibbling my ears. I no longer keep a prayer for myself. Should matters go awry and I perish here, then my secrets, my shame will perish with me and make a fitting end.

Come, Hunter. Come for your dead. Come at midnight like you always do, with the half-moon high, with your lackeys, your sack and spade, creeping past the watchmen with your lanthorn shielded.

Come, come, I am your lad. Your sweet Abe. And I wait for thee.

When your shovel strikes wood and you tear back the lid, then shall I make my repentance. For Harry and all of our sins.

Come. I long to see the same look in your eyes that I saw in his.

OF GENTLE WOLVES

'All wolves are not of the same sort'
Charles Perrault

FRIENDS, BEWARE GENTLE wolves. Never stray from the path. If you'd listened to your mother, girl, you wouldn't have been eaten. I wouldn't be hunting him now in the forest.

Josef, stay, my father said, old and fearful by the fire. *Let the woods and the wild look to themselves.*

The hearth echoes in my ears, cold under my hat, as I tramp up the crisp white hill. A robin watches, shaking its head. On the air, the scent and shadow of the beast. My axe rests over my shoulder. I ran back to the village to claim it, a broad, golden man barrelling through drifts and sliding down hollows, and then I was gone again. Big Josef. Kind Josef. A brave Christian soul all hereabouts would say, built for chopping and lugging wood. But a girl must be answered for.

Then take the stones, my father counselled, waving his cane at the cupboard. *The axe is only the half of it. A gentle wolf is a-roaming. Of all wolves, the gentle are the worst!*

I took the stones, all six of them. Wolf stones. Magic stones. Stones of binding and death. They weighed down my pack like snow on the branches, like my beard by the ice, but none so heavy as my heart. The poor girl was dead and there was no saving her. Well, only her immortal soul. Felling trees in the deep wood I heard it, the bright ring of her scream. Birds taking flight, outraged. Through the briar I thundered, winter and firewood forgotten. Breathless, steaming, I found my way to the cottage. Well my father might caution me; he has not seen the things I've seen.

The door stood wide, the embers aglow. By its light I saw the ravaged bed, the old woman lying there, her bonnet askew. Flakes danced over everything as if to hide the sight. Crows shrilled, interrupted at their feast. Eyeball in beak one flapped to the rafters, favouring the darkness there. The girl lay spreadeagled on the floor, her basket strewn beside her. Apples, cheese and oatcakes dotted the spill of her guts like a crate at some terrible harvest. The wolf hadn't cared for such comfits and taken the girl for his own. Half her face was gone, but I knew her for a villager. Blood and flesh painted the walls, none so red as her cape and hood tattered by the fire.

Did he make you undress? I'd heard of such things. *All the better to devour you...*

A lump rose in my throat at that, and one in my breeches to match, the thought of her hellish seduction, and the wolf, the beast who'd made it. I'd heard about him too.

A howl through the trees put me to flight, dashed the very blood out of me.

BEWARE GENTLE WOLVES. Never travel at night under a full moon. Childhood warnings sang in my skull, every snapped twig a bark, every gust a breath on the nape of my neck, rank with the scent of meat. What choice did I have, a poor woodcutter? The village looked to me for protection. Aye, I'd heard this tale before, the wolf come ravaging, the danger. As I climbed the white hills, it seemed it had been told a thousand times, spun like a web across time, and I tangled in the thread. Doomed to repeat my doom, you might say. The hunter and the hunted. The predator and prey. Who was who?

I climbed and I peered under the pines, my axe as keen as my eyes. I climbed until lights twinkled in the valley below, the dusk settling not long past midday. The smoke that curled from chimneys, the holy thrust of the church, an ocean, a world away. No icicle could match the one up my spine at the faint canticle afar, the distant howl of the wolf. A challenge. An invitation. Had the beast caught my scent too? I must reek of fear.

Father, I thought of you. For all your grey hair and crookedness, you might even come to outlive me. Annegret will feed you, no doubt, bring soup and bread from the inn. Zigmund, the blacksmith, who on occasion I dallied with behind the barn, will bring logs for your fire. What Franz the preacher would've made of it, how I let Zigmund into my mouth, hard as ironwood... How I suckled like a calf at teat, the longest draw for his milk! And I thought of rosy-cheeked mothers tucking in their children, all regretting their bedside tales now, of witches and wolves in the forest. There would be no tales tonight.

One, however, stayed with me, whispering in my ear as I built my paltry fire.

"A gentle wolf is made, not born," or so my father told me, back when the villagers still came to him for wisdom, for whiskey and wards. "One night many winters ago, a sleigh came a-riding through this valley. With every door closed and the watchman slumbering, a pack of wolves slipped out of the woods and fell into its speeding wake. Oh, such a howling you have never heard, boy. From the wolves. From the woman who rode on the seat. From the babe swaddled in her arms. The driver lashed at the horses and the farmer at the beasts, but naught could be done to dissuade them. When the pack at last overtook the sleigh, meaning to devour them all, the woman flung a prayer to the sky and her babe to the wolves, granting the party time to get away, gallop to the church. How she wept as the pack fell silent and the infant's cries besides.

Under the sainted beams, on the cold stone floor, she knew no God would ever answer her again..."

The story went that the child survived – at least so it sat upon some tongues – and was raised by a she-wolf in the briar. It accounted for the wiles of the beasts, they'd say, one of whom would sometimes walk under the moon on two legs and order a jug of ale from our very own inn. He was dark, they said, tall and silver-tongued, filled to the brim with charm. He'd tip the wench with gold, surprise the preacher by quoting verse and regale the whole room with accounts of travel in distant lands. But he'd never say where he came from, this man, and when he declared it was time to go empty his bladder, you'd never step outside with him into the cold. That was a gentle wolf, according to my father. That's what a gentle wolf was – one given to the devil and abandoned to the woods, and returning to both on four legs before dawn...

I'd never have believed it, old man, had I not seen the savage end of the girl and been spurred to plunge into the woods tonight. My regret grew deeper with the gloom. Why had I not brought Zigmund along? Summoned farmhands and the priest? There was a part of me, I acknowledged then, that wanted to see, to *know*. And to let no other detect my gaze, the curiosity there. Drowsy, aching under my skins, I looked up through the dying flames of my fire and saw a man standing under the trees.

Wolf!

Too late I reached for my axe. His foot came down, softly, on the handle. Only then did I mark his nakedness, his skin grey-gold in the embers, smooth as polished stone. A fuzz of hair covered his legs, which rose to his manhood between them. It dangled like ripe, forbidden fruit, and when I met his yellow gaze, my shame startled me along with my fear.

"Begone!" said I, abandoning the axe and scrambling away. Away from the fire, into the snow, for I knew at once who waylaid me. "Away with ye, Satan."

"Begone? Away?" the stranger said. "It was you who summoned me hence. The smell of you. Your need."

"Nay. Who are you that stalks the woods at night, putting fright to an honest woodcutter? Speak!"

"Does the wind have a name?" the stranger asked. Dark, he was. Tall and doubtless full of charm. "Do the trees that sieve it for secrets? Names aren't for the lost, Josef."

"Then what should I call you?" That he should know my name hardly surprised me; the servants of darkness snatch truth from a heart with sorcery and a wolf was a sorcerous thing. "The girl in the hood was innocent. I saw -"

"No one is innocent, least of all you," he said. "Not in your world, with its laws and traditions that leave no room for desire. The preacher would see you hang for them, but who am I to judge? Your God is not mine. I answer to the wild. If you must call me something, call me..." the man-that-was-no-man paused for a moment, plucking a name from the air, "Ingolf."

"I'll call you devil." If only I could wrongfoot him, dive for the axe. It was clear I had failed. I was going to die here on the hill, miles from home. There seemed no reason for courtesy. "I saw what you did to her, rakehell, and her grandmother besides. You ripped them apart like old cloth."

"Ah, Ingolf Rakehell. A fitting name." He smiled. His teeth had no place in a man's mouth, glinting between the fire and the moon. "All the better to make your acquaintance with."

"What manner of thing are you?" But I knew. Aye, I knew.

"I am of my nature. That is all."

"What's that, eh? Slaughter and ruin?"

"It is cold. I was hungry." The man, the beast, shrugged. How dare he look so fine in the firelight, a pillar of sinew and shadow? "As are you, Josef."

WATCH OUT FOR gentle wolves, friends. No wolf was ever gentle. They'll slip out under the cloak of night and flit from shadow to shadow like ghosts. So it seemed as I barrelled downhill, crashing through bramble and drifts. A branch whipped my cheek and speckled the snow like a prophecy, red foretelling red. I'd left my pack and my axe by the fire, and barely managed to grab my boots.

And the stones! Oh, the stones! Each one kissed by the village sage and graven with binding runes. *The girl will remain wandering the woods, butchered, bodiless and damned...*

As I plunged, huffing and sweating, I stole glances at the thicket on either side. The moonlight was most unkind. Sometimes I spied the man, his back and buttocks silver in the dark, racing between the pines in pursuit. A second glance and I saw nothing, nothing but the blanket of the hill, a virgin sheet for my blooding. A third and I made out the wolf, the coins of his eyes, his breath coiling from the brake.

There was no escaping this. Tales, I thought, are only good when one isn't in them.

As if prompted by the thought, by my pounding blood and the smell of me, the wolf came growling through the trees.

"There is another version of this tale, Woodcutter," said he. "In which I spare the girl and leave her a-weeping. But the wood in winter is cruel. Soon the girl ate all of the apples, cheese and oatcakes in the cottage. Starving, ravenous, she sought out rabbits and birds, but all were high in the boughs or asleep underground. By the end of the second day, while her grandmother softened and reeked, the girl turned her attention to the bed."

Wolf! Wolf! Every gasp, every step, seemed to shrill the same – *Wolf!* – but I couldn't help but hear him.

"Think of it," Ingolf went on. "Her little white teeth rending a heart, the blood hooding her hair. *Aaah.* And sweetmeats that she had no name for, sliding wet down her throat. And the tender muscle beneath, stewed with nettle and berry. And in time, the smallest bones she'd sucked clean. What of your laws and traditions then? The cold is the king of them all." The beast laughed, a snarl in the briar. "And a wolf is the king of the cold."

How I wished for the breath to beg him for silence! Or to offer a tale of my own, one father told me long ago, laying out the path of my fate. *Aye,* I might've said. *And a tale where the grandmother hides in a wardrobe and the woodcutter comes in time. With a swing of his axe, he slices you open from muzzle to balls, your wickedness undone. Then, with the help of the girl, he fills you with stones and buries you deep. All the better to keep you in your grave.*

There was no time nor the strength to say this. Nor would it have spared me from grief. As I reached a ring of boulders edging the bluff, there was nowhere left to run.

The wolf saw his chance and pounced.

GENTLY, HE TORE at me. Careful, his teeth. For though cuts marked my skin and I bled, it was my clothes that Ingolf shredded, peeling them off like a skin. In and out he darted, a fierce circle, swift under the moon. My coat lay in ribbons on my shoulders. My breeches a mere skirt of wool. Soon enough, the wolf had bared me to the cold and it was the cold I knelt to, exactly as he'd said.

"Finish it," said I, shivering on the ground. But Ingolf howled a laugh.

"How briskly you climbed the hills to find me." He

was drooling now, fixed on my naked bones. "How you slowed when you did. Is it death you seek, Josef? Truly?"

I thought of the girl, ruined on the floor. Why could the memory not hold me, douse the fire in my veins? Slaughter, damnation, quenched by desire. That's what a *man* was. A sob escaped me, a cloud like my soul swirling, adrift. I looked up at him then, my gentle wolf untouched by the cold. The way that the night etched him in silver... He was a man made of the wild and winter, bound together like hempen cords. It was a semblance, a mask hiding savagery. He was one abandoned to the forest, given to Satan and the moon. The buds of his nipples, hard on his chest. The throb of his manhood, lengthening now, blooded by the question.

He took a step forward. The snow hissed under his feet.

"The heat of you," I said.

"All the better to warm you with."

I gave myself to him then. There's no other way to tell it. I would've said the same to Franz the preacher in his confession box. But, as Ingolf closed around me and I melted against the fur of his chest, I know I would've sung it and laughed, glad to swing for this moment. All shame was gone from me, discarded like a cape and hood. Was this not why I had come?

Such a suckling commenced in the snow, the two of us folded, mouths to meat, a strange, eight-limbed animal. My head was full of him, his scent and the pines, the wet thawing earth, the wild. Ingolf nipped at me, my ears, my nipples, the nape of my neck. With each wound the hunger rose, blazing like doom in the forest. His finger, ice wet, slipped inside of me, into my burning hole. A calling. An invitation. I gave it no second thought. The hole with which I emptied myself would take something back for itself.

Panting, whining, I flung myself against the rock, my rump high, my legs spread to receive him, wide as a cottage door. Then came another blooding, the girth, the thrust of him painting patterns on the snow, the start of a new tale perhaps. Sweat-slicked, engorged, he worked his way inside of me. Together we rode like Selene in her chariot, out over the twinkling valley, out over the lands and the ocean beyond.

Come midnight, our song climbed higher than the wind. A chorus to crack the moon, bring her down from heaven.

Wolf. Wolf. Wolf.

FRIENDS, EMBRACE GENTLE wolves. Never listen to your mother. Always stray from the path. Travel at night under a full moon. Dally with the blacksmith behind the barn and laugh at village preachers. Give yourself to the forest, the devil and the moon.

Let the woods and the wild look to themselves.

On four legs, I run across the rise in the flood tide of dawn. Ingolf, my shadow, runs beside me. Yellow eyed, red tongue a-lolling, I see now and know. The breath of the night. The pulse in the earth and the sky. These are wonders, true, but oh, I have sights to show of my own! Down in the valley where the first fires glow there lies a feast that I shall place at his paws. Kind Annegret, plump and soft, savoury as her homemade soup. Zigmund, toughened by the anvil, toothsome as a tenderloin steak. Franz the preacher in his shrine of stone, a bitter pudding to cleanse the palette. Oh, and rosy-cheeked mothers and children in bed, all shivering and sweet, who'll feel no more cold come the end of this day.

And father, dear father, sat by the fire. Father with his wisdom, his whiskey and his wards, the last of which has proven true.

Of all wolves, the gentle are the worst.

ÍD⊙L⊙

THEY WERE UP in the mountains when the storm broke, under a clear blue sky.

"So what the fuck happened in New York?" Renzo asked him, thumping the steering wheel. "All this dancing around. Why don't you just come out and say it?"

He flicked his eyes, dark and full of Iberian fire, at Drew where he slumped in the passenger seat, his trainers up on the dash. They'd been driving for hours, west of Madrid and up into the Sierra de Francia, the massif that bordered the region of Extremadura and descended into Portugal. Low brown hills were giving way to the mountains proper, the road twisting, walls on either side. Since leaving the last remote, market-and-bar *pueblo* on their route, Drew had been sitting in silence, watching the miles slide by into the wilderness. The arid scrub. The bent trees. The occasional man with a mule. It was hot, even by Spanish standards. Irritation buzzed in the air like flies. Drew was trying to hide his pout. It was supposed to be a holiday.

"I've told you a hundred times," he said over the wind through the window. "Michael is a friend. The only reason we shared a hotel room was down to the budget. If you have a problem with that, speak to my agent."

Renzo, his fiancé, glared at the road. In the passing shutter of shadow and sun, he looked as fierce as Drew had ever seen him. *My bull. Mi toro.* Annoyingly, his strong jaw, brown locks and crooked nose still held the appeal they had the night that Drew had first met the photographer. In Soho, at a shoot two years ago. *Viral*, if he remembered correctly. Hadn't Renzo told him he shone brighter than his reflector kit, better in real life? English, blond, with the bleached smile that had seen him pose for several leading magazines, Drew could well believe it. His looks had never been in question. His behaviour, well...

"Oh, Renz. Drop it." He swallowed sarcasm, softening his tone. Best to get away from talk of Michael, the underwear model currently on trial – and *that* night. "You're going home. It's summer. You should be happy."

And I'm here, he thought, but didn't say. Drew rubbed the diamond on his finger as if to cast a spell. All he conjured was a snort.

"Mama is sick. Hardly time for a fiesta. It could be the last time I..." But Renzo wasn't ready to go there, biting back tears and glaring harder at the road. "I haven't been back since I left fifteen years ago."

Worms squirmed in Drew's guts. They'd been in Madrid when Renzo got the call, some relative or other passing on the news (Calaveras, the village to which they were headed, didn't have any reception, apparently. Shit, it'd never had a phone line according to Renzo). Meanwhile, Drew had been enjoying the bars of Chueca, revelling in cheap cocktails, cocaine and flirtation *sans* a punishing schedule for a change. He'd been drunk and building up to threatening Renzo to set a bloody date for the wedding when his lover had burst into the hotel bathroom, tearful and trembling. Stood in his jockstrap and looking forward to another night on the tiles, Drew had done his best to calm him down, making all the right noises, holding him. Shaking, Renzo had told him they had to make this trip into the mountains. Across fields of bony cattle, along a road that led nowhere. Who could live out here, he wondered? Who could stand the emptiness? Jesus, Renzo had done well to escape.

Drew reached over to the driver's seat, rubbed the back of Renzo's neck.

"I'm here for you, *tío*," he said. At least he'd picked up some Spanish in their time together. He'd even managed a smile when Renzo had said he'd booked a flight to Madrid instead of Mykonos. "It's going to be all right."

Drama. He should never have slept with Michael.

Renzo gripped the wheel and didn't smile.

AN HOUR LATER, high above the speck of Calaveras, Renzo pulled over to take in the view. The valley marched off into the sunset, a vista wreathed in a haze of distance, dotted by lakes and darting swallows. The smell of dust, peonies and pine was on the air. It was cooler up here. Drew suppressed a shiver of vertigo. No chance of a Mai Tai though. He went to pose on a rock, lizards skittering, but ended up cursing his phone. No reception meant no Instagram. How was he supposed to flex about his relationship sans social media? Their romantic-as-fuck road trip?

Gah. His stomach growled, but he didn't get his hopes up judging by the hovels below. Stew maybe. Sangria. Renzo was bored of him already, staring out into nothing. Nostalgic, probably. *He's such a dork.* Drew was about to bitch at him when he noticed the shrine.

"What the fuck is that?"

At the edge of the curve of dirt that passed for a layby, there rose a pile of rocks. On each, someone had painted a skull, adorning the mound with flowers, little wooden crucifixes, empty tumblers and coins. Atop the cairn was an effigy. Dusty and squat, the thing resembled the torso of a man, a scarecrow with sticks for arms. Faded ribbons fluttered in the breeze, its only attire. Photos and money too, pinned like trapped moths. Travellers must've left them here, paying their respects. Were the offerings for the lacquered face that crowned the figure? Under a wide-brimmed hat, a skull grinned, a cigar between its teeth. Candles, burnt down to stubs, peppered the figure's shoulders and the brim of its hat. In the deepening dusk, it was far from a pleasant sight.

"Ha," Renzo said, but he wasn't laughing. "Meet San Simón. The conquistadors brought him back from

Guatemala or so the villagers say. He's the patron saint of lovers. The guardian of marital virtue."

Drew half expected a look at that. Instead, Renzo crossed himself and kissed his fingers, then held them out to the idol.

"Yeah, he looks like he really cares."

"Hola, *abuelo*. I'm home."

Drew pulled a face. Flies were buzzing around the thing. It looked like living death.

Renzo was starting the engine.

IN THE LAST purple breath of dusk, they drove into Calaveras. The rental car was like an elderly chain-smoker, close to giving out. The road down to the crumbling rock shelf on which the village perched was a ladder of earth, stones like tiddlywinks under the wheels. There can't be more than twenty houses. Drew tried to count them, his nose wrinkling. Where are we supposed to stay? A banner with painted symbols, dried sheafs of wheat and small dangling objects hung over the main street – the only street – sun-bleached and tattered in the waning light. Elsewhere, Drew noticed ribbons on every balcony, pictures of nameless saints, the flat-roofed casas dark on all sides. Flowers lay strewn in the dust. There was no music. No chatter. Only the roosting birds.

"Four Seasons," Drew muttered.

Worst comes to worst, I can get Renz to get his camera out. He smoothed a sneer behind his hand. *Take some shots for National Geographic with me bare-chested and straddling a log.*

Renzo said nothing, his face unreadable.

Caught up in his homecoming. Me? I'd be pulling a U-turn and screaming.

A mangy goat staggered across the street, a bell around its neck. That was the only other living thing in sight until they reached the plaza in the middle of the village. In the dying light, Drew made out the glow of candles in the doorway of a large, gabled white building. A bent iron cross loomed from its lintel. *Ah, a church.* There were figures around the edge of the plaza, vaguely human, robed, stiff and unmoving. *More effigies. Great.*

They distracted him from the crowd before the building. Once he'd noticed them, he made out thirty odd people in the square. They were talking in low voices, shuffling in reverence. Had a service ended or was one beginning? He picked out rustic clothes and weatherworn faces, shadowed and inscrutable. Chatter fell silent as the car rolled into view. A palpable whisper, or maybe the wind, swept across the plaza. Also the smell of incense, sweet on the air.

Drew sensed every eye turn towards them. In the gloom, he saw that some in the crowd held instruments, bells, drums and tambourines. A girl with a trumpet. An elder with a guitar. Others were fussing around the feet of the idols, decorating the skirts of the resting *paso,* the large floats he'd seen carried like a litter through other Spanish streets in the past. Saint days in the country were far from rare. The preparations he was looking at could mean anything.

"What's with all the glitz?" The window was down and the villagers weren't far off. He spoke out the corner of his mouth.

"It's the Fiesta de San Simón," Renzo told him matter-of-factly. Funny he hadn't mentioned it up in the layby when Drew had seen the horror in rags. "We honour him at midnight."

We?

Renzo honked the horn, scattering birds and the chance of further enquiry. He shouted something in Spanish, loud and warm, a greeting that Drew didn't know.

"Hola," Drew said out the window. He gave a little wave.

The villagers stared back and said nothing.

IN A ROOM full of feathers and bones, Drew stood with his back to the wall and watched the old woman dying. And she was dying. Obvs. The room stank of it. The reek of herbs and smoke, remedies you wouldn't find in a chemist, was one thing. Dirty bedsheets and days' old vomit was another. It tested his gag reflex. It wasn't just the gewgaws dangling from the ceiling, the skeletal birds and the beads, a New Ager's wet dream in the candlelight. It was dim and there were too many people in the room, the atmosphere thick with anxiety and sweat. Who are these visitors? he wondered. Family? Renzo had never mentioned any siblings. Come to think of it, he'd barely mentioned Calaveras until he'd got the call in Madrid.

Some holiday.

Most in the vigil were weeping. Nobody spoke. The woman in the bed looked as parched as the effigy above the town, sticklike and small. Her eyes rolled behind spiderweb lids, the only animation in a husk of leather and bone. Spittle dotted the corners of her mouth. Drew found it hard to look at her. Christ, he wanted a cigarette. It was his turn to glare at Renzo, or at least at the back of his head. He was kneeling on the floor beside the bed. He held his mother's hand in his, enfolding fingers that looked as brittle as the things on the ceiling. He bowed his head as she mustered the strength to gasp something out, too faint for Drew to hear. Not that he'd understand anyway.

Suddenly, Renzo was a man he barely knew. He wasn't the hombre who'd pursued him from New York to London with phone calls, hotel sex and eventually a diamond ring. Strong, handsome, brooding Renzo, who struck him now as stubborn and selfish, uncaring of his husband-to-be who he'd torn away from all his fun to this dump. Why had Renzo insisted he come? He could've easily made the drive alone, reuniting with him later in Madrid. He sighed, restless. They both knew the answer to that.

The woman, Mama, coughed – long enough to make Drew fear that she was going to fall to pieces. When Renzo turned to look at him, with his sad, brown eyes, it took him a moment to realise that she'd spoken his name.

"Come. She wants to give you her blessing."

Drew returned a pained smile. At the sight of the corpse-in-waiting, her twig of an arm stretching towards him, he gulped in a lungful of smoke.

"It's fine." *I'm good.* "Please don't go to any trouble."

"*Venga!*"

Smile etched on his face, Drew obliged. Renzo took his hand and pulled him down – gently, though his expression suggested he wanted to wrench. Then he stood, leaving Drew perched on the edge on the bed. The old woman, Mama, took his hands. They were clammy in his, fish on a sun-warmed rock. Rotten.

"*Mi hijo,*" she said, with the same struggling breaths. "*Dígame. ¿Crees que Dios favorece a los fieles?*"

Drew turned his face up to Renzo. He didn't know what she asked of him. Didn't know what to say. Renzo made a sharp, encouraging gesture. But it was Mama who drew his attention back to her, her nails digging into his flesh. Her grip was remarkably strong.

"Ow," he said, his head turning.

That's when she spat in his face. Most of it went in his mouth.

"IT WAS A blessing, Drew. A bendición."

The two of them were in the bedroom at the back of the casa, no more than a cell with a slit of a window. Some dead flowers in a jug. A rusting double bed. *The Ritz.*

"Ew!" Drew, who'd been crying, pretended to retch. Then he threw the towel he was holding at Renzo. "Why did you bring me here? It's *hellish.*"

"Keep your voice down. Mama will hear you."

"Fuck you." It was unlikely that Mama would hear anything except her own splutters and croaks. "You've been acting weird since we left Madrid. What's up with you? Is this some kind of punishment?"

Renzo folded his arms. "Now why would you think that?"

Drew hesitated. Colour burned in his cheeks. He felt as transparent as glass.

"I told you -"

"I don't believe you. I've looked at your phone. You haven't answered any of his calls or replied to his texts. Why not?"

"Oh, so you're spying on me now."

"You cheated on me. Didn't you?"

"*¡No más preguntas, por favor!*"

No more questions. Drew shrieked it, childish in his own ears. Then he was crying again – real tears this time – unable to bear it out. The lie. There was only a need for escape. For a fucking cigarette. The hole in which he found himself was full of anger and death, sucking him down.

When Renzo spoke next, his voice was a flat, cold knife.

"Drew, I'm not going to marry you."

Drew reeled, the words like a slap. Renzo had become a blur, his eyes sombre, unblinking.

He means it. He means it.

"You brought me here to tell me this? At your mother's deathbed?" It was a low blow, but it thrilled him, rage spiking through his shock. "Fine. Go fuck yourself. Tell me the next bus out of this shithole and yours truly will be on it. You'll never have to see me again."

"There is no bus."

Renzo looked so calm, so unmoved by the ultimatum, that it spurred Drew to recklessness. Though he regretted it as he was doing it, he wrenched off his ring and threw it at the man before him.

"Keep it, *cabrón.*" His venom bounced off the peeling walls. "I'll walk home."

The ring sparkled on the tiled floor. Drew headed for the door.

"Maybe Michael will come pick you up," Renzo said as he fled.

BASTARD! PAYING NO mind to where he was going, Drew stormed out of the casa and into Calaveras. Alleys ran between the low cramped houses and the moon had risen, lighting cracked sections of weed-choked walls. It wasn't a big place; he soon found himself on the edge of the village looking out at the mountains through his tears. A hawk called in the darkness. The air was heavy with the heat of the day, fading like his sobs. Miles away, he made out the twinkle of lights. Probably another pueblo as remote and shitty as this one. His shoulders slumped as he accepted it; he was stuck here, at the mercy of Renzo and the hire car.

Shit.

"This is all your fault," he told himself. "You stupid bitch." He slapped his cheek for good measure, a habit carried over from youth when he'd lock himself in a cupboard and swear he'd get out, get away, become a star and shit on them all… He was already thinking about damage control. A break up wouldn't be good for his image, not now when so many had bought into the fairy tale. *20K followers!* Plus all those modelling contracts that Renz had promised him, a foot in the door with several top studios… As for love –

He was thinking of turning back, giving Renzo his best remorseful, blue-eyed look (and perhaps a reconciliatory blow job) when he heard the scream. At first, he thought it was a cat, some flea-bitten stray among the cacti and dust. But there was a tone to it, almost a lament, that pinged in his bones, making him taut. It was unmistakably human. A prayer? Some religious entreaty? The echoes seemed to come from the direction of the church.

Despite himself, his trainers swivelled in that direction. There'd still be people in the plaza, surely, and warmth. He was getting thirsty too, his mouth full of dust and unspoken reproach. Where better to calm down than in the large white building? He might even take in the midnight parade, pay his respects to San Simón with a glass of vino or five. Forget about Renzo for the night…

Drew was heading between the houses, the windows dark apart from the occasional candle, when he heard a scuffling behind him. Not too close, but close enough for him to stop and wonder. Some animal, rooting through the trash? He huffed and moved onwards, drawing to a halt at a crossroads between the huddled buildings. This time, he caught the sound of footsteps, echoes fading behind him. He'd have thought nothing of it except they seemed to stop whenever he did. Where the fuck was the main street? He could navigate from there. The closely packed casas were a labyrinth with no streetlights to guide him. The moon didn't reach down here and the shadows seemed thick, unfriendly. He took out his phone, but he'd forgotten to charge it. Suddenly, he seemed a million miles from anywhere. Even Renzo didn't know where he was.

Is he chasing after me? He shivered in triumph at the thought. *Yes, poor Renzo, heartbroken and looking for me in the dark, an apology on his lips...*

To test his theory, Drew moved on, slower this time. His heart was a techno beat in his chest and he found himself thinking of other things, things he didn't want to. The grin of the effigy up in the layby. The coughing old lady. The items dangling from the ceiling in the room. *Feathers. Bones.* He realised they'd been dangling over the street when they drove into Calaveras too, adorning the backwater fiesta. *Yes, little bones. From birds or God knows what...*

Instinct chimed in him, his guts twisting. Dashing sweat from his eyes, he flicked a glance over his shoulder. Again, he heard footsteps, the scuttling of someone in the alleyway behind him, stumbling in his direction. When he saw the silhouette pass between the houses, vague in the gloom, his heart leapt into his throat. *What the -?* Whoever it was, it wasn't Renzo. Not unless he'd shrunk by a foot and was sporting a wide-brimmed hat.

"Hello? Who's there?" He realised he should probably try Spanish; his nerves were making a fool of him. "What the fuck do you want?"

Did a place this small have street crime? In the dark, he heard a croak like an answer. A greeting? A laugh? The figure had stopped a few feet away. Stopped when *he'd* stopped, rigid in the dark. The tang of sweat carried on the breeze, along with something sweeter, the same incense as before. Then Drew caught the scent of tobacco a moment before a cigar flared in the darkness, a crimson eye that was closer than he'd thought.

The figure said nothing. There was a man. A dark little man, watching him in the alley.

It was all Drew needed to turn and run.

BY THE TIME he was jogging down main street, Drew was giving serious thought to calling Michael, after all. He didn't hold out much hope. A model who'd graced the pages of Esquire wasn't going to jump on a plane and then drive hours to save him. When he looked at his phone, the dead black screen, he remembered that there was no reception up here anyway. Fabulous. Reaching the edge of the plaza, Drew chanced a glance behind him.

All he saw was an empty street. The wind blew scrub and dirt across it. Hands on knees, he was recovering his breath, relieved without knowing why. So a villager had approached him in the alley? Big deal. Probably nothing else to do out here except bum cigarettes and cruise...

The moon was risen and full. Drew wasn't the outdoorsy type, but he judged the hour around nine. Where were all the people? The plaza was a cracked and empty expanse, surrounded by squat houses. They looked no more appealing than crates. The flagstones and tiles gleamed like milk. The night was warm, the heat in the air, but his blood cooled when he remembered the effigies lining the square. In tattered rows, they looked down on him from their *pasos,* the wooden platforms on which the villagers bore them garlanded with ribbons and flowers. There must've been twenty of them or more, the semblance of saints he didn't know in crinkled robes with paper crowns, veils and halos on their heads. Jewels hung around their necks along with crosses and beads, the knickknacks of some obscure Catholic ritual.

Drew fought an impulse to hide. It was their faces he didn't want to look at. Each one seemed lifelike under the moon, glazed in brown lacquer, granting the semblance of flesh. Some of the effigies looked fresher than others. Some looked old indeed, painted over many times, their hands like sticks and their cheeks peeling. Eyes like marbles stared unseeing. Teeth shone with the lustre of pearls. In rustling silence, the idols of the midnight parade waited for the hour of their worship.

Christ, I don't want to be here. He wondered if he could find his way back to Mama's house, though he hardly wanted to be there either, among the sickness and the bones. *Might as well click your heels three times.* It was dark and he was spooking himself. These people ate late and were probably at some dinner or other, marking their holy day. No one was going to hurt him out here, not in the Spanish wilderness. The country was famous for its hospitality – not that he'd seen much of it in Calaveras.

This'll make a good update. The idea made him snort. *The male model lost in the mountains, his Prada shirt snagged on a cactus.*

He could play it for sympathy, granted. Whatever happened, Renzo was getting flamed, and on all his social media. Sure, people went funny in grief, he knew that, but right in the middle of his holiday? Dragging him into this hole? *Bitch, please.*

Light from the church caught his attention. The glow was so faint he hadn't noticed it before. Now, with growing relief, he made his way to it, skipping over the flagstones under the blank eyes of saints. With a creak, he pushed the door inward. The first thing that hit him was the smell, the incense thicker than before. In quick succession, he took in the source of it. A little old man was working in the nave, the pews pushed back to give him room. Next to him, a large vat bubbled over a fire, flames rising from a small tiled pit under it. The liquid in the vat was thick and brown, and the man was applying it with a brush to the figure before him, a naked, life-sized mannequin clearly meant to join the ranks of the others outside.

It was an odd sight, but what wasn't in this dump? The old man hadn't heard Drew by the door. Pinching his nose, he meant to call out, ask for directions, a way back to the casa and Renzo. This was dumb. He should probably say sorry. But something prevented him from entering, something off about the scene. He was trying to place *what* when his guts twisted, a gasp escaping him.

No.

Drew stumbled back from the doorway, the sight imprinted on his shock. The flutter of an eyelid, the twitch of a finger – both had been unmistakable, tipping his view of the nave on its head. A hundred awful thoughts crowded his mind, the source of the scream he'd heard earlier pushing to the forefront. *Jesus.* Taking in the rictus of the idol, the hardness of its stare, Drew knew there was nothing it could tell him. He heard its terror all the same.

He spun on his heel. He had to get out of here. Someone barred his way, a shadow in a striped shirt. It was the little man from the alleyway, he saw, a cigar stuck between his teeth.

In the gloom, his grin seemed as wide as the brim of his hat.

"*Noches,*" the man said.

*

HIGH ABOVE THE crowd, Drew led the parade. For hours, he'd stood in the nave, drugged, naked and strapped to a wooden frame. The herbs they'd given him swirled in his blood. He hadn't felt much pain as they'd scrubbed and painted him, the resin hot on his skin. He'd slipped in and out of consciousness, fading and waking to prayers. There was a bitterness under the incense. Now, robed and jewelled, he was borne through Calaveras under the stars. It was midnight. The Fiesta de San Simón was underway.

On both sides of the street, the faithful flocked, throwing coins and flowers. Tambourines shook. Trumpets blared. Drums echoed off stone and the sky.

"Vaya con Dios!" they cried. And, *"Para los Muertos!"*

For the dead. His limited Spanish was still with him. San Simón had come to protect all in the village. Avenge himself on false lovers and vice, just like Renzo had told him. In fact, it was a parade of the lovers that Drew represented, he realised then. Some had been sublimed years ago. Others judged more recently. Hadn't the old man told him so in among his chants? Yes, Drew had heard him when his voice had given out, when he'd finally stopped screaming. Screaming was pointless, anyway. Who was there to hear him?

Dried flowers rustled on his head. Arms stiff and spread, the procession carried him towards the mountains. He'd have closed his eyes if he could, offer a prayer of his own, not that he was religious. It would've spared him the sight of Renzo. His former fiancé stood under the banner on the edge of town, looking up at him in the crowd and smiling. *Those dark, Iberian eyes...* Reverence lit his face like a lamp. *Mi toro.* Reverence at the offering, the sacrifice he'd brought home to the village. His anger, smouldering for days, finally had an answer. Seeing him encased in lacquer, Drew guessed he'd be free of it now.

A tear trickled from the corner of his eye. Would his rictus pass for a smile, he wondered? A grin of farewell? It was too late for anything else. No one knew he was here. How would they look for him? Up in the hills, he'd watch the days pass. At least until the birds pecked out his eyes. Until lack of water shrivelled him, made of him a husk like the other idols. Would the numbness wear off before that? He thought so. Even then, he'd remain, something for the faithful to stop and look at. Kiss their fingers and pray. Beg blessings of San Simón.

Drew was for the dead now.

Still, he was adored.

SULTA

THEY SAY THE camera never lies, but Tate knows that isn't true. These days, a tog like him has as many tricks up his sleeve as your average Instagrammer, from polarizing filters to adjusting white balance to colour saturation. It's no longer simply a question of how much light you let in through an aperture, the range of a lens or the power of the flash. That's why when he got back to New York, the pictures he'd taken in Mørkfjord puzzled him. The shrine on the isthmus, no more than a pile of old rocks, had been cramped and dark. Hell, all of Norway was dark, the days swathed in the depthless blue of the polar night. He's no amateur, but still. The photos shouldn't have come out as clearly as they have.

He's scowling at his laptop when Walt hunts him down in his study, a wineglass swinging under his nose as his arms close around him, a chin resting on his shoulder. They're together again, an Afro-Caribbean couple in New York. Their success against the odds.

"Are you gonna sit here all night? You've been gone

for weeks, Tate."

"Got a date with *Unseen World* in the morning." This is probably a good enough excuse; freelance photojournalism pays the bills and boy, is the mag going to love these shots. A Nordic Bronze Age shrine where no one has set foot for thousands of years? Where even the locals never set foot? Come on. "Took enough to get a pitch meeting. I want to straighten my pics up a little."

He remembers the little old man on the jetty. The knot of his face, his salt-stiffened beard.

No one goes out there, he said. *Some things* should *go unseen.*

"Mm. There's something *I* want to straighten up a little."

Tate laughs, but holds his ground. "Walt, it's kind of a once-in-a-lifetime deal."

And it is. The magazine is going to pay a heap of bucks for his snaps of Mørkfjord. But that's nothing compared to the exposure, the name he's on the verge of making for himself. *For them.* Tate Miller. The new Ansel Adams. He's wanted this ever since leaving high school in Queens. Walt can understand, but not *feel* it.

"Weren't you cold up there? Bet it made winter in the city feel like a sauna." Walt sets his glass down on Tate's desk, close enough to his Sony Alpha 9 that he winces. It cost him six thousand bucks, after all, and Walt isn't going to pay for a replacement on a Brooklyn schoolteacher's wages. His hands are moving towards his lap now, broad and smooth. "Don't you wanna warm up some?"

That's when Walt's head comes level with the screen and he sees her. Sulta. Sulta is what they call her in Mørkfjord, anyway. In lowered voices. With hooded looks. It means 'starving' as far as Google Translate goes. No wonder it took so long to tease it out of the villagers. A finger of ice from the isthmus creeps into his West Village apartment. Then under his cashmere sweater, his skin prickling like the day he found her.

"Jesus. What the fuck is that?"

The image on the screen should be a blur, considering the conditions when Tate reached the shrine, the sun conquered by the horizon for weeks on end and the afternoon gloom sinking into black. Remarkably, the carvings inside came out OK. The petroglyphs too, strange and looping, that surround the graven stone. The cracked disc of the idol's face, her hair snaking across the surrounding wall. Her mouth a broad slot of shadow. A hole through which the wind sings, arctic and shrill.

No one visits her now.

"Not a what. A who." Tate shuts the laptop lid, the altar eclipsed. "Sulta. She's a goddess. They call her the Hungerer."

Walt releases him. He's standing and looking down. To lighten the mood, and because the camera on his desk reminds him too much of that hollow mouth, he swivels in his chair and raises it before him.

"Smile!"

The flash goes off, painting Walt's revulsion in white.

★

ANYWHERE NORTH OF Trondheim is nowhere or so his guidebook tells him. It's November and the steep slopes, which are practically dayglo green in summer, only show in patches through the snow. Tate loads his hired jeep up with food, blankets and gas. The long road winding through the mountains makes him worry whether they'll be enough. He passes stave churches with layers of triangular roofs. Forests of pine so closely packed they form a wall of darkness. High twisted crags. Waterfalls and rustads, the little hillside farms. The place is a far cry from New York and the task ahead of him nothing like the fashion shoots or the urban scenery he's been snapping in the city, turning them over for a quick buck. When he caught wind of Unseen World's open call for a feature on 'hidden places', he bit his lip and bought the camera. Then a plane ticket. North of Trondheim is where he must go.

Walt asked him not to, but Kasper, the boatman, is more explicit.

"Even the Vikings avoided the place." His English is good, but he sounds edgy like everyone else's he's spoken to in Mørkfjord whenever he brings up the old tale. About the shrine. The Hungerer. He came across it in *Troll Country: Rare Myths and Forgotten Places,* borrowed from the Hudson Park Library. Now the book is well-thumbed and past its return date. "The standing stones on the headland," the old man points as if Tate can see through the mist coiling off the water, "warn against going there, each one carved with a rune. This is highly irregular. If the locals hear of it, they won't talk to me for months."

Bundled up in his Parka, Tate weighs the camera around his neck as if to convey the deal they've made. *Good job I paid you in dollars and not krone then,* he wants to say. *Made it worth your while.* The environs, grey ripples and shrouded land, don't lend themselves readily to sarcasm. It's a shrine he's going to and the air itself feels sacred, untouched. The cold grips him like a rebuke and he'll disturb it with his breath alone, ragged and steaming.

"I'll be ten minutes. In and out."

The keel bumps against shoals. A stunted tree emerges to greet them. The shallows lie as still as a mirror, reflecting cloud. Kasper has brought him to the isthmus.

"Half the village is empty and no one visits her now," the old man says, shivering. "Might be worth heeding the old ways, son. If you want something from her, maybe give something in return. That's the custom."

A joke to scare tourists? A way to get more cash? Tate can't tell. The boatman's beard, salt-stiff and white, is a briar of secrets.

"I'll give her the cover of a national magazine."

Then Tate is stepping from the boat, stepping into dreams and memory again. He doesn't hear Walt groan in the night, a warm weight shifting beside him. He doesn't hear the while in Walt's throat or notice the silence that follows.

Tate sleeps on, as oblivious as when he was straying onto holy ground.

*

IN THE OLD days, Tate heard, some cultures used to believe that the camera could steal a person's soul. Tribespeople would scream and duck out of sight on the plains, in the jungles, if an explorer tried to snap them. Did they think the lens would snare them forever, trap them behind glass? The idea springs to mind the next morning when he wakes up and finds Walt. It doesn't seem half as quirky when he lays eyes on his corpse.

"No."

Fingers gripping the arms of the chair, Walt is sitting in a rigid position before Tate's desk. The laptop remains closed. The camera is a black bug, watching. Walt stares back, dumbstruck and cold. Whatever he's seen has snatched the life from him. There is no blood. No sign of a struggle. Only ashen skin and gaunt cheekbones. Tate can see the veins in Walt's temples, blue like the northernmost skies after a Finnmark sunset.

A heart attack? A stroke?

It hits him. A gasp and Tate is falling into the bookshelf, airport bestsellers and 'How To' guides raining down. He lets himself slide with them, his gaze fixed on Walt. He sits there for a long time, counting his shuddering breaths. His thoughts ricochet. The smart thing to do would be to dial 911. Except it's 10am. He has the appointment of a lifetime with the magazine. Can he reschedule? Can he afford to do that? Really? Tate is on his feet and heading for the shower, second guessing his every move. Telling himself that he can't change anything. Walt isn't going anywhere, no. His camera, shiny and black, reflects him in miniature as he shoves himself trembling into his suit, picks up his kit and shoves the Alpha into his backpack.

"Fuck. I'm actually leaving the apartment."

Stupidly, he says this to himself in the elevator. It doesn't change his mind. His heart is a jackhammer, but Walt would understand, wouldn't he? He didn't go all the way to Mørkfjord for nothing. Later he can discover the body. Yes. Later, he can tell the cops he stayed with a friend near the airport, came home to his apartment from the pitch meeting, found his dead boyfriend. Later, he'd have sold the photos and have some kind of future ahead of him. Walt wouldn't want to stand in his way…

Yeah, a tog hears all the stories. In the old days, people used to believe you could scrape the very last image a person saw from the back of a corpse's eye.

Collar up against the rain, Tate wonders what it was that Walt saw as he shouts for a taxi.

IN THE BOARDROOM on the sixth floor of 67th Street, Tate sweats and makes his pitch. There's a large, framed picture on the wall of a breaching whale. Corny. Headshots line the room, each one the Photographer of the Year at some point. The envy Tate feels keeps him upright before the long polished table, braced against the judgement of the agents who sit there (and pushing his guilt about

Walt – poor, dead, abandoned Walt – to the back of his mind). There are three of them, two men and a woman. In their sharp grey suits, their faces are masks of corporate interest. The blinds are closed, but their eyes gleam in the glow of the widescreen TV. If eyes are the windows of the soul, then he can tell that they're already bored. He's one of a hundred that Unseen World will see this week. He has to knock it out of the park.

"Thousands of years before the Christian era," he begins, "we worshipped hungry gods."

He's hooked up his Alpha to his laptop and his laptop to the TV, courtesy of USB. Onscreen, the first shot reveals a huddle of snowy rooftops around the leaden Norwegian bay, setting the scene. Isolated. Below zero. The untouched places of the world. He tells them the village is called Mørkfjord and that humans have lived in the area since the Stone Age. Next there's a shot of the isthmus, a bleak narrow strip winding out across the mudflats and the water beyond. There's the boatman, Kasper, unsmiling. He clicks the wireless presentation pointer and reveals the exterior of the shrine, the low stone dome with the iron crosses around it (a later addition, he tells them. Sixteenth century). One of the guys is halfway to stifling a yawn when Tate clicks again and reveals the interior.

"Jesus."

"Is this some kind of joke?"

The agents sit back in their seats, aghast. In the split-second between Tate's faltering spiel and the realisation that something is wrong, a smile flickers at the corners of his mouth. The altar has stolen their attention. *Sulta* has stolen their attention, just like she stole his breath when he first stepped into the shrine.

'She is the wind. The sky. The sea.' That's what the old man said, repeating the story, the myth. 'She is an emptiness that cannot be filled.'

Tate's pride shrivels up as he turns to regard the image of the cold black stone, the carvings on the wall, and he sees the problem. Captured in HD, the altar, a slab of weatherworn, frost-speckled stone that he found on the day he entered (*trespassed,* a voice whispers in his head) is no longer bare. Instead, a riddle of flesh adorns the surface, naked and pale. He sees bodies stacked like sides of beef, their limbs entwined in what might've been ecstasy if not for all the blood. With a gasp, he makes out the torn remnants of breasts. Raw holes in place of eye and phallus. Caught in the glare of the flash, Tate sees legs hooked through arms, each one threaded together in a loose knot before Sulta on the wall, her howling mouth in 24.2 megapixels. He meets her graven eyes like a penitent and fights the urge to kneel, to beg. *Please.* It's the object in the middle distance, crowning the heap of offered meat, that stuffs his scream back down his throat.

God.

An infant rests there, shrunken and blue. It's this grim cherry on the gruesome cake that he guesses the agents are reacting to, one of the men climbing to his feet.

"I hope that's art," he says, a finger shaking at the screen. "Either way, we're not making a horror movie here, Mr Miller."

"Wait. I can explain."

Can I? A dark miracle is unfolding in the boardroom, because when Tate stepped into the shrine at Mørkfjord it sure as hell was empty except for the wind. Except for Sulta. How the fuck can this be?

Frantically, he clicks the pointer. He wants to erase the sight of the slaughter, the sacrifice. Could someone have meddled with his camera? Was it some elaborate prank? But Walt wouldn't know how. And besides, Walt was -

"Fuck."

The woman, hand over mouth, has forgotten her professionalism. Another photo has replaced the interior of the shrine, Tate realises. It's Walt. A closeup of Walt in the worst of all snapshots. His eyes are orbs devoid of pupils. His mouth a maw of silent agony. Veins stand out on his forehead, his cheeks. Tate can see there's something off about the image, a distortion that lends it a terrible weight. It's as if Walt is made of cellophane and someone has taken the end of a vacuum cleaner to it, leaving it shrivelled, sucked inward.

"Mr Miller, we've seen enough."

Agent number one reaches for the camera on the laptop stand. Before Tate can stop himself he's leaping forward, snatching at the device. It's more than possessiveness. More than the expense. Somehow he knows that. The woman yells, nonsensical. There's a moment of struggle, a ridiculous scuffle.

"Don't..." Tate forces the words through his teeth. "Don't touch..."

The stand tips over, the laptop crashing to the floor. The screen blinks out, a darkness that Tate would've found welcome had he paused to notice it. In his grip, the camera pulses. The flash goes off, lightning bright in the shaded room. For a moment, everything goes white. Tate blinks, his vision clearing, and he realises he's been released. The silence is so sudden it's profound.

The agents are on the floor. Unmoving.

OUT ON THE isthmus, Tate trudges across the spongy ground, his camera clutched to his chest like a second heart. The air is empty, but full of knives, each one keen to sink through his Parka, through his fleece and into his skin. A man could freeze out here in minutes and Kasper said he wouldn't wait long, his commitment palpably waning the closer the boat drew to the shrine. In turn, his muttering increased, crazy backwater talk of wind and sea and emptiness.

There's no path, he said. *The ones who came this way are centuries dead.*

This bears out as Tate makes his way to the dome up ahead. There isn't even a *suggestion* of a path, only brambles and tufts of sedge. Twice, he falters, wincing. Around the crumbling site, someone has driven crosses into the ground. Fifty, a hundred crosses surround the shrine. Lutheran pilgrims in the fifteen hundreds, according to his research. The crosses peep through the mist like raised swords, challenging his progress. Salt and time have rusted them black. *Snap. Snap.* Tate takes some pictures and continues, but he isn't watching his feet like he should be. He nicks himself on metal, once on his upper arm, once on his calf. He swears, but presses onwards. He doesn't see it, but blood speckles the frozen earth.

Steam coils off the grass.

DON'T TOUCH HER. That's what Tate was going to say to the agent. How crazy is that? Now, he's on Line 4 rattling under Greenpoint, sat in a crowded subway carriage and shaking his head. There are executives behind newspapers. A kid playing around a pole. With his gear hastily packed, Tate fled the building, leaving security to discover the bodies. He should've alerted someone, he knows. It was the same way with Walt. When he saw the state of the agents, withered on the floor, the terror on their faces, logic flew from him. How could he have explained it? How could he have told some secretary or other? Now dread was seeping into him, a touch of Barents Sea ice among the huddled passengers.

I'm not thinking straight. No shit. *It's the camera. Something got into it.*

Something... But it's true when he touches his precious Alpha in his lap – and he is always touching the Alpha – that his panic subsides, his heart slows, fading into a background hum of unease when he should be screaming, when his mind should be falling apart. Likewise, his feelings for Walt seem clouded. He loved the guy, didn't he? The guy who is currently growing stiff on the floor of his study. But no tears have come and the camera feels warm, throbbing slightly. A comfort.

He mutters to himself. "If you want something from her, give something in return."

Opposite him, an old lady who shares the colour of his skin looks at him like he needs help. None of it makes any sense. Except, in a horrible way, it does.

When the cops get on at Nassau Avenue, Tate climbs to his feet. There are two of them in black caps and jackets, guns holstered on their hips. He's sweating again, his breath coming hard. The old lady tuts at him. She's had enough of his nonsense and maybe she's right. There's no way he can tell if the cops are looking for him. No way to know if security discovered the bodies in the boardroom and dialled 911, spluttering out his description, his address. The route home he'd have taken. He can't know that for sure.

The cops are making their way up the carriage through the corridor of knees. The kid stops swinging on the pole, his mother's hisses returning him to his seat. One of the cops notices Tate, standing further up the carriage, a trembling, glistening figure. *Shit.* It's his stare, his tension, that's lent him a spotlight. The man reacts, an instinctive motion, reaching for his gun when he sees Tate raise the camera. There's a little distance between them. Can the cop even tell it's a camera?

The flash goes off before he finds out. Before the cop can shout, draw his gun. Electrodes spark. Xenon ignites. White light stutters down the length of the carriage, quick as a chameleon's tongue. There's a familiar split-second of nowhere, a world suspended in blankness. In its wake, Tate watches the cops fall to the floor. Executives lay in a litter of rags. The kid is slumped in his mom's lap, her head lolling on his back. *Every* head in the carriage lolls. It's as if everyone has fallen asleep at the same time, but Tate knows they aren't sleeping. The old lady has slipped off her seat, sprawled at his feet in a mess of scattered shopping.

The camera thrums as though sated.

Sulta. His head goes. *Sulta. Sulta.*

'The old ways,' Kasper told him.

The train rattles on and Tate wonders what the hell he's given her, what she's taken in return.

THE SUBWAY ISN'T safe. People are screaming on the platform. Other cops will come and soon. Before anyone can stop him, ask him what went down, Tate disembarks and switches to the M-Line, then jumps off at Marcy Avenue. He's back in Queens, but he doesn't mind. It's home, after all. Where he began. The buildings around him feel like shelter, grey and grimy wings. Heading west down Broadway, he passes under the shadow of the Williamsburg Bridge, the skeleton of some gigantic prehistoric snake or so he's thought of it since childhood. Now another monster has come. Older.

Traffic honks. Pedestrians pass by. He doesn't look at them. Feels guilty. He looks at his feet and clings to the camera around his neck.

Hush, she tells him, a whisper in his head. *Hush, my servant.*

Surely he's imagining it. Part of his breakdown. Lightly, his fingertips graze the buttons. The LCD display is a dull black rectangle, as inviting as it is repellent. Dare he look at the shots he's taken? Walt, petrified. The agents, fallen. Cops and thirty odd passengers on the subway, all of them drained. And whatever it is he snapped in the Mørkfjord shrine – the shrine that was there before there *was* a Mørkfjord. The altar. The petroglyphs. The one who dwelt within.

Sulta. The Hungerer.

At the entrance to Domino Park, Tate steels himself and clicks. The LCD display blinks into life. He's expecting to see his last shot, the interior of the train carriage, and his bark echoes through the day. Pigeons flutter, sharing his alarm. The screen, as it happens, is far from still. It's *moving.* Moving in a way no photo should move. Hands, white as the hilltops of Finnmark, are pressing against the inside of the glass, shrunken and tiny. The image teems, desperate, and beyond the scrabbling fingers and palms,

Tate thinks he can make out faces, little faces spectral and drawn, swirling in the depths of the camera. In the guts of the device, the Alpha. But that is insane.

"It isn't a camera anymore," he tells himself. "It's a mouth."

Yes, it is *fucking insane.* But that doesn't mean it's untrue.

Tate wants to get rid of the camera. It's an obvious decision. Sure, he could press 'delete all'. Somehow, he knows it won't do. There's a vampire hung around his neck, sucking at the world. Groaning, he hurries through the park to the railings, looks out over the East River, another grey expanse. The skyscrapers of the Lower East Side stare back at him, indifferent titans. An airplane pisses smoke across the sky. Tate tears the Alpha from him, winds back an arm to hurl the device into the water, into the depths where it belongs. Fuck the six thousand bucks. The camera throbs, warm and fleshy in his grip. Tate wants to get rid of it, but can't.

That wasn't part of the deal.

IN THE SHRINE, in the gloom, out on the isthmus beyond Mørkfjord, Tate sucks in his breath and raises his camera before the altar. Black stone regards him, shaped to resemble the face of a woman, raging and pained, her hair weaving across the wall. But it's her mouth, a broad black slot, that speaks with the wind, the air howling through the ingress. Flakes dance in the darkness. The granite rumbles. He's awed by the sight, an ancient marvel that no one has laid eyes on in hundreds of years according to the villager, the boatman. His heart is a ball of excitement, tight with the thought of the magazine's reaction, the fame and the money that must surely follow. He has travelled so far. To the end of the world.

The flash illuminates her worn features, her hollow glare. The wind is ceaseless and Tate lacks the knowledge to decipher her commands, but obeys nonetheless. The way she tells him to kneel. The curses she heaps upon him. *Do you not know me,* she shrieks? Can he not see down the tunnel of years, of centuries, to measure the ones she's devoured? Men, women, children – people who came to these shores in flimsy ships and laid flowers and stones as if either were enough to appease her. Before that, beasts who strayed into the shrine for shelter, wolves, seagulls and snakes. And before that, the stars, the cold accursed stars, the consumption of which led to her imprisonment. Into her, all of them have gone, all that she surveyed. Their souls siphoned, drawn down her undying throat.

Fool! Of course no mortal can see it. All they can do is witness the silence in the wake of her hunger, the divine emptiness, and keep a fearful distance. Have they written of her in their books, she wonders. As fragile, as fleeting as they. Are there tales and maps that have led the man to her, inviting him to stand here mindless and bold, so brazen before her tomb?

Will you release me, dust-bones? She is weak, it is true, and starving. *What shall I grant in return?*

Tate hears none of this. He only hears the wind. He points his camera and clicks, and clicks, and clicks again.

The light sucks at the shadows, a bridge from stone into glass.

THEY SAY THE camera never lies. Tate knows that isn't true. A tog like him has learnt plenty and now, standing by the river in Domino Park, he has learnt that some things should go unseen. That some things are unseen. The device does not see all. Neither does the eye.

He thinks of Walt. Sends him a silent apology for the death he brought into their home. But there's no time now, no way to turn back. Unspoken things have bound him. He has walked where no man should. The goddess has made him her own.

In his hands, the camera pulses like a heart, black and eager. Hungry. It boils with those consumed. And it will never be enough. Never enough for Sulta.

Cold, weeping, Tate raises the camera. Through the viewer, he can see the teeth of the city, the buildings holding up the sky. How far can her tongue reach, tangled, knotted in light?

All that she sees she will feast on.

QUEER
N⊙RM

In the wrong hands, clay is just dirt.

That's what Ferris used to say. And Norm is dirt, really. Dirt stirred by a few old words in an old book, shaped by gifted fingers. So Norm thinks as he wakes in a corner of the studio, a broad, hunched figure in shadow, rain tapping the skylights. He alone remains whole in the wreckage, the furniture, plates and statues left smashed and scattered by the Jackal gang. That was the first time they came for Ferris. Before... *Before.* Norm rouses and the violence swims back to him. And his purpose, turning the blocks of his hands into fists. Unlike Ferris, it isn't death he fears.

I must find them.

Does the Malach Hamavet awaken too, he wonders, black, feathery and waiting in the dark? Vengeance must stink like carrion and the angel, he imagines, circles over his head. Norm rouses come dark like he always does;

dark was the hour of his shaping. Whatever drives him, whatever ancient, lingering phrase, it is subject to laws the same as anything, mysteries beyond the reach of his function.

Protect.

With life, inklings come to him. In the warehouse-cum-studio, he pulls off his shrouds. He wrapped the plastic around himself to keep in the moisture while he slept. Even so, he senses that cracks have opened in him, the margins of ruin narrowing with every night of his search. It isn't as bad as the mess in the room. In the space where his heart should be there's the same dull ache at the loss of Ferris. It's been – what? – a month now. Later he'll go to the bridge like he always does, the only headstone left to him.

Nothing was the same after the attack. And the search is getting harder despite his efforts with the fettling knife and spatula. It isn't just the clay. For now, Norm is like leather, supple enough for his singular purpose. If he dries up, so will his efforts. The gang will get away with it. And the *shem* isn't going to last.

I'm all that's left of you, boss, he thinks, a mountain rising, the floorboards groaning. *Memories. Vengeance.*

And art. Ferris Cole was quite the sculptor, even made it into magazines. *Wallpaper. Renaissance.* Ferris with his quick, clever hands, his eternal frown in the studio. Slender and stooped, he'd given his all, both with his pieces and his work at the homeless shelter, helping the lost of London.

The girl, Eli. Isn't she why Norm is here, the seed of his existence? *And the old man, Stern...*

The memories might predate him, but he knows them, shares them with his maker as he shared his sacred space. The studio was a place for Ferris alone, where he sat with his pedestal, his rubbing plates and rollers, moulding and pressing pain into his work. His pieces adorned New York apartments. A Parisian hotel lobby. Time is the breath in the figures, each one life-sized, contorted or supine, their broken forms lining the room. Time trapped in a bottle, Ferris liked to think. That's what his patrons' wanted, blind figures of clay to remind them of beauty. To trap it. Norm isn't blind though. In the end, the time Ferris gave him is running out; a poisoned chalice since Ferris is dead.

Dead with only your breath in me. Fading.

Norm realises the thought won't help him. Not tonight. Or any. The rain sings, prompting him to upkeep, repair. He lumbers through the wreckage to the upstairs bathroom. Thankfully, the sirens had managed to chase off the gang before they reached it, Ferris cowering behind the door. Was it only a month ago?

Go away. Get out. His terror predates Norm too, but only by a day. *Please.*

Ferris had known the gang would come back. He assumed they'd break into the studio again. On some other night. When a match was on. Or a riot. The police couldn't be everywhere, he said.

Norm stands in the shower under a trickle, enough to begin the kneading of the nine hundred pounds of him into a presentable shape. The broad six-foot-five of him. It's important work. The city has eyes, even when it doesn't want to see. In passing headlights, he'll look like a man hunched under the smog, under debt and despair like everyone else. Up close, he'll look like something else, formed of earth and rage. Inhuman. Without upkeep, he'll become a mere lump of clay.

In the way that Ferris taught him, he pinches cracks closed and smooths over wear. Straightens limbs. Sharpens muscle tone. Assisted by the bathroom mirror, he uses the tools at hand to mend an eye socket, sagging in the night, and sketch a few lines on his forehead. It adds an impression of age, authenticity. Dabbing a pot of mica, he smudges shadows under his eyes, regarding his weariness in the glass, the dull routine caught in eyes of opal. Spruced and firm, Norm squeezes himself into the same old raincoat, tips the hood over his eyes and goes out looking for Ferris's killers.

This is how I go on, boss.

HATE HAS A scent. The city reeks of it. It isn't in the spew of signals alone, pinging between the satellites of murderous TV news channels. White noise. Digitised spite. No, hate seeps into the substance of things. It leaves a stain. Like garbage, like shit, it chokes the metropolitan streets. It clings to the billboards, the pylons, the bridges. It curdles with the shadows where some are forced live.

This particular odour, from capsized, derelict lives, Norm knows all too well. Sweat and tears. Stale bread. His nose tells him that this kind of hate is mostly self-directed. Ferris had done what he could, dishing out soup from his van. Blankets. Medicine. Advice. He'd tour downtown on most nights, looking for kids on the street, runaways, junkies, the poor, the lost and the broken. Most he'd encourage to go to the shelter, though he disliked the fact that he couldn't help them all. The triage of it. It was a *focus,* after all. To help displaced youth. The shelter had given Ferris a purpose beyond his sculptures, something that wasn't about him. He'd said that once in an interview.

Self-loathing, yes. Norm shares that too. In terms of Ferris, it had been expected of him, ingrained in him through a series of shitty inner-city schools and casual urban cruelty. He'd fought his way out, *carved* his way out and found a home in the arts – and in the downtown warehouse. Once, he'd even had a boyfriend, a flicker of light... But that kind of hate never leaves you. It *seeps.* It had seeped into Ferris by the end. Following his murder, the panic in the city made headline news, warning all of the spate of violence, the rising abuse, the late night attacks. It holds the same sour tang of fear. Acidic under the streetlights. In the echoes of footsteps. Women as they close up shop. Migrants who keep their eyes on passing police cars. Queers leaving nightclubs. Walking briskly, stumbling home.

Jackals watch in the darkness, waiting. The angel watches too or so Norm believes. Like a connoisseur, he stands on the corner and takes a deep breath. Rain. Petrol. Despair. A taxi catches him in its glare and he's glad of his earlier work with the fettling knife. He turns into the shadows between a betting and a kebab shop all the same, his head low. The scent is wrong. It isn't the strain of hate that he wants. The stuff he's after is sharper, more pungent, stewed in pressure cookers of resentment and reaching boiling point. The ingredients are blame and righteous disgust, spiced with an urge to do harm.

The scent of the Jackal gang. In his mind, a flash of crewcuts, braces and cross-daubed foreheads swim to the surface. Uniforms. Colours. *I will find you...* The cruel leer of a grin. The business end of a knife. Slurs like godless hymns, bouncing off brick. The thud of a boot in flesh. Blood, the starkest scent of all. Between sodium and shadow, the Malach Hamavet shuffles its wings and watches as always. Norm is watching too, neither so neutral nor patient.

I lack the talent for tears. As if to refute him, the rain drips down his cheeks. *But it hurts to see the things you saw, boss. At the end.*

It's all he has to go on. His fingertips leave impressions in his thick grey palms. Yes, their faces, the three of them with the little black crosses on their foreheads, ache in his mind, as clear as a snapshot. Ferris breathed himself into Norm and Norm shares all that Ferris was, all he'd been. Such was the bond between them. Death hasn't changed it, not yet. Norm, his creation, goes on. He'll go on for as long as the *shem* lasts. Go on until he finds them.

The city is vast and stinks to high heaven. How he longs to see their faces in the dark.

But it isn't just a question of that, is it?

"PLEASE," THE OLD man says on the museum steps. "Leave me be."

Norm hates that. Hates that he fills Stern with dread. It reminds him how Ferris felt in the days before the attack. After the graffiti and the emails, Ferris wasn't himself. Every street past eight promised God knew what. Every huddle of youths on a corner seemed a potential threat, ready to sprout fists and knives. Every footstep he heard behind him, climbing the ladder of his spine. Then only to resolve into giggling drunks running for a bus. It was no way to live. Ferris had become wired to the city, each one carrying a charge. No wonder he'd stopped eating in those last few days. No wonder he'd turned to the old man, to a forbidden art.

The museum is closed at this hour. Stern, the old man, climbs the steps for the light. He thinks that Norm will prefer the shadows and he thinks right. Norm follows him up to the portico, corners him against a pillar. When the old man takes off his hat, sweat gleams like silver in his hair.

"I won't hurt you." Norm has the voice of the pit from which he was gouged, booming off stone. He's a ghost in a raincoat, looming over his quarry. Behind the old man's glasses, all he reads is disbelief.

"You… look like him," Stern says. Norm can't tell if it's a compliment or not. In the depths of his hood, his own poor sculpting must make them look related, Ferris and him, despite the glitter of mica. The old man knows it isn't by blood. "You wear the face of the dead."

Stern spits. A rough ward.

"He helped you. Ferris."

"Why d'you think I gave him the book?" Stern snaps. "I should never…" His eyes dart at the square below, broad and empty of pedestrians. "Damn *goy*. So it is written. 'Covet not what is hidden.' I should've -"

"But you gave him the book. The *shem*."

The old man whines in his throat. "If only he hadn't found Eliana -"

"But he did. And she's recovering." Norm moves in closer, a wedge of a finger raised. *And Ferris is gone.* "Old man, your debt isn't paid."

Norm has no way of knowing what Ferris would make of it, the veiled threat. The sculptor had made sure that Eliana Stern returned to the land of the living. He'd brought her coffee and any words he could muster. Norm remembers that morning at the shelter, even though it was the week before he'd awoken in the studio. *All you have to do is try.* Eli had smiled. Smiled despite her track marks, her rattling withdrawal. She'd told Ferris that the medicine was helping. But talk was helping more. Addiction was like a scream, she'd said. She wanted it to echo into the past. Ferris had found her one night in an alley, a pale, dark haired girl fallen in with the wrong crowd. Who'd taken the wrong drugs. Needed money...

He drove you home the next day.

Norm remembers it clearly, although he was clay then. In the same way he knows that the man before him was once respectable. A rabbi. A teacher. Disgraced years ago for black rituals, offerings that no priest should make. *Cabbalism. Magic.* Ferris hadn't cared about that, so Norm didn't either. Ferris had returned his granddaughter to him. A bird with a broken wing, yes. But whole. Stern had been the first person who Eli called. That was good enough for Ferris.

But someone may have seen his van the night he helped the girl out of the alley. Someone was angry at her escape maybe. The sculptor could only guess at it, speculate to the police. *What did you do to provoke this?* they asked him. The hate mail was unspecific. Someone had taken objection to his work at the shelter or simply his sexuality. Either way, the Jackals, the gang, had come for him.

"I read about what they did to the studio." Stern rubs his face, looks like he wants to hide in his hat. He changes tack, seeking an excuse. "It was an old custom. An old way. Ferris needed protection."

"Yes."

"I didn't think..." The old man curses in a language that Norm doesn't know. "Chaldean wisdom. You can't ask any more of me."

"I can. I must. Undo my command."

Norm opens his mouth. It must look like a cave to Stern. The old man stares at his long grey tongue, the *shem* inscribed upon it.

Protect.

At least, that's what Norm thinks it means. He can read English, but the symbols are reversed in the bathroom mirror. Since Ferris left the world, Norm has discovered that he can leave the studio, roam beyond the locus of his original purpose. A little further each night, his feet growing heavier whenever he strays out of bounds. All the same, Norm can *feel* his moral limitations. The shackles. *Protect.* He can't do anything more.

Then Stern is running. His footsteps on stone, keys of terror in the night.

"It was a mistake," the old man shouts over his shoulder. "You should not be!"

Norm watches the priest stumble through puddles, across an upside-down city where hate, perhaps, does not exist.

HATE STINKS UP the city, the night. A bus sploshes by into the suburbs, mud forming on Norm's shins. A moving pillar of dirt, he's following the scent eastbound. Through the pedestrian tunnel where smackheads huddle and the angel loiters, ever silent and black-winged. Around the roundabout where traffic stalls. Beneath the photopollution, distant glaciers slowly melting as drivers punch wheels and curse. Past the bars where men laugh too loudly, squeezed into fashionable shirts. Where women join in, fearful of repercussion. The men emanate malice. An invitation. The way they fling chips, spit and swear... They want some poor fucker to reproach them, give them an excuse. Weak, weak men. Even this hate is bland. Everyday. Pathetic.

They fall silent as Norm trudges by. His shadow eclipses their grins.

Looking back, through memories not his own, Norm can see so much hate, a string of spite down the years. An uncle at a garden party, shrieking at a nine-year-old Ferris for turning up in his cousin's dress. Classroom slurs before Ferris even had a name to call himself. Strangers in a college canteen when he'd come out, smirking and asking the same old questions. When did he know? Did his parents know? Was he the girl or the boy? Stares in a hundred bars, a hundred apartments, a hundred parties. Train platforms. Waiting rooms. Offices. Shops and street corners. And the unsolicited rebuffs.

It's OK by me. I honestly don't mind. Just don't try anything, yeah?

Norm traipses through a park, growling. If God had shaped these people from mud as the Bible claimed, then what arrogance to think that a grain of it held any more worth than another.

Ferris hadn't shared such beliefs, of course. Primitive, he called them.

They're blind. That's what Ferris said. *Lost and blind.*

A being made, not born, Norm doesn't envy them.

*

LATER, HE HEARS a scream. No, it resolves into a fire engine, wailing over the river to the south. Out there, the sky glows red, illuminating the cell towers, wreathing them in fairy tale smoke. Norm halts by the railings. As the noise fades, he catches it. The piquancy. The cruelty. The murderous odour of the gang. Ignorance gone sour. A poison. How many lives has it seeped through, he wonders. Like cigarette ash through bedsheets, leaving charred regret. It drifts from a mile or so away, somewhere along the docks. Sirens are unlikely to venture there, light up the warehouses, the rusting cranes. But someone might, taking a shortcut home. Telling themselves that the rise in attacks is a story on the evening news. Exaggerated. No one wants to believe in a world like that, not really. Norm turns and lumbers in that direction. On feet of clay that should know better.

Ferris hadn't wanted to believe either. Even when friends insisted that the graffiti outside the studio was pointed, serious, the sculptor had put it down to kids. The day the first email arrived telling him that one night, when he least expected it, a razor would split him from ear to ear, he'd said it could be solved by adult conversation. Was he going to take hot cocoa to the thugs? a friend, a designer, asked him.

Some of the lost, Ferris, she'd told him and gripped his hand. *Can't be found.*

Ferris had hugged her and promised to call the police. Emails came every day after that. Each one described a nastier fate, threats of blades. Castration. A corpse that family members wouldn't recognise. One night, a downstairs window got smashed. There was laughter, shouts in the alleyway. Cruel names.

Ferris had dialled 999 during the break in. It had taken a matter of life and death.

"They smeared shit on the wall. The painting." He'd pointed at the mess, the slashed canvas. Black feathers. A flaming sword. A hundred watchful eyes. "It's the Malach Hamavet, the angel of death. My uncle gave me that."

A police officer had scribbled down a note, nodded. "Thank your lucky stars it wasn't you, sir."

"Two of those have been sold," Ferris told him, trembling, staring over the man's shoulder at the litter of limbs, the shattered statues lining the studio. He had thought he was going to die in the upstairs bathroom. "Thousands... Worthless now."

"But no broken bones, yeah?" another officer said, coming down the steps from the mezzanine. He made to clap Ferris on the back. Thought better of it. "They're trying to scare you. Don't give 'em what they want, eh?"

That was when it had started. In that moment, Ferris had stopped shaking. He'd clasped his clever hands to his chest. So much destruction. It brought tears to his eyes. He was a *creator*, damn it. If only he could tear the rage from his heart. Or knead it into a ball so small that it wouldn't matter.

That was why, when Stern showed up the next day with the book, Ferris had sat and listened. Taken the book from him. The old man had read about the attack in the paper. He'd wanted to show his gratitude. Repay him for Eli. Do something.

The look that Ferris had given the police.

"They broke into my home. This is a hate crime."

The officer had sucked in his cheeks. A radio barked on his chest.

"Too early to tell," he'd said.

THE PAST KEEPS Norm company, echoes of a world before his own.

I was a dream, boss, he thinks. *A whisper in words, written long ago on the banks of the Euphrates...*

All around, the water lies dark like his history, one of nonexistence and dirt. But the docks are not empty. When he turns the corner of a warehouse and enters a loading bay, he finds himself the audience to theatre. The silhouettes of cranes make a backdrop. Sodium lights the stage, under a crazed confetti of moths. Shouts sound like a tuning orchestra. The ring of metal on concrete arrests him in the gloom. He comes to a halt by a stack of crates, a figure broad and plain enough to merge with them, another block of cargo. No breath coils from him. Ferris alone has roused him, but he isn't truly alive.

It's the Jackal gang. *Gangs,* he corrects himself. Two of them, clashing in the night. The men closest to him,

Norm doesn't recognise. All wear green in some fashion, he notes, whereas the Jackals wear red. A tee shirt. A cap. A splash of paint on jeans. *Colours.* Some European dialect resounds in the darkness, under the streetlights. English answers them. More profanity than sense. Jungle calls. Urban omens. He makes out the little crosses on their foreheads. Their shaven heads. Braces. These, Norm has seen before. Knows like his own pain. His limitations. He has found the ones he's come looking for. Among them, the three who -

"This is our city, cunts!"

The gangs meet. Metal bars and knives swing, marking out the bounds of some unseen territory. A space that no one could want. Rusted machinery. Seaweed and rope. Saliva speckles the air. Fists wave. The atmosphere is rank with aggression. Then blood. A spinning tooth. A yell. Like shadow puppets against the warehouse walls, Norm watches a forest of limbs. They meet in a dance, brutal. Collapse into chaos.

Let them eat each other. His own fists ball at his sides. *Let hate consume them.*

That he could bear. An ouroboros of cruelty, feeding on itself and touching no other. *If only.* Instead, the cloddish sense of superiority. The self-righteous smiles. The faux disgust and the irrational fear. Instead, the injustice. The wheel of hate. And all the innocents crushed beneath it.

These men – if he can call them that – have failed at being human.

Norm has seen the rot in the world. It's what they did to Ferris that scars him. The same bloody knuckles. The same demeaning words. The clay he'd risen from to stop them, a guardian under a plastic sheet... In the end, it didn't matter, old custom or no. Norm wasn't there when they came for Ferris. One night, they found him walking home from an exhibition. He'd left his golem to watch over the studio.

Protect.

Wrapped in a scarf against the cold, Ferris hadn't seen the rot in the world.

The police were right, he'd told a friend, the designer, that evening. *I can't live in fear. I won't.*

He was shaking his head at the magic he'd performed. The creature he'd made with his quick, clever hands. He'd thought his heart was a shield. That an angel watched over him. But the only angel present that night had sported black wings. Had it smiled to embrace him?

It was midnight when the Jackals appeared on the bridge. Three of them, spilling from the throat of the dark. The memory is the brightest of all. It's stained in breath. Pinpricks of sweat. Panic. *Where're you going, sweetheart?* The camp imitation of Ferris. Laughter. Shoves. *Fuck you. I'm calling the* – The slash of a knife tore through his warning. Through tendons and flesh. Ferris screamed, echoes off the water. A brick rose to silence it, slammed into his skull.

Please, Ferris had spluttered. He knelt on the bridge, a hand splayed. His blood in his mouth. *Stop.*

The last sounds he'd heard – that *Norm* had heard a mile away, roaring under plastic – were cars sloshing past. Seeing and not seeing. In a wash of headlights, the gang had lifted Ferris, an offering. They'd carried him to the railings of the bridge. *Can you swim, faggot?* His blood had spattered the concrete as if in farewell. Then he'd taken to the air, his scarf flying. His heart like a burning bird. And then he went into the deep. The cold.

Was the Malach Hamavet waiting there? Did he fold you in black wings and take you into the dark?

In the here and now, Norm hangs his head. If only Ferris could've summoned up the magic and turned them all to clay. Let the rain wash away the dull malice of their lives… But no one can change the past. The past is dirt, like everything. Time is a journey from dust to dust.

Norm looms on the dock. He looks up and glowers at the gang. Sparks dance in the hollows of his eyes. He rises from the shadows like a wall.

Hate seeps. The world won't miss men like these. He is going to tear them apart.

THE FIRST THING that Norm ever saw was Ferris Cole. One moment there was darkness. Cold. Insensate as earth. Then there was the sculptor, the thin, stooped man with startled eyes. Norm awoke to Ferris with his hand in his mouth. Ferris had inscribed the shem upon his tongue. It was awkward, an intimate thing. But Norm knew why he'd been fashioned at once. The efforts that the sculptor had made. The instructions he'd followed. The hours he'd spent in his studio, fettling knife in hand. How he'd referred to his maquette a thousand times, the little wire man stood on the table. Measuring, carving and smoothing clay. Defining features. Tracing Chaldean symbols. Granting a name. A command.

"Norm is what we'll call you," Ferris told him, steadying himself. From a stool next to him, an old book with brown pages had fallen to the floor. Loops of wire, with which Ferris had formed his armature, glinted in the moon through the skylights. "Norm. After my uncle."

Like a ripple in water, Norm caught the impression of a wrinkled face. Hair whiter than hospital sheets, whiter that the bed the man lay on. A smile that was saying goodbye, apologising for it. For drugs that hadn't worked.

But Ferris had shaken himself from the memory.

"Look, it's the name that binds you, all right? Protect. Protect. Let no harm come to this place."

This place.

"Yes, master."

"Call me Ferris. Please."

Newly moulded, Norm had savoured the moment. And others. Many. Childhood memories, love and loss, had skipped through his mind in a heartbeat. The sculptor's in place of his own. His expression made Ferris laugh, a musical sound in the sheet-draped warehouse. It skipped over the wreckage too, the leavings of the break-in. Norm was aware of it in moments. The graffiti. The emails. The fear.

The sculptor had placed a hand on his chest, the clay damp enough to leave an impression.

"It's funny, isn't it?" he said. "Perhaps a little vain. I modelled your face on mine."

Norm sensed the sculptor's warmth. His loneliness. How isolated he felt in the city, down this street where so few ventured. Where lately some had come to hurt him, to shout and smash furniture. To drive him to this shaping.

Jackals.

Norm belonged to Ferris. And protect he would.

NORM IS UP on the bridge. Some time has passed. Time spent in memories, borrowed and warm. The sparse traffic pays him no mind, takes him for another statue along the railings. That's if people see him at all. An aeroplane roars across the sky, heading for somewhere better. Hate has grown stale. The same cold soup. Around his feet, chunks of clay lie scattered, debris from his fists. On the docks, fighting the shem, he clenched them so hard they cracked. The rain has made a mess of his face, a half-melted grimace. It has not doused the fire in his eyes.

I found them.

The anger in the night is his now. The Jackals fled when they heard a siren, ran off in a storm of blood. They hadn't noticed his presence. The magic abroad. The doom that hangs over them. The angel that watches.

"I can't break my bonds," Norm says to the river, black and sluggish below. He always stands in the same spot. The only headstone left to him. "I can't undo the command."

It's what he'd asked of the old man, the priest. Stern had refused him. 'Covet not what is hidden', he'd said. *What's hidden from me is justice,* Norm had wanted to tell him. The old man didn't share his frustration. He'd got what he wanted, hadn't he? Ferris had rescued Eli, nursed her back to health. Dark haired, troubled, but whole, she had gone home to her grandfather. But Stern's gratitude had its limits.

Norm needs help. Gifted fingers.

I can't do it myself, boss. If I could... He closes his eyes, picturing vengeance. The torn limbs flying. Their blood would paint the warehouse walls. The concrete. Dance in sodium with the moths. He imagines the screams. The pleading. Savours it. *If.*

"No," the Malach Hamavet tells him, from somewhere in the shadows of the bridge. "It is subject to laws the same as anything."

Norm opens his eyes. He sees nothing but the river, oozing by. The angel, all feathers, eyes and sword, doesn't like to show itself. It's a blur in his peripheral vision, always waiting for the end. Only Norm's liminal existence lends him the insight, the glimpse of powers beyond the world. And he knows the chains that bind him. The *shem* will not permit violence, allow him to bring harm. The Chaldeans knew what they were doing. So did Ferris Cole.

And the breath in him is fading, Norm can sense that too. Soon, he'll awake as a mere lump of earth in the studio. A heap under plastic, unable to move. After that, erosion. He'll be dust soon enough. Empty of rage. Swept up and forgotten. Forgotten like the book that gave him life, however temporary.

I could fall too, he tells himself. *Let the waters dissolve me. Carry me to the sea.*

Norm knows he can't do that either. It would also count as harm. How ironic in a city like this that his hands remain bound, the hate rattling through him like the endless trains. The platforms with their shoving imprecations. The passengers hiding behind their phones. Crammed like sardines, but miles from each other. All trapped like flies. Like him.

No, he'll return to the studio and sleep. Bide his time until dark. *Again.* Then he'll mend himself as much as he's able. Grab the fettling knife, the spatula and sponge. Reshape his broken hands. Mould his face into a human likeness. He'll throw on the same old raincoat. Go out with his hood up, searching for the gang. Like tonight. Like all the other nights. He'll find the Jackals, following their scent.

For Ferris.

It's all that's left to him. He is circling, circling. Powerless as dirt down a drain. A wind-up toy that's hit a wall.

And the hate, Norm thinks. *The hate that seeps through.*

THE SKY HAS turned a leaden grey by the time Norm reaches the studio. He's left a part of him behind in puddles. Small and unremarkable lumps. It wouldn't do to get caught outside. A slumbering statue. A monolith. Perhaps someone might recognise the sculptor's hand. He might wake up in a museum or a lobby. It's a foolish thought. And the dawn always tells him when it's time to return, the shadows chasing his steps. The studio is both his cradle and grave.

Pigeons scatter as he enters. The upturned furniture and the broken plates, the emptiness, have made the birds think the place fit for a roost. The Malach Hamavet too, the angel always here now, it seems. Like the darkness, the silence suits Norm and his purpose.

It's how I go on.

He's about to go upstairs, dampen himself in the shower, wrap himself in the shrouds, when he freezes in the gloom. There is someone in the studio. He can sense it. Someone stands among the broken statues, the figures that line the room. It isn't the angel. This is someone with breath and warmth.

He turns towards the shadows, growling.

"Please." A hand is held up, placating. In the grey light through the roof, he makes out hair, long and black. Eyes that have seen things, set in a pale face. A woman. Young.

Eli steps forward, trembling.

"My grandfather is old and frightened," she tells him.

Norm sees the book under her arm, recovered from the studio floor. What breath he has seethes from him.

"I'm not," she says.

THE FACTS
CONCERNING
THE FIRST ANNUAL
ARKHAM PARADE

BOSTON, JULY 1951

DEAR QUENTIN,

Forgive me for leaving without warning. I received an urgent phone call this morning and I guess I'm obliged to respond in person. Call it a question of decency. My trip north couldn't have come at a worse time, what with the backlog in our Pearl Street office, and my destination hardly amounts to a vacation either. Arkham! That ancient, mouldering Massachusetts town that legend tells us was cursed by a witch.

You'd have thought the Essex County tourist board would've made more effort to gloss over such crap! It seems little has changed since the '30s when, according to my old man, the *Herald* would feature articles about the torpedoing at Innsmouth in the winter of '27 and the disastrous Pabodie Expedition, which was funded by the town university. Lord knows there's zilch to recommend the place unless you like overgrown graveyards and salt marshes. My only saving grace is that the distance is short – forty-five minutes from Downtown Crossing – so I hope to head home in a day or two. With any luck, you'll read this note and skip thinking me a jerk.

The call came out of the blue from Wanda Olmstead, who looked me up in the Gardener-Athol directory. Mrs Olmstead is the mother of Walter O., my old roommate at the Miskatonic University. We're talking a good nine years ago now. Walter was a student of archaeology whereas I studied law. He was a bit of an oddball on campus, with his head often buried in books, and yet we became 'study buddies'. I guess he liked my practical nature, which might sound familiar to you. Walter never joined in on the hockey pitch, but he was useful when it came to homework! In fact. I was Walter's only friend. That's why his mother has reached out to me following his disappearance.

For reasons unknown, Mrs Olmstead appears to place no faith in the Arkham Police Department and has asked me to help her find her son. Two weeks ago, it seems there was an incident in the town. I hesitate to say a violent one – I don't want to worry you! Mrs Olmstead mentioned a parade that escalated into some 'ruckus' or other. Since then, my alumnus has been AWOL.

Sorry, Quentin. I know what you'd say. I'm sure you'd remind me I'm a humble tax collector and should leave the matter to the cops. I'm afraid that conscience won't allow it. If nothing else, I'd like to honour an old friendship and do my best to comfort his mother. I'll return to you with the job done and make it up to you.

Until then.

Jack

Letter #1. From the evidence file of the Boston Police Department, 154 Berkeley Street, Boston. Submitted by Mr Quentin G. Fields.

i. In the Rattling House

JACK ELWOOD WAS shaken and damp as he stepped into the squat stone building that passed for the Arkham railway station. The train that had brought him here had rattled along tracks laid in the last century and the tremors echoed in his bones. Most with business in the city lived in the suburbs these days or used a car on the old coast road. Too bad his was in the shop. He'd looked out the window, already missing Quentin and homesick. It wasn't hard to see why. Low, bleak hills had rolled off into the distance, the odd leafless tree on the rise. The landscape was draped in a greenish fog that rendered everything skeletal and dull, suggesting that he didn't even have the country air to look forward to.

Nevertheless, Elwood found himself mourning the wasteland the moment he stepped into myth-shrouded Arkham, strutting with valise in hand under Georgian eaves that dripped with gloom as much as the weather. Fog wreathed lampposts that had been quietly rusting since the First World War. Potholes made progress irksome for trucks and cars, which filled the air with a clamour equal to Boston, setting his teeth on edge.

Blank windows and empty drugstores regarded him, giving him the sense of being watched. Within minutes of stepping off the train, the hairs were prickling on the nape of his neck. In his immediate vicinity, all he saw was some Joe in a gabardine, smoke curling from behind a crumpled copy of the *Herald*. An old lady was feeding pigeons on a bench. When he looked over his shoulder, however, he caught sight of his spy. She was standing by a pillar in the station foyer, her eyes aglitter in a powdered face. She wore a lime green dress and was tall for a broad, he thought, willowy, if not Amazonian. Under her arm, she carried a yellow purse, so stuffed that it looked like a melon ready to burst. Atop her head, a pillbox hat rested on a mess of ginger curls. He frowned, puzzled by her glare, the pinch of her scarlet lips. Noticing his interest, she turned away at once, her high heels clopping as she fled.

What's your tale, nightingale? he thought.

He was a stranger in these parts and for all that unremarkable, a young man in a flannel suit and overcoat from Boston. Unable to land on a reason for the woman's attention, he shook off the zorros and headed for the tram. Once aboard the nigh-on medieval transport, he headed for nearby Water Street.

*

Elwood believed he'd made a mistake the second that Mrs Olmstead opened the door. Or rather half opened it, a face peering out in the mid-morning gloom. The woman's head seemed perfectly shaped to navigate such a portal. Her eyes, bulging and round, appeared to have evolved as a result of the passage beyond, abyssal thanks to the weather. Elwood had all but decided to light out for the station again when Mrs Olmstead flushed, becoming animated. His name was a hiss her lips, although there wasn't so much as a twitch of the curtains in the neighbouring houses and no apparent reason for discretion. Silently, he realized he'd missed his chance to skip the whole business, but he doffed his hat all the same. It was him alright, he told her, Jack Elwood, former roommate of Walter, her son.

Soon came the matter of Walter's disappearance, which left Elwood far more uncomfortable than the armchair the woman ushered him into, while she sat opposite on the couch. The living room curtains remained drawn, which he didn't blame her for, considering the miserable day. A floor lamp lit the space in an unwholesome glow, the colour of faded tax chits. In its radiance, Mrs Olmstead appeared to him a forlorn creature, with flaking skin in the folds of her neck and an oddly flat nose. Uneasy, he found he preferred to look around the room.

There were pictures of Olmstead Junior on the wall, the man as scruffy and pale as Elwood remembered, his eyes haunted by a surplus of dead languages and old stones. Walter was never going to be a dreamboat, but it might've done him good to pay more attention to exercise than study. He wasn't smiling in any of the shots. Elwood found he had no memory of him having done so, not even after he'd woken one night in the dorm from a bad dream – some nonsense about benthic realms and golden ingots, if he recalled correctly. Elwood had done his best to soothe him, the beginning of their brief fling, adolescent and boneheaded as it was…

The pang in his chest surprised him. Before he had time to examine it, Mrs Olmstead was handing him a cup of tea. At first, he thought that the saucer was rattling so much due to the poor woman's nerves. Then he realized the entire room was shaking. The pictures slapped against the clapboard walls. The lamp trembled, guttering. Cheeks flushed, Mrs Olmsted informed him that it was the eleven o'clock to Portland, the city thirty odd kilometres north. She went on to say, without prompting from him, that she'd had to move to a smaller place after her husband passed away six years ago. The only house that Arkham made affordable was the one down by the railway track.

"That was before Walter had his trinkets, of course," she said and shivered.

"Trinkets, ma'am?"

"Oh, he must've read about them in his books," she said. "Awful tomes. Ancient, mouldering and damned. He told me he was reading up on some cult over in Innsmouth. You now, the old seaport. Something about golden idols and human sacrifice. Ingots dredged up from the bay. A nasty business by all accounts. I wish he'd never bought them home!"

"Books or ingots, Mrs Olmstead?"

"He traded the books in Innsmouth, or so he said," the woman went on as if she hadn't heard him, her large eyes glazed. "This was a month or so before he... you know. Got his big idea." She smiled, apologetic. "Though who pays gold for old library books? Nothing in them but squiggles and symbols, as far as I could tell."

She told him there were six trains a day, passing either way, and that he'd get used to the noise. Before he could reply that he'd booked a room at the Excelsior, Mrs Olmstead – she insisted he call her Wanda, although manners forbade him – launched into the facts concerning the First Annual Arkham Parade. The widow spoke of her son with weary affection, but she never seemed to blink, no emotion lighting her eyes.

As if she noticed him staring, she lowered her voice and said, "You know how he is," to which Elwood gave a nod, remembering the books that used to litter Walter's side of the room on the Miskatonic campus. Were they similar to the ones he'd sold? He sipped his tea and hid a wince, the brew lukewarm and brackish, with an aftertaste that brought to mind the salt marshes north of the town.

It happened that the runaway (heaven forbid that Elwood should think him an 'abductee') had been frequenting some of the... less salubrious establishments in town. Most notably 'Pink Jenkins', a dive bar at the lower end of Peabody Avenue. "Over the river," the widow said and pursed her lips, which was all one needed to say about the area in general. Elwood was familiar with the joint, of course, and had reason to stare at the rug to hide the colour in his cheeks.

A haunt of rivermen, farmhands and factory workers, 'PJs', as it was locally known, was the only establishment in town that catered for men of a certain nature – and an illegal one at that – hence the faux mercantile frontage. Passing PJs by day, one would've taken it for a hardware store and never have imagined the bar in the back where local men gathered after dark, smoking and watchful in the shadows. Elwood knew better, having frequented the place on more than one occasion, and on the arm of Walter to boot. He'd even attempted a foxtrot to Ella, the recollection the source of his blushes.

"Why," Mrs Olmstead told him, "Walt claimed there was a 'shadow over Arkham'. He had him a mind to bring the fellas at PJs out of it, if you take my meaning. 'It ain't right,' he said one night, 'that we should live in shame when all we're doing is lovin' each other.'" Mrs Olmstead looked away, concealing her feelings on the matter. After stealing a sip of tea, she continued. "Walt planned to hold a parade, you see. Fifty men or so, marching bold as brass down Church Street on a Saturday morning, past the university and up to Hangman's Hill for a grand old cookout in the cemetery. And he wouldn't take advice, no sir!"

Elwood sat back at this, with a hankering for something stronger than tea. Such exhibitionism shocked him and not merely because it sat at odds with the Walter he'd known, the withdrawn and muttering student. Typically, the practical tax collector of Pearl Street came to the fore. "You'd need the mayor's say-so for such an event," he wondered aloud. "Not to mention dough from the council."

Mrs Olmstead was shaking her head like an echo of the eleven o'clock to Portland. The house creaked, settling. In a low voice, she informed him that not only had Mayor Armitage rejected Walter's proposal, he'd threatened to alert the local police. Usually, cops preferred to ignore the small seedy bar in the Merchant District and spare themselves the paperwork. A brazen display of licentious behaviour, she said, would shatter the thin veneer of tolerance that Arkham had deigned to muster.

"That wasn't going to stop my Walter." She leant forward, her eyes wide, and admitted that her son had sworn to go ahead with the First Annual Arkham Parade regardless. "A friend in need is a friend indeed, Jack. Will you help me find him?"

ii. The Statement of Samuel Wentworth

FOR THE SAKE of thoroughness, Elwood spent the rest of the day getting a slant in the local stores. Had anyone seen or heard from Walter? It took him an hour or so to confirm what Mrs Olmstead had told him (there was an outside chance that Walter was simply avoiding her, he'd thought) and to confirm that his search was going to take longer than expected. He considered getting on the horn to Quentin, to hear some reassurance, if nothing else.

Arkham was weirdsville and no mistake. The Federal-style buildings and the fog were one thing; the disposition of its residents another. In the cigar shop, he learnt of a 'strange violet twinkling' that was said to occur on occasion in the windows of Parsonage Street, but the shopkeeper clammed up on sight of the photograph that Elwood showed him, borrowed from Walter's mother. In the kiosk of the Sarnath Theatre, a broad muttered to him about the 'large deformed fish' that her husband had caught while out fishing on Gravelly Pond, yet she was much less forthcoming when it came to his quarry, informing him that she had business to get on with and that "fish aren't the only unnatural things in these parts," which he ignored out of politeness. When he stepped up to a pedestrian with his picture held out, he found a wad of tobacco spat at his feet, a passage from Leviticus squawked at him and his company abandoned on the sidewalk. Some, it seemed, knew Walter well enough. Knocking on doors wasn't going to help him.

Feeling much further than forty-five minutes from Downtown Crossing, Elwood had decided to give up for the day when again he sensed eyes upon him. He spun in the direction of the pharmacy, the gloom at the end of the street. There, he caught a flash of eyes, bright and glaring, and a blur of a lime green skirt as it vanished around a corner. Who was she, his stalker? What on earth did she want?

High heels echoed into the fog like the death knell of his inquiries.

QUEER GOINGS-ON IN Arkham were far from news, Samuel Wentworth, the general clerk of the Deputy Mayor's Department told Elwood in his small and caliginous office the following morning. Despite some garbled chitchat down the wire, Elwood had been unable to secure an appointment with the mayor himself and the secretary's tone had made it clear that Boston city tax collectors didn't merit special attention. Elwood soon found himself squirming in the presence of the bug-eyed clerk instead, who insisted on keeping the blinds drawn throughout the interview that he'd so reluctantly granted.

The wood-panelled office was dampish and allowed not the slightest draught. In minutes, Wentworth's pipesmoke shrouded the file-cluttered space, making Elwood cough and wonder why the fog was considered so noxious when tobacco was not. Curiously, the clerk had the same oleaginous look as Mrs Olmstead, the narrowness of his skull some hereditary quirk of these parts. Degeneration, perhaps.

Querulously, Wentworth confirmed that the First Annual Arkham Parade had indeed gone ahead, in June two weeks prior. And despite a rejected proposal for funding and repeated objections – both legal and moral!

"The youth of today," the clerk said and mumbled about the war and liberty and those who liked to take them. Pipe dancing in the corner of his mouth, Wentworth told the happenstance detective that Walter O. had informed the mayor's office he'd keep his 'protest' limited, for the most part, to the Merchant District where, 'it wasn't likely to upset anyone sensible'. Walter planned to lead the march up Church Street and past the gates of the Miskatonic University nonetheless. Then up to Hangman's Hill where he'd organized a band, fireworks and a grand old cookout as advised.

Here Elwood raised his eyebrows. The unemployed Olmstead had hired no less than eight farm trucks to serve as floats and adorned them with gaily coloured ribbons, streamers and balloons. Men and women, Wentworth said, squeezing the arms of his chair, had worn all manner of couture and painted themselves from head to toe. "Glitter. Lipstick. You name it," the elder spluttered through a particularly explosive cloud of smoke. "Men in ballgowns!" Some sported feathers and tassels, he went on, that weren't politely viewed outside of clip joints. Reportedly, some men wore undershorts and loafers ("and nothing else!"), leaving naught to the imagination and flaunting themselves before the good Christian people of Arkham in a kind of 'immoral assault'. There had been music and dancing, radios playing a 'barrage of rhythm and blues'. Astonished onlookers had to cover the eyes of children. Members of the local clergy blustered as men and women 'shared ungodly displays of affection', Wentworth concluded with a shiver. He explained that he quoted from the letter of complaint that Pastor Gideon Hawley had sent to the mayor's office the day following the uproar.

Propriety aside, it was the uproar that Elwood was interested in, having been the last time that Walter was seen. He squeezed the old man for further information, perspiring under his shirt at the description of the incident, a fracas that was unusual in a backwater like Arkham (though he'd have found it startling even in Boston). The rags were abuzz with the so-called 'Lavender Scare', which had seen some dismissed from government and was set to filter down into every industry and office, instilling in Elwood the utmost discretion, along with an undercurrent of fear. In these times, when men like him were deemed 'perverts' and 'criminals', he couldn't help but admire Walter's bravery, even as he shrank from its consequences. As Wentworth continued, Elwood put on an award-winning coolness to conceal his growing discomfort.

The trouble, he learned, had blown up on the junction of Church Street and Peabody Avenue where the warehouses sat closest to the river. A rumble had ensued between the fifty odd members of the parade and a mob of presumed 'factory workers' who'd crept out of the surrounding slums to mount an attack on the floats.

"Poured out of the warehouses, they did," he said, and again he shuddered. "All of them wearing these... masks. Strange, froglike masks, I heard. Must've been near double the number of the folks in the parade. Guns were fired on the floats. The mob wasn't dissuaded. By the time the police got there, most of the revellers had fled. Some folk were lying in the street unconscious. Truck tires had been slashed. Blood on the sidewalk. And the mob had retreated, slipping back into the gloom of the warehouses. The police weren't going to chase them down there."

Elwood, who'd walked through the district on his way to PJs, and never beyond the safety of the streetlights, could imagine why. The area known as Oldport was a maze of warehouses by day and brothels by night. If one happened to get lost in the backstreets, they'd risk a mugging or worse. On top of this, he suspected that the local heat weren't too put out by 'factory workers' doing their job for them. The parade had disbanded. No one had been seriously hurt, as far as Elwood could tell, and only a rube of a resident was missing, likely on the lam. It was hardly a priority for the Arkham PD. He was beginning to see why Mrs Olmstead had got him on the horn yesterday morning.

To that end, Elwood pressed on with his inquiries, drawing the clerk's attention to the matter that had puzzled him most during their smoke-bound exchange. If the council had refused Walter dough for the parade, he asked, then how on earth had he managed to hire trucks, fireworks, musicians and all the decorations?

"Oh, there's gossip," Wentworth told him, sitting back with a wheeze. "All I'm saying is that there was no parade along Pickman Street, which lies two streets over from Church. Nonetheless, someone broke into Levensky's at around the same time as the dust up. Turns out Walter O. had sold some trinkets to the jeweller the week before. Gold, as I heard it, though where a bum like him got it is anyone's guess. If you're fixed on poking your nose in, maybe start there."

Elwood tipped his hat and assured the clerk he would. To which Wentworth shook his head, vented smoke and concluded the interview by advising him against it.

iii. Watchers in the Mist

ELWOOD'S MIND WAS glittering with trinkets (the word *ingot* was nibbling at his mind) as he made his way to Levensky's, trudging through the mist. He didn't have to think too hard about where the gold had come from; Mrs Olmstead had told him that Walter had traded some old books over in Innsmouth, a queer kind of town beyond the salt marshes on the coast. As far as he recalled, there'd once been a refinery in the ancient seaport and whispers of treasures salvaged from the bay. Whatever the truth of it, the US Military had cordoned the place off in '27 to test torpedoes or somesuch, a matter that had contributed to the harbour's decline.

These days, most knew Innsmouth as a godforsaken place, near derelict after the crash of '29 and never recovered, the local industry sliding from boom to bust. Fish still came from Innsmouth – not as much as rumours though, even swimming to Bostonian ears. Most said that the seaport was cursed, bedevilled by bad luck and a haunt of vagrants and hoods, those who society couldn't find a place for. "They ain't like us, the Innsmouth folk," a drunk informed him on the steps of the Municipal Library in return for a buck to spend on hooch. "What yer askin' after 'em for, anyways?"

That was the best result from the inquiries that Elwood had made downtown. No one liked to talk much in Arkham, but he learnt that no trains travelled directly to the coast, preferring to shoot north for Newburyport and Portland beyond. "Demand don't warrant it," a shopkeeper said before turning her attention to another customer. "Nor sense." Whatever Walter had been up to, it seemed a straight up black market trade, enough to raise the funds for his parade certainly, and courtesy of some shady Innsmouth source.

None of which explained the boarded up window of the jewellery store. The trays behind the patch-up job were empty, he saw, and the space beyond them dark. Most of the glass had since been removed, the frame all splinters and fangs, dull under the weather. Shards crunched under Elwood's shoes and coupled with the stench of the Miskatonic, his nerves were soon doing the rhumba again. An unpleasant thought was forming – about theft, revenge – but Levensky's wasn't offering answers and the jeweller in question had refused all his calls. No wonder if the guy had been up to no good. Last time he checked, receiving stolen goods was a criminal offense. The smash and grab had taken place during Walter's parade, someone (or some*ones*) getting the bulge from the uproar over on Church Street. He didn't kid himself it was a coincidence; Walter had fenced his gold at this store and none of the others had been ransacked. Whatever business had gone down here, ingots for easy greens, it had clearly gone south.

The notion was an omen. Hearing footsteps, Elwood turned, half expecting to see the same lime green dress, the powdered face that had dogged him from the train station. Instead, he made out figures in the fog – two or three silhouettes that made him wish the hour were later and the streetlights on. Scrawny they were, and moving in a peculiar fashion, lurching towards him as if they weren't quite comfortable in their shoes, a thought that slipped hands around his throat. There were no pedestrians around and he had no reason to think the strangers a threat. Menace emanated off them all the same, causing him to take a step backwards.

"What's the grift, fellas?" Elwood managed.

A growl cut him off, the nearest member of the gang hastening his steps, his heels scraping. He made out a cap, a narrow face under it, the features masked by a scarf. Did they intend to mug him right here on Pickman Street and in the middle of the day? They'd make off with his Bulova watch, a gift from Quentin on his thirtieth birthday (an ache in his chest made him wish he'd got his partner on the horn now) and a handful of dimes. But he didn't think so. He wasn't far from French Hill, the wealthy suburb of

Arkham, with its rows of impressive yet decaying houses surmounted by the spire of a church. Oldport was streets away and even if these were factory workers on the warpath (his next breathless thought), what business would they have with him? He noticed more of them now, shapes further back in the fog, approaching.

"Fellas..."

It appeared he was wrong about being attacked. The nearest gang member made a grab for him. In a blur, Elwood glimpsed a ragged sleeve, clawed fingers on the end of it. The sight tore a cry from him, along with the water that speckled the ground. It appeared that his assailant was soaked to the bone. The stench of the river made him gag. Arm raised to fend off a blow, Elwood shot a look around him, seeking escape. One heavy he might tussle with. Six would see him counting bluebirds in seconds. He was no more a brawler than he was a detective. It was time to make like a tree, he thought. His attacker lunged for him again, a knuckle sandwich darting past his shoulder.

The next moment, a squealing sound was filling his ears, a wash of radiance lighting up the street like Christmas. Hissing, the figures cringed in the headlights blazing through the fog, the harbinger of the car that came tearing around the corner. It was a Cadillac, he saw, a beat up coupe with bullet-shaped fenders and a chrome grille. In a blink, the bucket was screeching to a halt beside him, rubber greasing the tarmac, exhaust fumes billowing. He could only gawp as the driver shouted out of the rolled down window, her pillbox hat and lime green dress a beacon of salvation in the gloom.

"Get in," the woman told him, wheeling a glove at the passenger door. "Unless you fancy a trip to the bottom of the river."

Elwood needed no encouragement. Wrenching the door open, he hoisted himself into the wagon, the vehicle roaring off down Pickman Street the second his soles left the sidewalk. Illuminated by the headlights, he drew some satisfaction from the factory workers – or whoever they were – leaping out of the Cadillac's way. It snuffed out the moment he took in their faces, no more than flashes in the fog. Each was a strange, unearthly green, their eyes bulging from narrow heads, their skin squamous, covered in scales.

iv. The Plight of Miss Lillian Crow

FOR A WHILE, they drove in silence, Elwood gathering his wits. Taking his bearings from the bare hills and cadaverous trees, he realized that the woman was driving out of Arkham and into the open countryside. Traffic was light and telephone poles waltzed across the flats of sedge-grass and shrubbery. It was late and dark wasn't far off – if it ever truly left this corner of Essex County. Embarrassed, but grateful for rescue, Elwood asked his most pressing question. Who the devil had attacked him?

"Cultists," the woman replied, her voice husky and low, perhaps due to lack of sleep or too many cigarettes.

Suit rumpled, Elwood pulled himself upright, glaring. She sat with her gloves on the steering wheel, her eyes fixed on the road. "Second generation hybrids. Guess they're hoping to score brownie points with the Order by getting their idol back. They must've reckoned you'd lead them to it. To me. You can hardly blame them, sweetheart. You've been shooting your mouth off all over town."

This admission, bizarre as it was, washed over Elwood like drizzle. He leant in closer, peering at the woman's profile, her powdered cheeks, her sharp nose and the wild ginger curls under her hat. Spying a trace of the familiar, he sat back in his seat with a gasp.

"Olmstead. Walter Olmstead. I'll be—"

"Hey, now!" He – she – shot him a glance. "That cat is dead. Or as good as dead. It's Lillian Crow to you, buddy. Capice?"

Elwood snorted. With her wig and paint job, his rescuer looked a world away from the scruffy student he'd roomed with at university. Gosh, but he'd been wasting his time flapping his photograph around and didn't this take the biscuit?

"Look, *sister,* your mama set me sniffing on your heels and it hasn't exactly been a boat ride. Seems you've caused quite the ruckus in town. I don't blame you for the disguise, but..." He shrugged without a shred of nonchalance. "You and I need to have a little chat."

"Firstly, Jack, that isn't my mother." His alumnus shot him another glance, a knowing one. While he digested this, remembering the Widow Olmstead's bulging eyes and the brackish cup of tea she'd given him, Lillian hit the brakes and swung the Cadillac to the side of the road. She parked in the shadow of an old blasted tree. Birds took flight, squawking. Then she turned to him, the engine rumbling. "Secondly, you need to listen up. *Walter* was the disguise. I wore him for thirty odd years until the morning of the First Annual Arkham Parade." She held up a hand to check interruption. "Honey, just nod once for yes. Otherwise, keep your trap shut, OK?"

Reluctantly, Elwood gave a nod. Such things weren't unheard of, of course. He'd been to PJs enough times (along with some well-appointed basements in Boston) to know that guys and dolls could play 'musical chairs' if they wanted to. What was it to him? No one would think him a model citizen if they happened to find out about Quentin, an African American employed by the Pearl Street office... It was shock talking, he realized, and thought of his partner helped him to saddle it. Christ, he needed a drink.

"I got no beef with that," he said. "Like I said, I came up here to find you. And though I ought to bust your chops, I'm glad to find you alive." She smiled at that, but he plunged on regardless. "Look, unless you want me to hitch a ride back to Arkham pronto, you'd better start spilling the beans."

In response, Lillian reached for the purse in her lap, a lurid yellow, and flung it over to him. Elwood caught it, heavily, and found himself staring down at a pair of bulbous eyes and fat, drooping lips. The hideous visage

– which one might call *batrachian* – leered up at him, the idol sculpted in gold. Its flanks resembled fins, the look of some forgotten, thalassic god.

"Dagon," she explained. "Say howdy-do."

"What the heck is this?"

"The Father of the Deep Ones," she told him. The idol gleamed despite the lack of light, some strange alloy rendering it chromatic, alive. "Folks worship him over in Innsmouth. They reckon a city lies under the reef. 'Cyclopean and many-columned *Y'ha-nthlei*," her tongue tripped over the name, which surely had no place on human lips, rouged or no. "I don't know about that. I do know those freaks have a truckload of gold. I read about it at the university, some discovery back in the '20s. Never thought I'd catch the bug myself."

Elwood pushed back his hat and scratched his head. Archaeology and dead languages had never been his forte. Piece by piece, he was putting the puzzle together.

"Books. Old books. You traded—"

"I got greedy," Lillian said, as if he'd accused her of something. "I should've stuck to ingots, sure. But why stop at a parade? I had me a mind to open a coffee-shop in downtown Arkham. You know, somewhere for folks... for folks like us to go. And that costs dough. So..."

"Where...?" Elwood's mouth was dry. The idol stared up at him, making him squirm. Blind condemnation glittered in its gaze. "Where did you get this... Lillian?"

"I took it from the Innsmouth Masonic Hall."

"You... took it?"

Lillian flapped a hand. "Jesus. Are you a cop now? It was left on the altar. It was night and no one was around. I'd come from the Old Marsh Refinery – Bobby Williamson keeps a pawnshop there, not that it's advertised – and the hall doors were open, the congregation down on the shore. Before I drove back to Arkham, I thought 'Why the hell not?' No one was gonna miss an old statue."

"You were wrong."

Lillian looked at him. Her eyes betrayed her sentiments, as did her trembling voice. "Jack, they're not gonna stop." She didn't need to say who; he'd seen them for himself. "I only took a down payment on it. How was I to know they'd come looking, attack the parade and smash up the store? I'll have to settle with Levensky later… Oh God. Jack. My mother…" She sobbed, panic climbing into her voice. "You have to help me."

Elwood swallowed. "Help you do what, Lillian?"

"Why, I have to go back to Innsmouth. I have to give the damn thing back."

Elwood let that sink in for a moment. Then he offered her a humourless grin.

"Oh, I don't think so, lady," he said. "My job was to find you. If you want my advice, you should high-tail it out of here why you still can."

"They're not gonna stop, Jack," Lillian repeated, reaching over to squeeze his arm. A little too hard, he thought, making him doubt the damsel-in-distress act. "Don't you see? If they don't get what they want… well, they've seen you. They know who you are. The Miskatonic isn't the only river in Massachusetts. There's the Charles River too. The Mystic and the Neponset, all flowing through Boston. Let's just say that the Order prefers to keep its secrets… secret."

As she spoke, Elwood stared at her with growing horror. Quentin! His mind went skating over ice. What about Quentin? His dread mounted as Lillian reached over and flicked a switch, the glove compartment popping open, mirroring his jaw. Inside, he saw a small, pearl-handled revolver. Loaded, at a guess.

Before he could say another word, Lillian tutted and put her foot to the metal. Lurching back in his seat, Elwood began to object. The squeal of tires cut him off. The car pulled out and ripped along the road, heading for the coast.

"Terrific," he said.

"Hell, we all make mistakes," she said. "Buckle up, hon. Time to kiss it better."

v. Frog Soup

CONSIDERING THE ATTACK on the parade and the way that the 'cultists' had come for him, Elwood proposed that a joyride into Innsmouth probably wasn't the best course of action. Lillian hushed him. "I told you I had a contact, didn't I?" To that end, she pulled up at a rundown gas station that emerged from what seemed like an ocean of marshes, flat, grassy and reeking of brine, stretching to the town and the sea beyond. After tapping him for quarters, Lillian's high heels clopped across the forecourt to a rusted payphone where, she told him upon returning, she'd fixed up a meeting at the Old Marsh Refinery come midnight. "Williamson will get the idol to the Order," she said, checking her hair in the rear-view mirror with a calmness he found hard to credit. "No harm. No foul. Then we can get on with the business of living, such as it is in these parts."

Elwood didn't share her confidence. There was something about her that niggled him, but he was too shaken to put his finger on it. And he was in too deep to turn back now, knowing if he did he'd never sleep again, starting at the drum of rain on his North End apartment window, every gurgle of the drain. The muddy stretch of the Charles River would never look innocent again. And it sure as hell wouldn't be fair to put Quentin at risk. Or to tell him about this unfortunate jaunt, what with his nervous disposition. Pouting at his ashen face, Lillian said that he knew what to do if things went south, nodding at the glove compartment. Then she fired up the bucket for the last mile or so into the seaport. High above, the moon rode with them, gibbous as it rose in the sky.

Innsmouth wasn't much to look at. On the outskirts of town, stately old mansions rose from overgrown lawns, the weed-choked statues and boarded up windows blurring like ghosts as they passed. The faded opulence soon gave way to strangled streets and cramped, unremarkable houses, most of their windows dark, the odd one lit by a feverish lamp. Heeding his advice, Lillian refrained from taking the main road into town, turning off at the Ipswich Junction instead. She headed north along what a rusted sign told him was Adams Street. Where it met Bank, Elwood noticed a rumbling in his ears, louder on every bridge they spanned. The Manuxet plunged through the town, carving a series of waterfalls through the terraces of streets to the shadowy harbour. At their mouth stretched the sea, a vista of ink at this hour. Out there lay the bay and the rocks which Lillian informed him were known as 'Devil's Reef', her voice a murmur over the engine. According to her, it was the font of all myths, tales of mad sailors and ancient gold. The reef gave way to the sunless and saliferous depths of the Atlantic Ocean.

Lillian pulled up on the corner of Federal and Paine, selecting the lone bar and grille for supper, a joint called Gilman's. The hotel, a Georgian monstrosity, lurched over the square like a penitent. A tug on Elwood's sleeve drew his attention to the Masonic Hall. The building sat on the sparse triangular green at the end of the labyrinth of streets. Its belfry and pillars looked ordinary enough, he thought, though he saw no cross, or for that matter, any recognisable religious symbol on its spire. Instead, he made out the sculpted waves and a Grecian pair of eyes set on its architrave. Its archaic gaze watched him like a portent. He shook off his misgiving, putting it down to the fact that the building was the source of his woes. In this godforsaken place, it no longer struck him as strange that some might cling to the beliefs of old, forgotten sea gods and idols, but the realization didn't give him much cheer.

Along with Lillian's manner, her looting bugged him too. It was the casual way in which she'd confessed it, Arkham parade or no. He could understand her reasons well enough. Men like him were considered roaches by polite society and few had qualms about stepping on them, not to mention what they made of those who dared to flout gender. The notion rattled the walls of their tidy world in the same way that Lillian rattled his. He'd grown too accustomed to life in the shadows. The truth was her defiance shamed him. Likely due to her theft, the doors of the Masonic Hall were shut, locked against the cloud-strewn sky. And women in lime green dresses. Could they undo her mistake? Make amends for her crime?

The atmosphere dripped with abandonment and penury. Half of the stores looked empty. The few pedestrians along the sidewalk darted from streetlight to streetlight, collars up in the glare of the Cadillac. When Lillian killed the engine, Elwood spared a glance for the eaves above him, elegant at the turn of the century, now cracked and sagging under the fog. He'd come here out of altruism, he reminded himself, to honour his alumnus, the friendship they'd once shared. The glow of the restaurant window, a cancerous yellow, did little to assure him it was wise.

*

INSIDE, ELWOOD ORDERED the soup of the day – in truth, a clam chowder – and he wasn't surprised to find it lukewarm and brackish, flakes of unidentifiable herbs afloat on the surface. Still, he was hungry from his tussle in Arkham and the long drive, and he slurped it down in the hope of reviving himself. Then he wiped his lips and subjected Lillian to another round of interrogation.

"What happened to Mrs… to your mother, Lillian? Were you suggesting—?"

"If only I knew," she said, putting down her fork. She'd only been playing with her salad anyway. "When I went back to the house after the parade, my mother wasn't there. Or rather, whoever *was* there, wasn't my mother." She grimaced, recalling some unpleasant memory. "They're in the town, which won't come as news to you. They've been creeping in for months now, I guess."

They, Elwood loosened his tie. He was feeling queasy, out of sorts. The room was cramped and empty of diners, the windows shut against the weather. All the same, he experienced a chill. He recalled the widow in the rattling house, her glassy and bulging eyes, her talk of golden idols and sacrifice. "A nasty business by all accounts", she'd said. And he remembered how she'd pointed him to Mayor Armitage and the clerk he'd been presented with, who'd sat in his gloomy office and coughed, his narrow head wreathed in pipesmoke. The whole thing had been a set-up, sure, a way to find the missing thief. But—

"The cult." He suppressed his dread with practicality. "What do they want? Sounds like more than a stolen statue."

"Who knows?" Lillian said and her shoulders fell. "Expansion of the Esoteric Order of Dagon? That's what they like to call themselves, anyway. To establish churches from Portland to Boston, perhaps…" Lillian fumbled for a cigarette in her overstuffed purse, lit it and went on through a veil of smoke. "As to what they *believe,* well, that's more complicated. According to the books in the Miskatonic library, there's some unholy union between Innsmouth and the folks of Essex County. They say that ambassadors came, rising from the drowned city of *Y'ha-nthlei*, fathoms under the sea. There's more than gold down there, Jack, or so I read. There's old things. *Old Ones.* With the right incantations, sacrifice, the Cult of Dagon hopes to establish the Deep Ones on land. And make way for the oldest of them all. Great Cthulhu, who in his house at R'lyeh waits dead and dreaming. *Fhtagn!*"

"Come again?"

"It's something they say. The cultists. In the old tongue."

"Boy, you've done your homework." Elwood steepled his hands under his chin, impressed. Lillian was frowning, an echo of the student he'd once known. It dawned on him that her dress and make-up wouldn't have changed that and he found he couldn't dismiss her claims as easily as he'd have liked. Shaken, he slurped another spoonful of soup to hide his expression, wincing at the taste. The revolver, pearl-handled and cold, dug into the small of his back, a small comfort. "You sure did wander into a snake pit with your blasted parade." He held up a hand at her protest, offering a placatory smile. "I'm not saying I blame you. What those bastards think, all scripture up front and cruelty behind doors, well... it ain't right. But you know there are people out there who'll hurt us. You gotta be careful." He sighed, wearied by his words. "Let sleeping dogs lie, isn't that what they say?"

"Sleeping *gods* in this case," she told him and pursed her lips. "You know, there are worse things a girl could do. We're all equal in God's eyes. We all cry, laugh, shit, bleed and die. Judge not, isn't that what He said? Well, all I see is a whole heap of judgement. You're damned straight it ain't right. That kind of shit is *inhuman.* We have to show them. They have to learn. That's why I wanted my parade. What else do you suggest? Hiding forever?"

"Spare me the sermon. We're not the only ones in the shadows in these parts. You'd have thought the Arkham PD would've done something. The townsfolk. Anyone!"

He recalled the lack of response from the department in question, the day of the Church Street parade. How deep did the conspiracy go? How much had the cult infiltrated? What in blazes was going on here?

"Like frog soup," Lillian told him.

"Huh?"

"Frog soup," she said, as if addressing some chump. "You know, from science class. Put a frog in boiling water and it'll jump right out of the pan. Put one in cool water and turn up the heat..."

"Yeah, I get it. The frog won't notice. So that's how..."

He belched, cutting himself off. The chowder churned in his guts. Regretting his appetite, he looked across the table at Lillian, tasting salt and alarm. The woman was swimming in his vision. Blearily, he watched as she stood, a hand climbing to her breast, her eyes wide. Following her gaze, Elwood turned in his seat, squinting at the figure who'd entered the dining room. At once, he fumbled for the revolver in his belt. He attempted to stand, his chair skittering from under him. Leaden, he dropped to one knee, the gun sliding away on the floorboards. The room was full of fog, the walls rippling.

"Thank you, Jack," the Widow Olmstead said from the doorway. "A friend in need, yes?"

Spluttering, Elwood stared up at Lillian. In his mind, the pieces snapped together, making a terrible sense. Her lack of grief for her mother, for starters. Her peculiar knowledge of the cult and its aims. The idol in her purse, simply 'taken' from the hall. The way she'd followed him to Pickman Street... She was a wolf in sheep's clothing, all right. Or in this case, a lime green dress.

"You... you brought me here on purpose..."

He tried to say more, to rebuke her for her double-cross. All he caught was a blur of ginger curls before the waves closed over his head.

*

vi. Upon the Black-Sailed Altar of Dagon

SACRIFICE, LILLIAN HAD said. Elwood sneered at the memory, the world swimming back into focus. A senseless span of time had passed. He'd been lying on a floor somewhere, drifting in and out of consciousness. A door had opened, closed. Footsteps had come and gone, echoing on stone. When he came to, his hands were bound and he was upright, a pole pressed against his spine. A groan escaped him. Anger simmered in his guts at the trick for which he'd fallen. Yeah, he'd fallen hook, line and sinker. Lillian must've spiked his soup. How could she do this to him? He'd come all the way from Boston to find her (it was forty-five minutes from Downtown Crossing, but he might as well have crossed an ocean). His former friend had only plucked him from the clutches of the cult for her own nefarious purposes. To offer him up, no doubt, in place of stolen gold…

The roaring in his ears, a hubbub that he placed as the sea, made his suspicions hard to pin down. The wind was heavy with salt, the spray on his cheeks rousing him. He heard music, the deep drums and the chanting all around, some flute-like instrument assailing the starless sky.

"*Iä! Iä! Cthulhu fhtagn!*"

Hardly daring to credit his eyes, Elwood drank in his surroundings. The first thing he noticed was his elevation. He stood several feet above the street. The night had deepened, the moon wreathed in scraps of cloud, but it was impossible to orientate himself in Innsmouth. The crowds didn't help much. Shadowed forms lined the sidewalk or hung out of windows above, arms waving in time with their cries. There must've been a hundred or more of them, their godless chants thrumming in his head. The sight of them made him reel, threatening to snap his mind. Was he hallucinating? The dope was still in his blood, after all...

Chowder rose in his throat, the aftertaste of betrayal. His flesh cooled to match the fog and he knew that what he was seeing was real. Every eye on him was sallow, orbs in narrow amphibian skulls. Every face was a pale, pelagic green. *They ain't like us, the Innsmouth folk.* He recalled the drunk at the Municipal Library, grasping the understatement. Yesterday, he'd taken such features as some hereditary quirk of New England. Now he suspected a different reason, some ancestry in Neptunian depths, the unholy union that Lillian had spoken of. The dwellers of Innsmouth were anything but human...

"Iä! Iä!"

Like a bird tossed on the queer cry, Elwood's gaze was drawn to the heavens. Whatever god reigned here, he feared it lurked in the darkness of the bay and wouldn't deign to help him. The black sail that billowed above, coupled with the lurch of the ground under him, brought home the fact that he was mobile. The mast at his back, the boom and the rigging overhead, left him in no doubt which vessel bore him. Shivering, dazed, he realized that he was in a boat of some kind, a schooner or ketch on the back of a truck. The draped seaweed and shells above, weaving and clacking like banners, spread a ball of cold through his guts. In some grim, benthic distortion – a mockery of the incident that had drawn him to Arkham in the first place – it dawned on Elwood that he was in a parade. *A parade of all things!* The boat was bedecked like a float, navigating the crowded streets. He had been bound to the mast, the blasphemous procession winding down to the harbour and the ocean beyond.

It was then that he noticed Mrs Olmstead – or whoever aped her in this (he shuddered at the thought) strange backwater ritual. The woman, lanky and wild, stood at the prow. It was she who was whipping the crowd into frenzy, her tall hat bearing a freakish, clerical aspect. Gold glimmered in the murk, her beads bringing to mind the golden statuette, lustrous with the same strange alloy. Her vestments, long and green, belonged to no orthodox faith. Even in the gloom, her aquatic visage was unmistakable. She swayed like an ancient reborn, some latter day priestess of the sea. What hair she had left was a sketch on her skull, her bones elongated, narrow. Her skin, a tattered mask, had peeled away from a toadlike mouth and the same round and watery eyes regarded the scene unblinking. Close up, Elwood noticed the gills on her neck. Between webbed hands, she clutched a wedge of solid gold. He recognised the object as the same foul statue that Lillian had shown him on their way to Innsmouth.

"The Children of the Deep shall never die!" the imposter shrieked, the idol held high. "We kneel to Dagon who birthed us, who gave us breath. Hearken to

us now, father! Open the gates to sunken *Y'ha-nthlei.*
Accept our sacrifice!"

The crowd roared – *Iä! Iä! Cthulhu fhtagn!* –
incomprehensible words from a time long before history
as Elwood knew it had begun. It didn't take a genius to
realise who the priestess meant by 'sacrifice' either, no
more than it did to see where the float was heading. The
boat crawled along the harbour wall, the black waves
rolling beyond. The knowledge wrenched a groan from
him, lost in the hubbub. He had never been more than
a fish on a hook, lured by the bait of his conscience. The
cult intended to give him to the sea, to the seething waves
of Devil's Reef and whatever lay beneath it.

Another groan answered his, closer than the celebrant
creatures and their raving, foam-lipped doyenne. The
mast shook with his efforts as he struggled for release,
rope burning his wrists. Craning his neck, he saw her.
Lillian! The woman had been bound to the mast behind
him, her pillbox hat lost to the chaos, her curls streaming
free. She looked up, her falsies aflutter. Taking in the
scene with mascara-streaked eyes, she appeared more
troubled than shocked. She had seen these abominations
before. Hell, she'd done business with them.

All but cheek-to-cheek, her lips a smear, Lillian
caught his glare.

"Jack! You're alive. Damn it, the frogs did a number
on us…"

In that moment, he knew that his capture wasn't down
to her. Lillian had seen a way to elevate herself along with

her fellows – men, women such as himself – and bring them out of the shadows, to confront the prejudice of Arkham. In a surge of relief, Elwood forgave her at once, for her thievery, her cause, grinning despite himself.

"Lillian!" He had to shout over the crowd. "I thought you... the idol... the soup..."

He shrugged, helpless, but she took his meaning.

"Well, thanks for nothing." She shook her head; neither of them had time for reproach. "Can you reach my leg? I'm wearing a garter. There's a nail file..."

Elwood didn't think such a weapon would save them. Nevertheless, he strained against his bonds, his wrists smarting. As luck would have it, his captors had appeared to rely mostly on the dope, his restraints giving way enough for him to reach her thigh. As if handling china, he teased out the thin metal tool, gripping it between slick fingers. Like he'd seen Lex Barker do in a *Tarzan* movie, with Quentin sat beside him at the drive-in, Elwood turned the blade upward. He began to saw through the rope.

"Open the gate, Father! Accept our meagre offering!"

Her cry skimming over the waves, the Widow Olmstead spread her arms and spun to face her captives. The boat had reached the wharf now, reaching the top of a launch. A slope of stone led down into the water. The crowds thronged the harbour wall, chanting, joyous. They were too far away to see Elwood's efforts with the rope. The priestess, however, was not. Her eyes flashed as his bonds snapped, Elwood wresting free of the mast. At his back, Lillian sagged, released. Like a matador, Elwood lashed out with the nail file, swift under the moon. He might as well have wielded a paperclip. The priestess snarled, revealing a row of tiny teeth, each one piranha sharp. Dropping the idol, she lurched towards him.

"Jack, the crate! The crate!"

It took him a second to grasp what Lillian meant. Then he was darting forward, reaching for the mess of equipment on deck. He'd managed to fling the lid open when the priestess fell upon him, her fingers – claws – sinking into his shoulders. Crying out, he sprawled on his back, arms raised to keep her at bay. The creature snapped at him, drool peppering his face. Her gills seethed, her back a hunch of spines, designed for the lightless fathoms. He only hoped it would give him an advantage. The priestess, or whatever she was, had strength to her. Elwood knew he couldn't hold her off for long. In his ears, her vile croaking, doubtless summoning disciples to her aid. Faint splashes confirmed his fears, the creatures diving off the harbour wall in their haste to reach the boat. If they did so, he was finished.

Then Lillian was there, a lime green blur. Lips a fierce moue of red, she raised the oar in her hands and brought it down hard on the priestess's hump. With a crack of splintering wood, the fiend wailed and slumped to one side, giving Elwood time to leap for the flare gun that Lillian had spied in the crate. Grabbing it, he climbed to his feet, dizzy and tipping along with the deck. The truck was slipping into the water, the driver giving no thought to drowning. The bow of the boat, which overhung the roof of the cab, met the blackish waves. Despite the sails above, it was plain that the vessel only served a ceremonial purpose, some foul oblation to a heathen god. The boat had meant to see the both of them into the bay, soon sinking them drugged and bound into the waiting depths. Lillian and him were merely bait, fodder for the blasted sea.

Worse, the inhabitants of Innsmouth, hideous to a one, were swarming through the water. Some began clambering up the sides of the boat. *'Iä! Iä!'* In seconds they'd reach him, a hundred claws to tear him to pieces. He'd never see Quentin again, never bask in his smiles in the Pearl Street office or feel his warmth next to him in bed… It was this that spurred him to action. He shouted at Lillian to stay back. Recalling how the creatures had shirked the Cadillac's headlights in Arkham, Elwood raised the flare gun over his head. With a cry, he pulled the trigger. Light blossomed over the bay.

In the crimson radiance, the priestess shrieked, shielding her face. As one, the creatures hissed, the would-be boarders falling back, crashing into the water. Half-blinded, Elwood grabbed Lillian's arm and pulled her to portside. He had no idea what he was doing – he was a tax collector from Boston, damn it – but it was clear that it was time to disembark. There were other boats nearby, bobbing in the gloom. One of them must surely have an engine…

The flare was fading, an arc of phosphorescence over the bay. Before Elwood took the plunge, the deck shuddered under him, the shells rattling overhead. It reminded him of the eleven o'clock to Portland, shaking the house on Water Street, an event that seemed an age ago. The tide was sucking at the launch, drawing back over shingle and sand. Something out in the bay was approaching, he realized, something larger than a train. It swept close to the shallows, rising from the Atlantean depths.

As soon as he thought it, a tremendous bubbling filled his ears. He looked beyond the prow, the waves churning, a whirlpool troubling the surface. The reflections scattered and dimmed, the flare winking out overhead. The fog closed in, dousing the waves in darkness. Waves sloughed on the bay, lashing at the harbour wall, carrying the odd creature with them. With the disturbance, the sprawled priestess raised herself to face it, gazing with adoration at the tide.

Elwood looked at Lillian, his dread mirrored in her pale, streaked face.

"Dagon," she breathed.

The sky shook. A submerged bellow thundered through the depths. Rigid as stone, Elwood saw a great fan of spines break the surface of the bay. Scads of seaweed and fish poured from the slick membranes between them. The muck slopped from anaemic flesh, from the jagged titan who came, silt sliding off its bulk. Its shoulders, each the size of the Masonic Hall, thrust its colossal skull from the sea. Scaled and horned, its snout narrowed to a black grille of fangs. Caught in the glare of a gargantuan eye, Elwood howled, his brain fit to burst. Mortals weren't meant to see such things, the understanding spearing through him. How long had the beast waited, its name remembered by only the damned? Had it lurked for aeons, patient and hungry under the sea? What chaos did it bring, summoned from slumber by the Order? Under the leviathan's claws, the buildings and bridges of New England would crumble like matchbox toys.

As if to echo Elwood's dread, the priestess prostrated herself, her head to the deck, her claws clasped in prayer.

"Nog!" she murmured in the same dead tongue, hushed and reverent. *"Nog ng vugtlagln vulgtmm!"*

Gazing over the harbour, Elwood witnessed a similar scene, the crowds falling silent, their toadish faces pressed to the ground. His heart, a drum, cringed to see them. Some deep, unplumbed part of him longed to sink to his knees before the giant, to beg Dagon for mercy. To spare his pathetic, landbound life...

Lillian didn't share his awe. Taking advantage of the lull, she grabbed Elwood's tie, wrenched him towards her.

"I don't regret it, you know," she said. "Any of it."

Elwood met her defiance. "I know."

In her eyes, he could tell she'd lost her taste for gold. She had probably heard enough dead languages to last her a lifetime. There was pride and then there was survival. Before he could stop her, Lillian grabbed his shoulder and pushed him, the two of them crashing into the water.

*

PORTLAND, JULY 1951

DEAR QUENTIN,

How can you forgive me? I'm sorry for leaving the way I did and it sucks to send you another farewell. By now, you'll have read all the facts concerning the First Annual Arkham Parade. I sent my report to the Herald and the rags are doubtless ablaze with the news. Please take this letter as a postscript, which should help you to make more sense of things. You'll be pleased to hear I'm as well as can be expected. I'm heading west with Lillian Crow to a 'safehouse' in an undisclosed location.

How did we escape from Innsmouth, you might ask? Well, it wasn't easy. While the inhabitants were distracted by the horror in the bay, Lillian and I managed to swim to a speed boat and fire up the engine. Navigating the reef was a horror in itself and I'm afraid to say we were pursued. Needless to say the creatures swam fast and we rounded the headland narrowly, barely missing the rocks. Once we'd navigated into Plum Island Sound, with dawn breaking the horizon, we found ourselves alone, left to either drift or drown. Instead, we made it to Newburyport and there I was faced with my godawful choice. The writing of my report and this letter.

Please believe me. The Esoteric Order of Dagon is real, as real as anything I've put in my account. You may think that I've abandoned you; I ask you to remember my practical nature and ask yourself whether I'd lie. If only my trip to Arkham had concerned a missing friend!

To my regret, I've come to learn that an inhuman cult, some ungodly spawn that dwells deep under Essex Bay, has infiltrated New England. Arkham has fallen under its sway, presumably with Boston soon to follow. Wise to their plans, Lillian and I find ourselves hunted. Though it weighs on us daily, for now it's best we keep to the shadows.

To return to the city would lead our enemies straight to you. The reason for my continuing absence is for your protection, my dear, and I beg you to respect that. DO NOT CONTACT THE AUTHORITIES. Don't show anyone this letter. Throw it on the fire and mention it to no one. Take what you can from the safe in the Pearl Street office and head west as soon as possible. Under no circumstances come looking for me. Steer clear of Innsmouth!

This isn't over. Somehow, I'll make my way back to you. One day, Quentin, all the shadows over us will pass.

Until then.

Jack

Letter #2. From the evidence file of the Boston Police Department, 154 Berkeley Street, Boston. Submitted by Mr Quentin G. Fields.

VĪVĪSEPULTURE

VĪVĪSEPULTURE (NOUN):
the practice of burying someone alive.

THE GHOSTS ARE loud tonight. Eric hears them howling around the house in the wind, but mostly inside his own head. If you asked him, Eric would say he doesn't believe in ghosts. Like a million other folks, he's far from special in that. He believes in emptiness though. Ask him and he'd tell you that a ghost is just a memory, a vacant lot filled with the debris of dead feelings. Paul said so once, after reading some book or other. And Eric has thought that way ever since Paul passed three years ago, leaving him to wash up alone on the shores of his late forties, clutching the crushed tin can of his heart and wondering, wondering how the hell he's supposed to start over. Now that the flat stomach of his thirties has become a bowling ball under his shirt. Now his hair is streaked with grey. Now he doesn't have the ready, fuck-it-all smile that made Paul fall for him all those years ago, that cold sweet year up north. None of which saved Paul John Rodriguez (1979 – 2024) from the car crash. A coal truck had skewed on ice, flipped and crushed the roof of his Ford. Crushed them both, even though Eric was miles away choosing tiles for the bathroom refit and didn't know it until the police showed up at his door an hour later.

'Your husband is dead,' they said. Just like that. Didn't even ask if he wanted to sit down first. A faint air of disdain had hung over the porch. They'd have preferred a wife. Normality. It showed in the officers' faces. Somehow, Paul's death was less to them. And Eric was less than that. You can forgive Eric for not having a particularly spiritual outlook. Eric knows what it means to be alone.

But tonight the ghosts are loud, he's weary of TV dinners and his own sorry company, and so he decides to go out.

THE TROUBLE IS it isn't the house that's haunted. Maybe a couple of Cuba Libres will silence the noise. He isn't expecting much. Enough to wash down the taste of processed mac 'n cheese and Xanax, and send him into sleep where (he thinks) the dead can't touch him. That's on his mind when he steps off the subway and, collar up like a cartoon crook, slips into the downtown gay district. To a bar he's never been before. A bar without memories.

A bar with a name he won't later recall. Music rumbles, a dirge through the floor. The place reeks of *Le Male* and cigarettes. There's a toilet that he reckons stinks worse. Probably a dark room that stinks worse than that. Whenever a guy walks by his booth, Eric sucks in his gut, not that anyone is looking. Most folks are looking at their phones. Eric is invisible. How ironic is that? Haunted *and* a ghost. He's forty going on fifty and on the scrap heap along with the rest. The gay living dead. He tells himself it's a place that Paul would hate and that makes it better somehow. He'll order another drink, then head on home, he thinks.

He's thinking it when the guy slides into the booth and sits opposite him.

"Drowning your sorrows?"

The guy makes a joke about the necessity of hooch in a place like this. He's trying to take the edge off it, but Eric is too in shock to laugh. Noah was hammering nails into wood the last time anyone approached him like this. Even guys in the office only approached him with documents and sales figures and tedious chat about their weekends. Mundane, hetero lives.

He manages to cough out a reply. It isn't a good one.

"Or myself."

The guy nods. It's disarming enough for Eric to take a look at him. The guy doesn't get up to walk away. Not yet. A second later there's the fear that this might lead somewhere. Lord, they might even fuck and how the hell is he supposed to remember how to do that? A second after *that*, he realises that the guy is a corpse.

"I hear drowning isn't as bad as they say. Try being smashed in the face with a claw hammer."

He has Eric's full attention. Eric is sitting bolt upright against faux red leather and choking on his rum. He can see that the guy is his type, sure. Or at least he *used* to be. His fringe was probably blond once. His denim jacket sings 'top', but it's had its time in the sun. He's what? Thirty, thirty five? Hard to tell. Pallor mortis is quite the makeover, he thinks like a dick. Bloated lips smile at him, a shade of blue that Eric knows isn't... Uh. That word again. *Normal.* There's the noticeable stink of him too, an earthy sweetness that's far from sweet. When the guy takes a sip of his drink, Eric can see the straw through a hole in his cheek, the hint of tendons and a black tongue. Rot is eating him away. And, like the guy said, half of his face is toast.

"Get over it," the guy says, watching him. "Name's Bobby. And yes, I'm dead."

Eric can see that.

Bobby tries to explain. "Some arsehole did it. Six months ago. Bad date or what? Shit, *I'm* still not over it."

Murders in downtown aren't rare. Every day there's a new smiling face on a milk carton. A woman missing on the news. It's a running theme in every major city, but Eric has been distracted of late. Paul has kept him busy. The emptiness.

But Eric hasn't met the dead before.

"You're a ghost." Shock prompts him to state the obvious.

Bobby pulls a 'duh' face. His wounds squelch a little. He flicks back his hair, a sarcastic punctuation mark. From his left cheek up, he's all crushed bone with an eye missing. There's this hole there, crusted by blood. The aftermath of the blow, Eric thinks. *A claw hammer,* he said. It looks like an open grave.

Then Bobby reaches over and grabs Eric's hand. His touch is like an icepack.

Eric pulls back but there's nowhere to go.

"I'm dead and I need your help."

ERIC HAS SEEN Horror movies. Who hasn't? In Horror movies, you run. How the fuck he's out here on the street with the guy – shit, the corpse – isn't something he'll ever be able to put into words. But he knows why. Bobby saw him. Bobby chose him. And Bobby, dead or no, is better to talk to than an old photograph of Paul, the TV or himself.

These are the reasons why Eric doesn't run: A cold bed waiting. The lack of a cat. No taps on any of the apps he's cruised like some creepy uncle (not even when he used a profile pic from college). The crushing knowledge that tomorrow will just be an echo of today and him fading along with it. It's a humdrum cycle. The office. The evening call from Mom and her ever-sad tone. The gazing at the pillow where Paul lay his head. The masturbation. The tears. And the ghosts, of course, howling around the house. His head.

Run? Run *where?* Bobby, at least, he can see. And besides, a psychotic episode might break up the tedium. It's clear what's happening here.

"... any ordinary Friday night," the dead guy is saying, trudging beside him. "You know how it goes. You're lonely and horny and looking for some. I've met jerks before. Shit, I've met more jerks than I *have* jerked, you know? But this guy was different."

"Because he murdered you?"

Bobby snorts. It's meant to sound caustic. The fluids that spray from his nose kind of spoil the effect. He wipes it on denim. Looks sheepish.

"No. I mean he was different in a nice way. A maybe-you'll-mean-more way. You think I follow every rando out of a club?"

Eric doesn't answer. He's painfully aware of the fact that not only has he followed a stranger out of a bar, the stranger stopped breathing months ago. Who's he to judge?

"Silence speaks volumes."

"Sorry," Eric says, offers a smile. "I mean yes. I know what you mean. When I met my husband in Uni, I -"

"Wow. Did I ask about your love life? Go brag somewhere else. I kind of got zeroed here!"

"Sorry," Eric says again. "That was insensitive." Then he decides it isn't and says, "Actually, my husband died too. Three years ago now. Car crash."

"What was his name?"

"Paul."

Bobby asks Eric which district.

Eric tells him.

Then Bobby rolls his eyes. Eye. And he snorts some

more body fluid and what look like gobbets of clotted blood.

"Jeez, Eric. It's like you think we all know each other or something."

Then Bobby laughs, bumps his shoulder (squelch) and leads him to the club.

The last club that Bobby ever went to.

AT SOME NEBULOUS point around forty, a tipping point occurs. The pink portcullis of the scene comes down and the pop songs get muffled behind it. But there are other changes as well. Not just a runaway waistline and hair in the plughole. There's more to it than that. More than finding yourself short of breath on the stairs or suffering a hangover that lasts all week. Or going to bars and grasping the fact that men no longer notice you. That the noticeable part of your life is over. For the most part, you become invisible. When you're invisible, the dead can see you though. Or so Bobby tells him. It's an explanation of sorts.

Cocktails and cadaverine, that's how it starts. A few drinks under neon that speed up and ripple with each gulp (you better believe that Eric is drinking). That and the faint, ever-present reek of his... date. Can he call Bobby that? After all, they're out on the scene. Their secondary world. A postmodern Narnia complete with bears and otters and queens. They don't belong anywhere else. Society has made sure of that.

Desperation perfumes the air. Perspiration, gum and cologne. And something else. The rot. Eric looks around and he sees them like headstones in the crowd. Pale faces. Blue lips. Hollow eyes. Can the *living* see them too, he wonders? The truly alive. The ones under thirty, anyway. The slick jocks with the fuck-off eyes. The anxious looking twinks at the bar. The drag queen who slips and shrieks on the floor, heels high, wig askew. Men make out in the shadows. Men stare like a wall. No one stares at Eric though. Everyone here has an emptiness, he knows. Everyone has a *want.* It comes with the territory. But no. Tonight, it's Eric alone who can see the dead.

Again, he didn't note the name of the place. Who gives a shit? Time has become a shutter in blacklight. One minute he's downing shots with the rancid Bobby (sambuca dribbles from a hole in his chin). The next he's ordering another round. The last time Eric did this, the first birds were crawling out of the Jurassic mud, having evolved from dinosaurs. And here he is two hundred million years later, flirting with a corpse.

It's inevitable. The two of them take to the dance floor. Their hips sway. Rum splashes their shoes. Lady Gaga beseeches folks to stop telephoning her as the club throbs and spins. They're up close, the corpse and him. Bobby. Their groins all but brush. It's only when their lips do that Eric snaps out of it. Worms on the guy's breath. And Eric realises then that he's *thinking* about it. How it might feel. A cold nipple on his lips. A blue tongue in his hole. Does the blood still pump, turgid and black? Can the guy even... get hard? There's more than zombification at play, surely. Bobby, by his own admission, is a ghost. And no ghost has been louder than this. Will Eric take his pleasure here, down in the disco of the dead? There's a word for that too, he remembers. A long one beginning with N. And what does that make him, exactly? He thinks he's going to be sick.

He's fortysomething and more than tired. Eric forces his way to the bar. Then the quietest corner of it, which is far from quiet.

"Why... why do you look like that?" he roars in Bobby's ear. He should push him away. Leave. But he can't. TV dinners tell him he can't. So does an old photograph.

"Like what?"

"You know. Like..." Eric flaps a hand.

Bobby takes his meaning. Shrugs. He's a little hurt though. Eric can tell.

"It's how I remember myself. It's how I am now... Somewhere."

Somewhere.

"I thought... Well."

"That I'd float from the ceiling in some glowing white form? Uh uh. Not in the rules."

"There are rules?"

"You don't think being born and dying is a rule?"

Eric considers. It's a fair point.

"Bobby, why are we here?"

"Another rule, hombre. We have to retrace my steps. If we want to get there."

"Where?"

"Through the wardrobe door. To Oz. Stop asking stupid questions."

Ice closes around Eric's hand. Bobby leads him towards some steps. He wants to correct him, but doesn't. *Oz.* There's nowhere to go, so he follows.

Over the threshold if not the rainbow.

WHERE DO THEY go, the gay living dead? The ones with widening waistlines, thinning hair and no fuckbuddy or husband. The ones whose runway has run out and plunged them headlong into the swamp. Where do they go when Narnia has closed her doors to them? Do they gather on some island, druid style, and sacrifice Prada shirts that no longer fit and try to muster up the long lost names of all those they've fucked and ghosted, mournful under the moon?

No. Eric knows where. They kind of fade into the background. They bask in the light of flickering TV screens. They feast on lukewarm microwave meals. Every night is a ritual of phone calls from elderly mothers and every morning means waking up in a bed like an ache, half of it forever pristine. A space that was never filled. An emptiness. Eric knows that emptiness. And he knows that when you finally see it, when you realise that the emptiness is all you'll ever know from now on, then you become invisible. When you're invisible, then the dead might come for you. Why waste any more time?

Tonight, the dead have come for Eric.

The two of them walk past the bars, the takeaways and taxi stops. Where the hell are they going now? Eric doesn't kid himself that this is a normal date with a normal guy. Normal. Nothing is normal! The night isn't going to end with clumsy sex and false promises. Even if they fucked then Bobby would probably fall to pieces on him. The thought returns his hand to his side and widens a distance between them. When they reach the corner, Bobby's face lent colour by the streetlights, the guy stops and looks embarrassed. Then he points between the buildings at the dark end of the street. At first, Eric only sees shadow. Then he makes it out. A vacant lot. His flesh crawls as the penny drops.

This is where it happened.

"This is where it happened," Bobby tells him.

Ah, but there's a resonance here.

"A ghost is just a memory, a vacant lot," he murmurs.

"Excuse me?"

"Something Paul said once. Ignore me. I'm drunk."

"I miss getting drunk," Bobby sighs. Then nods at the dark end of the street. "I was drunk the night he brought me here. Joe or Jack or Jonathan. This was his idea of a romantic spot. How dumb am I?"

But Eric knows that dumbness too. Hell, he pictured the guy sticking his dick inside him like an ice pole. It hardly makes him a saint.

"Show me," he says. At this point, he wants to see. He wants to understand. Plus, grim as it is, the last time he had company, the formation of basic elements was taking place in the wake of the Big Bang.

He bet the truck made a bang when it flipped and landed on top of Paul.

Eric winces. Regrets the last shot.

The ghosts laugh in silence.

THERE'S NOTHING REMARKABLE about the lot. There's the hole in the fence you'd expect to find. The same ripple of worn-out concrete. The same weeds creeping through the cracks. The same litter. At the back of the lot there's an area that nature has conquered, all brambles and wires and earth. A patch where the streetlights can't penetrate. A place where men like Bobby could penetrate, however, and go their separate ways. One Friday night six months ago, Bobby found himself penetrated by a hammer to the face.

"I thought he liked me," Bobby says. "Even as I knelt in this dump and unzipped him, I thought that. And I guess he did."

"You think so, huh?"

Bobby eyes him in surprise. "Sure, as a trophy. A spirit fuck or whatever. Because that's what I am now. Just hanging around. Until…"

"Bobby?"

"It's dark, but there are blood stains here. Right where we're standing."

Eric shivers. Suddenly the night is cold. The rum is

running out. He's a coward at heart. Paul said that once too, during some row or other.

Oh, Paul.

"And shards of bone. The eye I guess he took with him."

"Too much information."

Bobby grins (squelch), but it's a sad one.

"Look, you didn't have to come."

"No."

"I'll tell you one thing. It hurt like hell."

And despite the smell, Eric holds him. There's probably all kinds of muck dripping onto his shoulder, but Eric doesn't care. Somewhere out there, there's a mother and a father waiting for a son. Friends who'll never see him again. A future of roads never taken. And Eric wants the comfort. The last time Eric hugged someone... Well, you get the picture.

"Eric." After a while, Bobby sniffles, collecting his deceased self. "Why did you come?"

Because you saw me. Because you chose me. Because there is nothing waiting.

Eric doesn't say any of that. It doesn't matter that Bobby is dead, it's still awkward.

"You know why," he says.

IT'S EVERYTHING THAT Eric imagined. Bobby is like an ice block inside him, the question about the blood answered. Or there's a memory of blood. Bobby brought a condom and lube, still in date where Bobby is not. To add to the irony, Eric is bent over a rusty refrigerator, but the smell of the trash is better than the smell of Bobby and he thinks that makes it OK. Cold or not, his body answers like it never forgot. There's the pain, sure. Then the butterflies, snow-coated in his belly, up his spine. Nerve endings rejoice and sing. At last! At fucking last! He grits his teeth. Closes his eyes. Imagines it's Paul on their third date, that cold sweet year up north. He pushes down the morality of it. Fuck that. It isn't the long word beginning with N. Bobby is a ghost, not a – oh! Oh. For a minute or so all thought scatters. His ring clenches around frozen flesh. All the butterflies go up in flames. Then Bobby gives a grunt, savage in the dark. For a few fleeting moments, Eric goes with it. For a few fleeting moments, feels loved.

Not long after, they sprawl on their backs in the dirt, staring up at the photopollution. Up at the lack of stars. The emptiness behind them.

"That was better than… you know. The night with the other guy."

It's a bad joke and Eric pulls a face. A face that Bobby doesn't see, but nonetheless conveys the fact that he knows this isn't love.

But it isn't a TV dinner either.

NIGHT OF THE gay living dead. They're walking again. Drifting. A little closer, if not holding hands. Eric thinks he's getting used to the smell. Wonders what that means. He could ask Bobby if there's a heaven or a hell, but he doubts the guy knows. There's not much difference between them, he thinks. One having stepped beyond. The other bored in the waiting room. Both invisible. A thin sheet between them. Spring ice on a lake. Not much.

They walk and Eric looks in the windows. At couples. Families. Kids. Once he'd had a taste of that, what it felt like. To come home to something other than ghosts. To cook for someone. To bounce stupid ideas around. Memories. Plans. To curl up on a couch too small for them and watch movies while one or the other snores. To hug. To fuck. To share the bills. To take out their worst childhood traumas on each other. To fight. To fuck again. It was hard, at times. But it wasn't empty. It held the emptiness at bay.

"This is it. The end of the story."

But it isn't, not quite. The final scene is the cut of a railway track that runs behind the houses, through the litter-strewn bushes and thorns. There's a slope. The glitter of broken glass. Enough barbwire to put off the most reckless of teens. And there's the risk of the trains, of course, slicing through the bland, smug heart of suburbia. Not even the dogs shit down there, Eric thinks. It's an overlooked place. Invisible. A good place to hide a body.

"This is where he put you," he says.

"Yup. Rolled up in an old carpet from his van. Not that I knew he *had* a van. Or a hammer for that matter."

Bobby laughs, a wet sound. A comedian he's not.

And Eric gets it. He does. He's seen Horror movies. He's read spooky stories. There's no point stating the obvious.

"There's evidence down there. DNA, maybe. Under your fingernails. Is that it?"

That's why you brought me here.

Bobby frowns. Then he understands. Typically, he shrugs.

"I don't give a shit about that, man. I just want what we all want."

"Right."

To be found. To be seen.

"Guess this is the part where you tell me about the rules again," Eric goes on. "They find you and you're at peace, right? You can move on elsewhere." *Heaven. Hell. Nirvana. The Big Gay Orgy in the Sky.* "That's why you came looking for me."

"Yes."

"Specifically me?"

"I... think so. I think you only get one. It isn't as if there's a guidebook."

Eric nods. Chews it over. It's no big deal to dial 911 and report a body in the briar. He can do so anonymously, he thinks. The police are duty bound to respond. He remembers the officers on his porch that night and yeah, he has a doubt about that, but he can always keep calling. Persist. He could send an email to the papers too. Give no details. No one has to know it's him. Somewhere, a mother and a father are waiting for a son. Somewhere, friends are hurting.

But tonight, for once, the ghosts are quiet.

Tonight, Eric has drank and danced and even fucked. And maybe Paul was right about him, after all.

"Hey!" It's Bobby, calling out behind him. "Where the fuck are you going?"

Despite the awkwardness of it, Eric finds himself on the move. His blood and bones – still warm, yes – are taking him back up the street. Back towards the city and the bars. The light. And he can't believe he's smiling. His smile quickens his steps.

Sure, he's down among the dead. But there'll be no emptiness tomorrow.

Bobby, having come, must follow him.

THE CICATRIX

LONDON, NOW

YEATS ONCE WROTE that the world was full of magic things. And magic was on Becket's mind this morning as he creaked from another restless sleep and into the bathroom of his cramped Balham flat. His mouth was stale with rum, cigarettes and the taste of burnt moths. With a hangover worthy of Nero he stumbled for the khazi, disgorged the slop of yesterday's supper. His locket, a dull gold, hung open at his neck. The picture inside it flashed a smile, guileless in a young brown face. Becket couldn't remember when it was taken. Seb, his former apprentice, had been thirty years in his grave. Vanished. Like everything was these days.

A shit. A wash. When Becket rubbed the steam from the bathroom mirror, he reflected that he no longer saw magic things at all, not unless the magic was black. But he saw his seventy-year-old face in the glass. Once, audiences across Europe had called him 'magisterial', but he could see no trace of that now. His eyes had guttered, snuffed out by bitterness. His lips held no wryness. His skin had grown haggard, a map of an ill-lived life. Of too many cocktails and meaningless sex. *Of murder,* his conscience croaked, strangled as it was.

No magic things. Strange for a magician to admit that, a rejection at the end of things when fame, friends and money had gone. When no lovers remained to lick his balls and a demon stared at him from the mirror.

"Sad," said Ormenus, the Author of All Calamities. In the glass, the demon looked as blue as his mood, cherubic and levitating. "Ladies and gentlemen, witness the fall of the Great Magus, Becket Ward. Once the rival of Marzan the Magnificent. Now blind to his own summoning."

Fuck. Becket shut his eyes. Like a streak of piss, last night came flooding back to him. The diagram on the living room floor. The grimoire (*De Occulta Philosophia*), open before him. The candles, the bowl and the dead moths. The *khetem* clutched in his fist. And the demon, Ormenus, who'd come at Becket's bidding moments before he'd blacked out.

"Gah," Becket spat. "*Exi seductor.* I've changed my mind. Fuck off back to Hell."

Ormenus, all fangs and tail, chuckled.

"Oh, magus." Its voice was salt and gravel, resounding from beyond the world. "Do you imagine words alone hold power? Those heady days are gone."

Becket growled, his knuckles white on the edge of the sink.

"We all do things we regret."

"That's putting it mildly," Ormenus replied. "Thirty years you've had from me. And a pretty price you paid for them too." The demon jabbed a claw at the locket around the old man's neck. "Isn't that why I'm here? *Seb* was the name on your lips last night."

As if made of clay, the creature shaped itself to resemble the youth in question. Into the face of Becket's shame. The slick black hair. The dark eyes that had first arrested him in Cairo, back in '82. And his smile, dazzling as moonlight on the Nile. Forever frozen in a photograph.

Seb Hassan Samir. Long dead and buried. *Dead, yes, and burning.*

As if he could forget.

Becket's face was a sphincter, puckered with pain. He snapped the locket shut, a defensive, futile gesture. The demon knew his heart. Outside, a car horn blared. A train rattled past, the passive-aggressive business of London a million miles away. Rage climbed up his throat, exploding in a shout. It barely echoed in the cramped space. Then he flung out a fist, the mirror crumpling inward.

The demon grinned in the webbed shards.

Seb. Where it all began. Damnation.

"The black star is back," Ormenus told him. "Will you make your peace with God, magus? Or with me?"

*

LONDON, 1972

ALONG WITH HARRY Blackstone Jr. and Marzan the Magnificent, Ward had been considered one of the greats. At his peak, he was the toast of clubs from Moscow to Madrid. It didn't start out that way though. Not long after graduation, a blond haired, tall young man with a bright future ahead of him, he'd abandoned a promising career in the sciences, seduced by Magic School. Magic, that was, that had nothing to do with the paranormal. As far as Becket understood it, the art involved illusion and sleight-of-hand, that was all. Practically minded, he'd applied himself. By autumn of his gap year, he'd collected enough books in his bedroom to block half of the window. The birds in the tree outside had been mindless to the trials that he was about to subject them to.

A talent for vanishing pigeons soon taught him that there was money in it. And a few quid had rolled in, first at the parties of friends, then later in a small Northampton theatre. While he was treading those boards to modest applause, Evander Marzan (not so 'Magnificent' back then) was entertaining the backstreets of London. Neither of them knew it, but both had fortune hanging in their stars. Marzan, the young prodigy with his proud Greek looks, black top hat and mysterious smile was on his way to the big time.

"He *is* admirable," Becket had told his father, the old man scowling at Marzan's appearance on breakfast TV in their Fen Ditton cottage, a place left to them after Ruth, his mother, had succumbed to cancer years before. "It does take a certain skill. As it happens, I've been thinking of moving to London myself. Make a go of it."

"And kiss your life goodbye, idiot. Do you know how much it cost me to send you to Christchurch?"

Becket, who'd found a new hero, had left his father wheezing at the box and embarked for the city in question. He'd rented a room in Camberwell where the traffic shook his window all night and filled the tiny space with fumes. He'd practised rope tricks. Shuffled cards. Produced doves from handkerchiefs. When he got bored he went into Soho, drank and laughed like a loon. He went home with policemen and dancers, all good-looking, all forgettable. His heart was set on the stars.

When he read in the *Stage* that Marzan was holding auditions for his upcoming show (*Fantastikós!* the posters screamed from Paddington to Poplar, the magician gathering steam in the city), Becket went along, borne on the hope of becoming his apprentice. And on rattling nerves.

"A clever act of restoration," Marzan told him from where he sat in the auditorium, a silhouette of curls and broad shoulders through the footlights. His voice matched his aura, rich and deep. The magician looked fit to burst from his shirt, all Hellenic muscle and fuzz that didn't much help the butterflies in Becket's stomach. "What else can you show me?"

Becket had tried to vanish the blush in his cheeks as if that's what Marzan had asked him. This was on Long

Acre, deep in London's theatreland. Stood on the verge of greatness, Becket had taken his chance. Gently, he'd set down the remade bulk of the phone book on the table beside him. He'd closed his eyes. Focused. Flourished. He fancied he heard a gasp and cracked an eye open to see the book floating off its surface.

"Impressive!" Marzan clapped his hands and laughed. Then he dismissed his manager and agent, and fixed Becket with a brilliant smile. "How about lunch?"

Later, after too much wine, Marzan had left his top hat propped on a bedknob in his hotel room as the two of them fucked, the magician and his prospect. Grunting into a pillow, Becket had imagined that every thrust of those strong Greek thighs brought him a step closer to triumph. His old man would be so proud of him! Perhaps he could send some money home, once *Fantastikós!* was up and running, and he was the talk of the West End.

Becket Ward. Apprentice. Protégé. *Magician.*

Marzan had soon left for the theatre, citing further auditions to get through. Standing in a rain-washed Leicester Square, Becket had wanted to joke that there was no point now, surely. Instead, he'd scribbled down his number on the back of a tube ticket and handed it to Marzan.

"Promise me... Evander." He'd dared the name, squeezed the magician's arm. "Call me?"

His heart was like wax, melting under those fierce eyes. It beat in time with the traffic and the rain, the particulars of a world from which he was ascending.

Magic, magic things...

As promised, Becket got a call three days later. He'd barely slept, barely eaten, waiting for the telephone to ring. In a crisp monotone, a man who identified himself as Marzan's agent told Becket that sadly, he hadn't made the cut. The phone cord had bitten into Becket's hands, twisting like him in the hall. Wings of shadow had fluttered through the room.

"To be honest, we're looking for someone younger," the agent told him. "Better luck next time."

THERE ISN'T A joy the world can give like that it takes away, Byron once wrote. An older version of Becket, successful, adored, had liked to scoff at that. It was his party piece. He'd dismiss the poets he'd read at Cambridge with a thousand bon mots in a thousand bars, the drunkest (and most obsequious) in his coterie laughing at every one.

"Why, one can always seek out new joys," he'd say, his Mai Tai swinging in hand. "Cocaine. The horses. Buggering a fan. Byron certainly did."

Then, with a skill as slick as any he displayed on stage, he'd make his drink disappear like a rabbit in a hat and call out for another.

Wisdom, Becket had found, came with age. Years slipped by between his days in London and his eventual fame, a decade filled with performances, nameless lovers, puff pieces and fathoms of drink. And magic. *Real* magic. At first, it had been the odd séance with friends, the petitioning of the dead for favours. The location of a buried chest. The power of fear over an audience. Such amusements had fired Becket's mind and led him to unmapped bookshops in Glastonbury and York. In a couple of years, he'd read everything from *The Discovery of Witchcraft* to *The Book of the Law.* A year after that he'd purchased an antique volume from one Justin Margrave, a portly critic (and queen) in Covent Garden, and things had taken a turn for the better after that. Soon enough, Becket was practicing ritual from tattered tomes, adding colour to his shows, drama. He drank rum and smoked cheroots. Stuff what the critic had said; a little incantation never hurt anyone. He was a seeker after the truth. The orgies, the bacchanalia came later. The press had lapped up his mystique.

Besides, why shouldn't he feel proud? He'd shed so much blood, sweat and tears, not to mention the hours he'd spent to prove himself worthy. For a while, the magic had worked like a dream. Seen him scale to new heights. Money had rolled into his bank account.

And Marzan had his rival.

LONDON, NOW

HUMILITY HAD BEEN a cruel lesson. When one could no longer get up the stairs in one go and sex without payment was a faded dream, one tended to soften one's crowing. The years had climbed up Becket's back and twisted it, bending him like a bishop's crook (though he'd never been so holy). Time had spun his locks into silver, raked over his skull. The stride that had carried him before the footlights of Paris and Rome had become a shuffle, accompanied by the applause of his cane.

And the black star, as the demon had told him, was back.

"It was inevitable," he said to the here and now, the living room of his Balham flat. He regarded the debris of last night's ritual with a cringe. Around him, books towered with their wealth of knowledge, from *The Key of Solomon* to *De Nigromancia*. A skinned dead cat. A cracked ball of glass. A cup that Judas was said to have drunk from. All seemed useless in the face of it. It had all come down to the *khetem*, after all. "The house always wins."

Doctor Sallow had told him as much in his High Road practice last Tuesday, the X-rays spread out on his desk. He hadn't used such flowery speech. The cancer, in remission for decades, had returned, a black star over his heart. The tumour, of course, was malignant. *Hungry.* How could he tell the dour, perfunctory man behind the desk that he'd staved off the disease with spells, his offering? With innocent blood, no less. Sallow attempted a commiserating smile, indulging a septuagenarian who refused all advice and still smoked twenty a day. When he'd given him weeks to live (six at best), Becket had nodded. It *was* inevitable. Death was coming for them all. Even bargaining for time hadn't succeeded in sparing his youth and its innumerable pleasures.

At least you know where you're heading, he'd thought.

He shuddered, a chill that the drapes were unable to check. Then he sought out another bottle of rum, half-rolled under the living room couch. Instead of clearing up as intended, forgetting the whole infernal idea, he grabbed a packet of Viagra from the escritoire, downed a couple of little blue pills and bent to relight the candles.

Where was I? He found his spectacles under the armchair, turned his attention to the grimoire. And the *khetem,* the relic snatched from the shelf.

Ah, yes. Seb.

CAIRO, 1982

TIME WAS THE true magician, he knew. It made all things disappear. People, cities, empires... Memory was the great decoy, the wave of a pristine glove on stage, the flutter of doves from a cape. Still, one couldn't stave off death forever. Shakespeare was right. What was done could not be undone. Or so they said.

Becket hoped to change things if he could.

"We were in the Scarab Club in Cairo," he told the circle he knelt in, the candlelight and the drawn curtains kind to his nakedness. He pouted at his belly with its ladder of silver fuzz, his swelling cock beneath it. He'd always been a tall man, well hung and rugged. He'd never felt smaller than this. "The summer of '82. I was badmouthing Marzan at the bar, the greasy, money-grabbing fraud. That was the first time we met, Seb and I."

"Tell me," Ormenus hissed.

The Author of All Calamities was lying on its back on the ceiling, its gaze fixed on the renewed ritual. The *remembering*. Becket had taken up the thread of the spell, a homespun combination of Egyptian sex magick, Solomonic diagrams and Enochian chants. In his mind, the invocation was a bloom of power, hieroglyphs and Latin winding like thorns, keeping him sharp. The floorboards bit into his knees.

He focused on his avatars, the sigil of the god Atum who'd wanked the world into existence. The Theban statuette of Min, he of the constant erect phallus. And the sketch of King Camara, torn from Dee's *Heptarchia Mystica*, to represent the angel of summoning. Each one was set in the circle. His was a dark and masculine sorcery. In his blood, the drugs sang.

The demon watched, enthralled. Had Ormenus tracked his withering over the last three decades, the breadth of their fiendish bargain? More likely it merely saw a man, a soul wavering in the darkness. With every breath, Becket drew nearer the Gates of Hell, his body betraying him as Time betrayed all, no matter their ambition.

"He never laughed at my jokes," Becket said, his voice thickening along with his cock. In his mind, etched as deep as the *khetem*, Seb Samir stood beside him in the crowd. He was a slender figure in a pinstripe suit, the fez atop his head like a night boat upon the Nile. Steve Miller was singing *Abracadabra* on the bar stereo, annoyingly. It was the young man's eyes that had stuffed all the witticisms down his throat and caused his hangers-on to drift away, in search of more eloquent amusements. "Oh, what a distraction he was. I recall I was rather rude to him at first. Told him I didn't have any money." Seb had smiled and touched his elbow. "Then he asked for a job."

"Yes. He was your apprentice for ten years, before the black star arose. He helped you into cupboards. Sawed Barbara in half." The demon flapped a claw, impatient. "Get to the good bit."

Becket choked. Demon or no, he wanted to tell it that he hadn't taken Seb to his hotel room that night. That he hadn't plied the youth with promises and rum. That they'd gone for a walk instead. Yes, that was a better story. A pleasant walk past the Al-Azhar Mosque or through the maze of the Khan el-Khalili. How they'd discussed Bolingbroke and Paracelsus, the two of them almost touching, wary of strangers in the Saharan night. It was an image that Becket had sold himself for the past thirty years, vivid enough to hold the ring of truth. A way to tell himself he'd been a better man.

There was no fooling the Author of All Calamities. Lies were its oxygen, its daily bread.

"Truth is, I never thought I'd see him again," Becket confessed, stroking himself. His balls dangled like bruised plums, ripe with the pills. "At first, his naivety bored me.

I simply wanted to show off. I told him how I'd read the poets at Cambridge. Got into magic. Parlour tricks at first. Then... the real stuff. I was going to fuck him and kick him out of my room." He coughed, throbbing in his hand. "Hell, I'm only human. It was the sex that made me think twice. And the talk of tombs."

"*Tell me.*"

And he did. With mounting jerks and shortening breath, the magician wanked out the memory.

SEB WAS ON his knees in minutes of entering Becket's hotel room. He'd barely taken in the fittings on the four-poster bed, the gleaming, if tacky, touches that had adorned the Marriott Ramses before they'd torn the place down in the 90s. Printed pharaohs stared from the walls, kohl eyed. Outside, palm trees hissed in the wind. The traffic on the Nile Corniche wafted into the room along with the heat, the sand and the stink of the river. Becket paid it no mind. He let the youth unzip him and pluck out his cock – it'd needed no help to stiffen in those days – and taken him in his mouth. Seb had sucked at him as if he were parched, his tongue tracing the underside of his shaft, returning to swallow him once more. Deeper this time. Harder. His fingers, smooth, formed a tightening ring. The rhythm had matched the magician's breath.

A better man would've told Seb it wasn't necessary. The thirty-six-year-old Becket *did* need help, both off the stage and on. He could afford to pay for it too. Seb, he thought, was no different from any other prospecting Cairene. He was poor, streetwise, keen to escape his sand-and-camel shit world. He knew about magic too – *real* magic – but Becket didn't know that at the time. All he'd known was the spell underway, his fingers tangling in the young man's hair. When he'd pulled Seb away, spit dotting the carpet, he'd looked up at him with eyes like burning stones.

"Use me," he'd gasped. "Master. *Sidi.* I'm yours."

"Don't talk." Becket had wrenched Seb up by his hair. He'd tweaked his nipple, the bulge in his pants. "That's my first stipulation. Shut the hell up and take off your clothes."

Seb had obeyed. Cotton tore under trembling hands, smooth brown muscle under it. A thick, circumcised cock had sprung from his yanked down trousers. Buttocks, firm as gourds, had willingly parted. At that point, Becket recalled, Seb couldn't have talked if he'd wanted to. Both of them were gasping for air.

Talk would come later, through cigarette smoke on pillows. The youth told him about the wonders of the desert, the ghosts, the djinn and the demons out there (and the treasures they guarded), lost in buried tombs. The resources waiting to be tapped… On that distant, fateful night, the 'Magus' had thought himself the teacher. He'd taken Seb roughly – the same way he'd fucked any lad in the Christchurch dorm – the bedstead banging against the wall while Becket had ploughed him to a barked conclusion.

It was no more than sex, he'd thought. The rest would come later, much like a curse.

Like the black star. His cicatrix.

London, now

WITH A CRY, Becket came on the floorboards. Jism spattered the circle. Already growing cold. Tears leaked from the corners of his eyes and not merely with the effort.

This is the worst part. Under his ribs, his heart flopped like a fish on land. *Remembering Seb. What I did to him...*

Atum, Min and King Camara looked on in dispassion. Sweat stung his eyes, blurring the scene. Christ, he needed a cigarette. Rum.

"Are you... satisfied, demon?" The creature sat in the royal box of his memories, watching them play out with relish. Wasn't that why he'd summoned it here, to feast on the meat of his past, devour it in exchange for... what? One last glimpse before the end? Peace? Had he the breath, Becket would've laughed. "Haven't I shown you enough?"

"You're pathetic," Ormenus told him, like gravel crunching under boots. "Do you think the joy of a dying old man holds any weight with Hell? Look at you now, Ward. Lower than the belly of a worm."

Candles guttered, strewn by Becket's outstretched limbs. With the last of his strength, he rolled onto his back and glared up at the Author of All Calamities. The cherub leered down, its tongue lolling. With fat, judgemental eyes.

"Let me see him. *I beg you!*"

His cramped Balham flat dulled his roar. Once he'd relied on such theatrics. Smoke and mirrors. *The good old days...* Time had left him no puff of smoke, no trap door to escape through. The demon saw him for who he was. And yet still he put on this performance.

"It isn't joy I want, magus. It's *pain.* The most painful memory of all."

"Please..."

Ormenus laughed, a scatter of knives. The demon was melting into the plasterwork, a scaly Cheshire Cat. Doubtless called back to Hell for some awful task or other. With a flick of its tail, it was gone. But not before Becket had gauged the depth of its mercy, as shallow as a young man's grave.

Between his knees he clutched the *khetem*, its glyphs impressed on his skin.

In his eyes, an unseen spark.

CAIRO, 1982

THE SAQQARA SANDS swirled with mystery. And memories buried deep.

"'Come ye, blower of knots,'" Seb had said in the Ramses Hotel, the morning of their trip to the necropolis.

Becket knew it as an ancient term for 'magician', one who worked with cords and charms to heal (or inflict) pain back in the Old Kingdom. The innuendo was clear, borne out by the wink that Seb had given him. The youth was growing cheekier by the day. One too many fucks had made him cocksure, convinced of Becket's infatuation.

But Becket had made no promises. As he climbed into the jeep that would take them down the Western Agricultural Road and into the Governate, their faces wrapped in scarves, the magician had made a mental note to slap him down at the earliest opportunity. Physically, if necessary. His *shabab* was getting ideas above his station.

Who does he think he is? Something in his chest ached at the question and he scowled at Seb's grin. *Does he think I'm in love?*

It was only later, in the excavated heart of Saqqara, a labyrinth of pits, crumbling valleys and wind-gnawed mastabas that Becket had thought twice about it, awed by the surrounding ruins. The rubble of Memphis stretched under the sun, the catacombs sacred to forgotten gods. Along the Nile, the palm trees seethed in the dust. The site was famous for its tombs, its gilded coffins and idols. Who knew how many caches of mummies – not only human, but cats, cobras and scarabs too – had lain here unearthed for centuries? All gutted and pickled for the Duat (the present day Becket could empathise), the Ancient Egyptian underworld.

On that day, he'd been younger and less cynical. Most finds at Saqqara, their guide informed them as they climbed a rocky slope, had been sequestered in the Museum of Antiquities, riddles locked behind glass. But not all. There were tombs, the man said, known only to the wise. Some had been plundered, yes, and plundered again over the years. And some where no robber would go, deterred by the curses carved into their doors, the threat of a hundred violent deaths.

Becket, with an English conceit, was keen to put his own spells to the test. In one crumbling scroll, procured from a merchant in the Khan el-Khalili, Seb had assured him that they'd found a key. The guide led them down a shallow trench (where, the man went on, the archaeologists had stopped digging in the 70s), Becket swatting at flies and half listening. His shirt was damp, his teeth on edge. At last, he stood on the brink of greatness. He could feel it with every expectant breath. A pharaoh's mask. A chest of jewels... He was going to be rich. Rich beyond his wildest dreams. Forget the West End. He'd be the talk from New York to Sydney. Folks would flock to him instead of his rival, the so-called 'Marzan the Magnificent'.

When they came to the hole in the ground, it doused his excitement somewhat. The stone had rolled back, the curse dispelled by his grumbled chant. Then Becket had regarded Seb's chagrin in the beam of his flashlight. Hieroglyphs on the wall beyond fluttered along with their shadows. He saw no gold. No jewels. No *dead*. Only chambers filled with dust. Caskets long rotten. In the gloom, Seb had failed to notice his fist, shaking and anchored at his side. Becket had wanted to strike him then. The guide hadn't dared to come within ten feet of the tomb and wouldn't have heard it anyway. His hand was stayed by the object his companion held.

"Look, *sidi*. Look what I found."

With a scowl, Becket had taken in the find. He made out figures in bone – ivory, he thought – carved along its length, capped by gold at either end. Anger had melted into greed. Bright eyed, he'd reached for the thing. The wand or the -

"It's a *khetem*. A cylinder seal," Seb told him. "From the Old Kingdom."

"Only this?" Becket asked. His eyes darted around the tomb, along with echoes of resentment. "Is it worth anything?"

"Master, please. Respect the dead..." He held up a hand at Becket's snarl, then shrugged, changing tack. "A relic like this means more than money."

Becket sighed, dry as the air. "This better be good."

"According to the *Book of the Dead,* this was used to summon demons."

At this point, the memory grew fuzzy. It curdled with wishful thinking. In his Balham flat, Becket Ward, the onetime Magus, clung to the dream anyway. Hadn't he given a bark of joy, pushed the youth up against a wall? He'd pressed Seb's face to Anubis, the blind, dead gods of the past. Why, he distinctly recalled his sacrilege, unbuckling Seb's belt and yanking his pants down. Becket had dropped to his knees. Seb had gasped as stubble rubbed against him, Becket forcing his buttocks apart. Grunting, he'd drank of his *shabab* – *his* – his tongue drilling into the depths of him.

The image rippled, a mirage. Sand whispered through the cracks, pouring into the tomb. Every grain bore a weight of guilt, collected over decades. *Seb. Oh, Seb...* The chamber was filling up with the stuff, the desert swallowing them whole. Caught in the lie, the young man's scream was drowned out by sand, along with his glittering eyes. Into the darkness the two of them spun, sucked into the Saharan womb like empires and memory, Time both real and imagined.

What did it matter now?

LONDON, NOW

NAKED, COLD, BECKET clutched the khetem. Hell wasn't through with him though.

"A fine morsel," Ormenus said, flames dancing in its eyes. Impish, the demon was edging the boundary of the circle, licking its inky lips. "But that wasn't the day he died."

"Nor was it the first time I wanted to hit him." The magician sat cross-legged, drunk on the living room floor. Night had fallen during his second attempt at the summoning, the relic placed under his arse. Come what may, the demon mustn't see it, lest it suspect a ruse. Streetlights leaked through the curtains, the orange pall of London. Shadows draped the knick-knacks in the room, souvenirs from his travels. A Hand of Glory he'd found in France. A crystal ball from Prague. None were suited to this particular task. "The first time he..." He coughed, a pain in his chest. "The first time he cheated on me, I did. Some businessman from Saudi. Said he was a prince." He gave a laugh, sharp in the gloom. "Oh, Seb didn't know about my scrying. I saw the whole thing, you know."

"And it made you hard."

"I'm a man, demon."

"That isn't what I meant," Ormenus said. "But such memories are the bruises around the wound. Let me get my tongue in there, Ward. Let me lick up the pain."

"All right. I'm getting there."

"No. You're stalling."

Yes, you fucker. Indeed.

The demon hungered for anguish. Why else would it have heeded his petition, abandoning the torment of the damned to attend a washed up magician? Their previous business had concluded thirty years ago, the granting of time in exchange for blood. Some memories were humdrum fare. Some were *haute cuisine.* Despite their agreement, the temptation had appealed to the demon. But it wasn't obliged to grant him his wish.

"Thirty years," Becket muttered, longing to cling to the last of them.

"You had your time," Ormenus said, fingernails down the inside of a coffin. "From London to Rome.

And beyond. Come the millennium, you had surpassed Marzan himself."

Evander, you cunt. Mention of his rival, svelte where Becket was seen as forbidding, was a knife through his heart. Marzan had worn his stupid hat as if to convey that he was the taller. *You might be food for the worms, but you owe me. I paid such a high price...*

The demon, of course, relished it.

"Longevity was a gift. But you were headed for Hell regardless." The demon grinned, swinging its tail. "This is late in the day to... alter our arrangement."

"I'm still on this side of the gate."

"Not for long, Ward. So let's cut to the chase."

ROME, 1992

THE ARRANGEMENT, AS it happened, had been to postpone death. 'The carriage held but just ourselves', Dickinson wrote. In this case it had been Becket on the seat, rattling to the Gates of Hell. In autumn of '92, he'd collapsed in Rome, passing out in a mess of paper flowers, some tawdry conjurer's trick. The stage hard under him. Before darkness claimed him, he'd heard the audience gasp. It was entertainment, nonetheless. At the end of the tunnel was a spotlight, bright in his frozen gaze.

Barbara was still in her leotard, her makeup smeared, when she got him to the hospital. She'd only ridden in the ambulance out of politeness, he thought, some tenuous sense of duty. On a couple of occasions, the knives during the throwing act had struck her. Once, he'd nicked her thigh with a saw, the result of too much rum in his dressing room, for which he believed she held a grudge. The girl looked exhausted when he emerged from ER. She'd likely been crying over the thought of lost pay. Becket muttered his thanks and Barbara didn't stay long. In fact, she never came back. Not merely to the hospital. Ever.

Poof!

Where was Seb, he wondered? He was drowning in sedatives, sucked into the polyester pillows as if they were Saharan sand. Perhaps his *shabab* had stayed at the theatre, handling the fallout, the complaints... but his collapse had happened yesterday. If Seb were here, he'd talk to him, he told himself. Ten years had passed since the Scarab Club. It was high time. He'd pluck up the courage to tell Seb he... cared about him, insist he was still his *sidi.* To prove it, he'd clutch the young man's hand, bring it to his crotch under the covers – it was incredible how *horny* a near-death experience could make one – and offer him a modest pay rise. It was the closest he'd come to an apology.

The next day, a mouse of a man called Doctor Capello had sat like a mourner next to his bed and showed Becket the X-rays. That had been his first glimpse of the black star, the shadow over his heart. Capello had spread the radiographs like Tarot cards. Death. Death. Death.

"*Cardiac sarcoma*," the doctor told him in English. "You've been overdoing things, *signor.* This tour of yours..." Capello flapped a hand at the grimy square that passed for a window, dismissing the sold out venues in a way that vexed him. "You're forty-six years old, Mr Ward. Perhaps it's time to quit smoking, yes? There were traces of cocaine in your blood. I'm sure you could afford treatment."

Drugged or no, the magician hadn't taken it lying down. People were relying on him, he said. He had appearances to honour. He couldn't simply perform 'Becket Ward's Great Vanishing Act' and fuck off into some clinic. Didn't the doctor know who he was? *Europa Arcana* was the talk of the continent. He'd been on the front page of *La Repubblica*.

The memory had become as hazy as the rest. But he'd said all of these things and nowhere near as politely. Capello had left him to his curses, his tray flung against the recovery room wall, and retreated into the gloom of the hospital. Next time, he'd sent a nurse.

For three days, Becket had sat in his hospital bed, troubled by more than the cancer. Oh, he'd had ample time to think on his sins. An elderly father he'd never called. Employees he'd never paid. Animals he'd sacrificed. All those he'd cursed.

And a young Egyptian he'd treated like dirt. Who he'd never told -

Oh, Seb.

Like the tomb at Saqqara, the walls threatened to crush him. Above him hung a picture of the Pope, the avatar of smugness. For three days, Becket Ward, the

'Great Magus', had sat in his own piss, considered his demise and wondered where the fuck Seb was.

London, now

"This is cruel, demon."

"Why, thank you," Ormenus said. He was genuinely flattered, affecting a bow in the candlelight. "Self-pity is sweet. But that wasn't the half of it."

Becket gagged. Partly it was the bottle in his hand. Partly the moths, crisp in the bowl. The taste was supposed to aid concentration. It couldn't compete with his ire.

"What Hell..." Around his neck, his locket swung, a sad pendulum, "could be worse than this?"

Ormenus chuckled. "Wait and see."

Rome, 1992

Becket checked out of the Gemelli Hospital the second he could stand. A stooped Icarus on Francesca Vito, he waited for a cab. Doctor Capello had insisted he remain for further check-ups with all the politeness of one who doesn't want guests to stay for dinner. The magician had turned his tumorous skull on him and blown smoke in his face.

No, grazie.

Death was in him, a living part. But the black star was not without power. He'd make the best of the weeks left to him. *Yes!* There was no longer reason for restraint, he thought. He waved the doctor farewell, the butt of his fag bouncing off tarmac. A snatched infant, say, on the right altar, at the right time, could gain him influence, a special place in Hell. What fear of repercussion now?

First, he had to find Seb.

There were journalists outside the Palazzo. He'd had his agent book him a suite. How they pecked like crows in the rain! Cameras flashed. Onlookers gawped. The sordid details of his private life were often smeared across the press these days, titillation for the gibbering masses. Once, he'd been a youth in London looking at the stars. Now his dreams sickened him. In all likelihood, the news of his collapse had been greeted by religious types as proof of his wickedness, his reward for dabbling in the Black Arts. In hindsight, he found it ironic. He had yet to make use of the *khetem* or attempt anything *truly* demonic. In an odd way, the days following his diagnosis had held the last of his innocence.

"No comment," he snapped at the hacks outside the hotel. "Give it a rest, will you?"

He cursed under his breath, wishing them all a sudden end. His carriage was heading straight to Hell. There was plenty of room on board.

In the hotel lobby, he met his agent, Ted Culpepper. The man had flown in from London, growing ever more frustrated the longer the magician procrastinated, sequestered in his suite. For days, Becket refused to speak to the press. He rejected statements written on his behalf. There was the business of a porter who claimed that Becket had harassed him – nothing a cheque couldn't fix. Venues kept calling. Culpepper fumed. Ticket holders wanted their money back. The show must go on.

"If you don't fix this," Culpepper hissed at him one morning over breakfast, "then Marzan will. He's in Rome, by the way. I'm sure a call to his manager could secure an appropriate stand-in."

Culpepper was red-eyed and balding. More so of late, his head resembling Becket's boiled egg. His words were anything but wise.

"Nice to see you too, Ted." Becket smirked, raising his tumbler of rum. "Thanks for the flowers you sent to the hospital."

Culpepper had sent no flowers, no more than he'd enquired after his client's health.

Becket had banished the man from his presence. The next day, he'd fired Culpepper and called off the tour. *Europa Arcana* was over. What did he care for the yelling at his door? His former agent would give himself a coronary. Robed in silk and soothed by opiates, the magician's attention was on the crystal ball he'd packed in his suitcase. A disembowelled cat lay in the kitchenette, blood pooling on the marble bar. Dark wings were folding around him. He had no time to spare.

His *shabab,* his lover, was missing.

*

LONDON, NOW

"I FOUND HIM in Greece." He was coming to it now, the crux of his undoing. The error he'd made. "He ran off with that bastard. Can you believe it? After everything…"

For a moment, Becket was young again, squinting through footlights. A handsome man smiled at him in the audience. *What else can you show me?* He remembered how Marzan's agent had called days later, the sting of the phone cord in his hand. As if his words had been a prophecy, the years had crawled over him. He shivered on the living room floor.

"He gave you up for dead," Ormenus said. It was amusing to him, to watch these mortals and their endless fuck ups.

Grizzled, his hair in his face, Becket gripped his locket. He'd had it made in Copenhagen years ago, not long after his *shabab's* death. A *memento mori.* Or an albatross. His other hand fell to the floorboards, the bottle rolling away from him. It seemed just as keen to escape him. He was drunk… but not too drunk. In his mind, symbols danced, invisible and bright.

With the tip of a finger, he stroked the *khetem.*

It seemed strange to say it, amid the feast of memories. "Yes. He forgot me."

*

ATHENS, 1992

A SPELL TO drain power. A word of death. These were on Becket's mind as he went through customs at Ellinikon International. The caution he'd taken throughout his career, avoiding outright diabolism, had fled the second he'd spied Seb in the glass. Since then, he'd been up to his eyes in the Codex Gigas, The Heptameron and The Book of Abaddon. There were few effective spells to extend life. Plenty to end it. Longevity involved dealing with demons, the servants of Hell. Thus he'd embarked on a new education. Marzan, the so-called 'Magnificent', had stolen something from him. Something precious. He wanted it back.

The bastard wanted to hurt him, kick him while he was down. Perhaps Marzan had cast a spell of his own. As for Seb, well, his apprenticeship had made him lean, his daily routine of pulling ropes and hefting props. His boyish looks had given way to broad shoulders and an iron arse. And, Becket thought with envy, few could withstand those depthless eyes. When he recalled his beautiful cock, screws tightened in his chest. To think of other hands upon it, especially – *God!* By all accounts, Evander Marzan was no stranger to men, the preening, bearded wolf. Thinking of his ridiculous hat on posters in Warsaw and Amsterdam, Becket's nails bit into his palms. Huddled in the back of a cab, a grim-faced rake in an overcoat, he whisked down Piraeus Street for the theatre. He couldn't imagine his *shabab's* abduction as anything but sorcerous.

"Can't you hurry up? The curtain falls at ten."

December rain lashed the windows. The windscreen wipers were better than the crap on the radio, some squealing girl band or other. The Athenian night swept past, a blur of neon and traffic. The odd museum and statue flashed by. Above all, the Acropolis blazed, golden in the dark, the realm of tourists these days instead of ancient supplicants.

I'll squeeze out what magic remains...

The black star throbbed, feasting on his heart. *Christ, I'd kill for a cigarette.* He hadn't packed more than a small case: a change of clothes, a grimoire, the *khetem*, chloroform and a pistol. He didn't intend to stay long in the city. If he couldn't release Seb from the spell, spirit him away from this land of gods, then he'd be gone in a day at most...

Thanks to his scrying, Becket had gleaned enough of Seb's movements to judge his location come the finale. Dutiful as he was, he'd stick to his schedule like clockwork. Disgorged from the cab, the driver sped off in a stream of expletives. The magician leant on his cane (the skull atop it no consolation for its necessity) and wheezed onward for the stage door. Rain belched from gutters. The fire escape had become a cascade. Shadow and neon winked in the puddles. A black car, a Mercedes, crouched at the end of the alley. The lights out. The driver seat empty. *Good.* The place wasn't much for a reunion. It was private though. That's why his *shabab* had parked here.

When Seb emerged from the stage door, his head swung this way and that, checking that the alley was empty. Once upon a time, he'd done the same for Becket. The weather had seen off the press and the most determined of fans. He didn't notice Becket at first. Then he tensed, frozen. He spun towards the gloom by the trash cans. The car keys he held splashed into a puddle, the echoes softer than Becket's greeting.

"Why, Seb?" It was all he asked, shaking his head. "Just tell me why."

Seb took a step backward. He knew the power of the man before him, sick or no. He wasn't about to put it to the test. In his eyes, Becket could see he knew exactly what he'd done, the pain he'd caused. There was space for a hundred things, a hundred excuses that Seb might've given him, from sorcery to blackmail. In his wounded gaze, Becket only read scorn. A longing for freedom, perhaps. And something else. Something so horrid it had threatened to explode the star in his chest, as fierce as a black supernova.

"*Sidi.* Ward. I -"

"You were seeing him before, weren't you?" In a flash, the understanding came to him, Becket stooped over his cane. "For how long? Tell me, do you...?"

Thankfully, the question went unanswered. The stage door opened again. Out came Marzan the Magnificent, his top hat tipped to the rain. He almost walked into his apprentice, Seb like stone in the alley. His beard, trimmed and slick, parted in a rebuke. Time held the space in its grip, the neon a smear of purple. Marzan followed Seb's gaze to the shadows. He straightened at the sight of Becket raising a pistol, a black-gloved finger on the trigger.

Spells. A word of death. In the end, Becket simply shot the man, the alley resounding with the noise. The night had slammed shut on betrayal.

Marzan's hat flew off and landed in a puddle. Red joined the reflections.

BECKET HAD SEB drive. One didn't argue with a man who happened to hold a pistol. Twice, his former apprentice – his former lover – tried to reason with him. Becket hushed him. What the hell could he say? Infidelities he'd learned to overlook. He'd done so on several occasions. But he'd known them as meaningless, symptoms of the road. Marzan was different. On that night, he was beyond talk, a spindle of rage in the Mercedes. He sat in the backseat, the Reaper made flesh. He watched the glow of Athens give way to the foothills as the car sped north.

Oh, there'd been a storm in him, fierce as any simoom. Memories strained to prick his conscience, dissuade him from his course. Seb in the Scarab Club, a hand on his elbow. His gasps in a forgotten tomb. With the same concentration he used for his rituals, Becket distanced himself from them. Seb was merely a tool now. He would pay for his crime. The magician had found the method in his book. The *khetem* was the key.

This is all your doing. Your fault.

Trembling, Becket had Seb pull up to the cave on the mountain road. It was near midnight. Mount Parnitha loomed above them, snowcapped under the stars. The Tatoi Forest creaked on all sides, a restless hush in the darkness. When Seb killed the headlights, he seemed to sense his fate in the gloom. Tear-streaked face turned to his captor, he chanced an entreaty.

"*Sidi.*" His voice was raw, his muscles bunched like a caged tiger. "Please. Don't do this."

"You're begging the dead." Becket's eyes were burning, damn it. He couldn't afford to lose focus. Not now. "I'll have one last kindness from you."

Seb gave a sob, turned in his seat. Was there a remnant there, a ghost of affection? Or did he merely weep for himself? Finding nothing to help him in the darkened road, he hung his head, sniffling. Ignoring the pain in his lungs, Becket leant forward. He tugged the chloroform-soaked rag from his coat pocket – *hey presto!* – and clapped it over his *shabab's* mouth.

There was a struggle. Then silence.

IN DAYLIGHT, TOURISTS knew the site on Parnitha as the Cave of Pan. In fact (and verified by Becket's research), it had once served as a shrine to Hecate, the goddess of the witches. In books that one couldn't find in a library, he'd read how the ancients had made sacrifices here, chickens, goats and suchlike, beseeching

Hecate for favours. A place of power was vital for his summoning, even if the deities were not. The magician had learnt as much. Gods were masks, nothing more, imposed on the chaos on the world. And Becket had his own preferences.

This in mind, Becket lit the candles at the rear of the cave. He painted symbols in cat's blood. Seb, he stripped naked, a sign of oblation. As he worked, he numbed himself to the task. The body on the slab was simply a man. His cock, a mere lump of flesh. His eyes were closed, their magic lost.

There'll be other lovers, Becket told himself. *A future filled with them.*

His apprentice would secure it for him, another three decades of life. His offering was the crux of his bargain. He would tear the black star from its zenith.

"Oh, Ormenus, Author of All Calamities." The echoes bounced around the cave, his knife shaking in his fist. Under his knees lay the *khetem,* fuelling his invocation. "I summon you forth. *Venit seductor.* Accept my sacrifice."

He gave himself no time to hesitate, to hold the knife from its purpose. Uttering a binding word, he plunged the blade downward. Blood danced in the candlelight, painting the cavern walls.

There was smoke then, and laughter.

Through it, Becket looked up to see a small blue form.

*

London, now

"How utterly is flown every ray of light." Becket sat drunk and naked on the living room floor. The ritual was complete, his seed and the memory offered, a potent, bitter feast. "Brontë wrote that. How right she was. Your gift was no gift at all."

"Come now," Ormenus said on the bookshelf, replete with the magician's anguish. "A score and ten. That was our bargain. And it's fair to say you made the most of them. You saw your name in lights at Madison Square Garden. Drank an ocean of rum. Fucked from Toronto to Timbuktu. If it hadn't caught up with you, who knows what you'd have achieved? A lasting legacy, perhaps."

Becket hadn't expected sympathy. Hell didn't know the meaning of the word. And for a while, he'd enjoyed his success. Since that night on the mountain, he'd cited 'divine intervention' whenever he met the astonishment of doctors, his cancer shrivelling to nothing, the black star dispelled. He'd stood beside Marzan's grave (they'd placed his top hat on the coffin) and closed his eyes at the sound of dirt on wood. Hid his smile behind his scarf. No one suspected him, the Great Magus. He'd covered his tracks so well, thanks to a simple obliviating spell. *A lover's tiff,* they said in the papers. Seb was nowhere to be found. (Before dawn, Becket had rolled the Mercedes into the Marathon Dam, thirty miles to the east, and then hired a private driver. He'd returned to the Palazzo with the staff none the wiser).

But he couldn't change universal law. Over the years, as the footlights faded, the crowds dried up and age closed its claws around him, his suspicions had come to fruition. Regret was a poison. Memory a curse. That was the cruellest lesson of all. What was done could not be undone.

Or so they said.

At his side, his fingers closed around the *khetem*. Hieroglyphs pressed into his skin.

"I loved him, you know," he said. And Seb had been with him every night since, a shadow in the wings. In every hotel room as the magician lay in the foetus of this or that hangover. With this or that whore, none of them an inch of what he'd lost. "In the end."

Why would a demon care about love? Such passions appealed as sustenance alone. Or rather the pain left in their absence.

"We would not have answered you otherwise."

"And so? Have you considered my plea?"

"Indeed." Ormenus grinned. How it enjoyed dragging out the moment. "What will it change? I'll grant you your window, magus. Make your apologies brief."

A swish of its tail. A raised claw. Heart pounding, Becket watched the floor take on a liquid quality. The chalked circle rotated, a vision that had naught to do with the rum. The candles guttered, the bookshelves eclipsed by a deeper darkness. The room shook. His crystal ball shattered on the floor. His avatars, Atum and Min, sank into the portal as though into sand.

King Camara fluttered up to the lampshade, borne on a scorching updraft.

Yes. The living room was giving way. With a shudder of triumph, Becket found himself on the brink of Hell. *At last.*

His hair, sparse as it was, flailed and crisped in the heat. He paid it no mind. The circle would protect him. Clutching the *khetem*, Becket breathed in the ash and looked down.

If he'd expected fire and brimstone, then he was disappointed. No classical Hell for him, it seemed. No fields of lava and blasted rock. No sinners suspended over flames. Instead, like a dubious god, he looked down upon a ruined town. Through the miasma, the place was a stain on a black savannah. He made out columns, Romanesque and crumbling. There, the flyblown awning of a theatre. He saw a half-buried pyramid. A broken cross. The riddle of streets were scars on the emptiness, aswirl with twisters of ash. The wind wailed, a lament.

In the back of his mind, glyphs from dead languages spun, the spell within the spell. He wondered at the vista. The town. He'd read that the damned envisioned the Hell that awaited them, reflecting their own transgressions and crimes. As he thought it, he found himself cringing at the wreckage of his past. Yes. The wasteland was a mirror of his soul. Egyptian ruins. A sleek Mercedes... Why wouldn't each inferno be different? In the distance rose a palace that he didn't recognise, many turreted and black. His heart shrank at the sight. That, he reckoned, never changed. He looked away, back to the streets below.

This is nowhere, he realised. *The end of all ambition and lust.*

But not memory, no. The thought wounded him. The wanderings in this place, parched and alone. Endless. This is where he'd sent Seb. His soul.

As if drawn from the ash, the magician spied the man in question. He was staggering down the street. *Or what remains of him. What he remembers of himself...* The youth was naked, his physique devoured, withered by the shifting waste. His hair, like night, matched the rest of him. The man was less than skin and bone. A ghost, consigned to a place where time held no meaning.

"*Seb!*"

Becket's cry was swallowed by the wind. Now he was here, prostrate on the threshold, the words he'd rehearsed in the bathroom mirror, his apology, dried up in his throat. In his chest, the black star swelled, threatening to engulf him. Around his neck, his locket swung. His albatross. He wiped his brow, his spectacles dislodged and falling, spinning into the storm.

Still, Seb looked up.

Sidi.

The ghost below recognised him. No joy lit his expression.

"Make it quick, magus." Ormenus spoke between the boundary of worlds. "I have other fools to attend to."

Becket ignored it. *The fucker.* Aching, he reached through the hole in the floor. He reached for his *shabab,* the same way he'd reached for him for thirty years, drinking the venom of regret. And Seb was reaching for him too, he saw, spurred by the hope of release...

"Stop that." On this side of the gate, the demon shifted on the bookshelf. Loose pages took to the air, charring above the gulf. "I granted you a moment. No more."

Becket closed his eyes. With the last of his strength, he struggled to his knees. In his skull, the wisdom of the ancients flowed, guiding his veiled conjuration. Seb's hand was in his now. *Firm.* He was dragging him, inch by inch, from the clutches of Hell.

One last magic thing...

Nursed in his mind for hours, buried under rum and regret, Becket uttered the words of power. He thrust out the *khetem,* the relic shaking in his fist. He flung the spell against the bookshelf. The walls shook, the room shuddering. The relic, recovered years ago from a Saqqara tomb, throbbed in his hand. This was its function, the summoning of demons.

And their *binding.*

It was to be his greatest trick.

He tightened his grip, fastened on the memory below, the ghost of Seb Samir. With their reunion, the wasteland rippled and seethed.

Ormenus hissed. The magician barely heard him. Ichor splashed against the bookshelf, washing over Paracelsus and Fludd. Becket gritted his teeth, the spell ringing in his skull. They were reeling, him and his *shabab,* cast like stones across the surface of Time. On a stage in Rome, the magician leapt up from the boards, his blackout undone. A thousand shows, a thousand applauses, all blurred past like playing cards. The Sahara churned, unearthing tombs and gold.

"*Desist!* I command it."

The demon roared, outraged. Behind his eyes, Becket was back in the Ramses Marriot, lying on Egyptian silk. Breathless, he dashed away a tear... and found himself looking up at the youth. The past and the present crashed like waves, colliding. It took a moment for Becket to grasp his new perspective, the change lurching in his guts. Seb was kneeling in the living room now. Becket dangled over the abyss.

The light was fading. The *khetem* waning, its intervention all too brief. Despite the heat, Becket shivered. There was laughter coming from below. The relic slipped from his fingers, spinning away in the dust. The demon, Ormenus, sank its claws into his leg.

"Have it your way, magician. One soul is much like another."

Becket wanted to scream. Instead, he looked up. Seb gazed down at him through the portal. He smiled. Smiled like he had in the Scarab Club, back in '82. A fez-crowned youth, touching his elbow at the bar. The sands of Time shifted and swirled.

And he smiled up at Seb. "Seb. I..."

In the end, what could he say? Becket had made his choice. He closed his eyes. Let go of Seb's hand. Even as the wind took him, howling in his ears, he smiled.

He knew this place. He'd walked here for thirty years, through the shadows and the waste. It was the landscape of his heart.

Ormenus, the Author of All Calamities, dragged him into Hell.

END TIMES
IN PARIS

WE WON'T ALWAYS have Paris, my love. That old movie lied to us. Who could argue with that now, after the trumpets sounded and the seals broke and the beast and his armies marched forth, leaving the city of light in darkness? You only have to look at the rubble where Notre Dame once stood or the arrondissements, the streets broken, black and littered with bones. Or the nameless things that walk in the night. Or the spire of La Tour Eiffel, crooked after the quake, her beacon circling through the haze of ash to know that it is true.

We'll have Paris for a hundred odd days and no more, won't we?

"YOU MUSTN'T BLAME yourself."

It was hard to say, I admit, with the smoke in my throat and my lips cracked from the lack of water and food. I was on my way home from foraging in the wreckage, my sack half empty and the fact plain. The city was dying. Thanks to you and your kind. But it was the first thing I said when I found you on the Pont Neuf, a span of black teeth across the mired waters and the night. You were in your uniform, your once-white robe, standing on the wall and looking down. Your shoulders were slumped. Your wings folded, coated in dust. The flaming sword you held in your hand was smouldering but limp.

"It's over," you told me, a whisper carried on the wind. "They're gone."

I didn't need to ask who you meant. Days before, I'd been to the boulangerie and found the ovens hot, the bread stale, the shop empty. Discarded clothes, watches, wallets and jewellery lay on the floor. It was the same story in the supermarkets. The galleries. The parks. Headphones and underwear, garters forgotten. The odd pacemaker. A gold tooth. While the damned were still shuffling through the ruins – the politicians, the bankers, the lawyers, the drinkers, the poets like me – the faithful had gone to the sky as promised. Been spared the Tribulation, the end. Chapter four verse one. The gates had opened and closed. And here we were in chapter six. Paris was a graveyard and we alone endured, bony figures on borrowed time. We scratched like dogs in the dirt. Raided the abandoned vending machines in Gare du Nord. Boiled whatever shrubs remained in the Tuileries.

"I didn't know," you said and shook your head, "that it would be like this."

"Who did?" I replied. "No one listened. Revelations was just a... story, right? And you were only doing your job."

It was a stupid thing to say, I know. Insensitive even. But I had no more to offer. No job at the school since the quake struck. No students since the clouds had parted and snatched up all the kids. Instead, I wandered the bars in the Latin Quarter, sifting through the rubble in search of intact bottles, determined to wash away the ash, the loneliness. There was no reason to pretend anymore. Tears softened the shattered sight of Paris. I stumbled on by, half blind to the chaos. Restless sleep half drowned out the sobs. The screams.

You grunted something. Something about the burden of it, I think. *Holy orders,* that's what you said. You stood golden eyed, staring at the waters.

"The fall won't work, you know." I'd found something better to say, after all. "I can't speak for what's in there."

You snorted, watching the worms writhe under the surface of the Seine, perhaps wondering how their teeth would feel as they dragged you down, a ball of brown limbs and dusty feathers. Or perhaps you thought I meant deeper than that. Down into damnation.

"My name's John," I said. "I'm a teacher. Or I was."

You said nothing to this.

"Religious studies," I explained with a cough.

Then your shoulders shook and your wings along with them. At first I thought you were sobbing, but you wiped your face and turned to look at me. The Tower lit the streaked gold, tears through the ash on your cheeks.

You arched your eyebrow in amusement. The irony of it.

"Uriel," you said.

Then you sheathed your sword. Came down off the bridge.

I took your hand. I took you home. To my small apartment in Le Marais, a once-shared place on la Rue de Picardie. I was reasonably sure that my flatmate Simone (who, despite the cigarettes and the absinthe, really had seemed to want to be a nun) had gone up with all the rest. Her cat, Louis, had never come home. If I'd known you were coming, Uri, I would've cleaned the place up. Instead, we sat on the living room floor among the books scattered by the quake, the pages of philosophy and fictional exploits, Descartes, Dan Brown and what not. There was an art book of nudes that I kicked under the couch. Au revoir, Mapplethorpe. There was a picture of my mother in Somerset, England. I picked it up, blew ash off the glass, and set it back on the mantelpiece. I'd never had the chance to tell her the truth of who I was or why I'd run off to Paris in the first place.

And I'd brought an angel home, against my better judgement.

Well, judgement was coming, I thought. I didn't much fancy my chances, so what the hell?

"She would've accepted it, you know," you said out of nowhere and I realised then that you could probably see *everything*. The nudes. My secret. My shame. And I supposed you could see through my jacket too, tattered as it was, to my sinning little heart. How hard it was beating for you. That your salvation hadn't been entirely altruistic. "I think."

I made you tea, the saucer rattling. You didn't drink it. I don't think your kind do, so I overlooked the slight.

"Here we are in the *hell époque*," I quipped. "Paris in springtime. The stuff of novels, movies and songs. Our last days."

For a while, you were silent. I wanted to light a candle. To see you better, I suppose. But I didn't. Too churchy, I thought.

Then you said, "A time, times and half a time. No more."

The echoes were a bell in the room, sounding the depths of conviction.

You wept then, your feathers shaking ash on the rug. Drops of gold shone on your cheeks. I crawled across the floor and reached for you, to comfort you but hungry too. If we have so little time, I said, then why not make the most of it?

"We have each other," I told you. "It isn't the End of the World."

Not quite.

LATER, I LEARNED how much you welcomed damnation. Then, I'll confess to a little vanity, that you saw something in me. The idea is still hard to let go. With the eyes of

Heaven averted, I didn't hesitate. On the strewn books on the living room floor, I pressed my lips to yours, tasting gold through the ash. Your hands were on my shoulders, pretending to resist. Your robe came loose, dirty laundry on the rug. Then your wings closed around me as I shed my rags, my flesh burning against yours, milk to umber. Your wings spread like the tree in a razed Eden. Sheltered, I ate of your fruit.

Did I tell you I wrote poetry? Of course, I could write that you fucked my brains out on the floor while I'm sat here at my escritoire.

In the night, the blood moon rose as we lay together in the dark. The small hours brought a swarm of locusts, the rush of their wings clattering outside. They were too large to get through the windows and didn't trouble us much. There were plagues, you murmured, as if I didn't remember. Then Something Not Of This Earth shrieked in the darkened streets and people ran screaming before it. On waking, I wasn't sure if I'd dreamt it. I'd slept so deeply, so safe in your arms. Roused, resurrected, I turned to you again.

It wasn't just the movie, my love. The Bible lied too. It isn't true what they say about angels, is it? There in the ruins, we joined. As any man joins to man. Even if you weren't one, not really.

Cast out and careless, rolling, damned in the dust. *Heaven.*

*

"You mustn't blame yourself," I said again, this time over stale croissants in the ribcage of a restaurant on Rue de Turenne. Le plat du jour. "At least, you can't take all the blame. I saw it on TV."

We weren't receiving TV anymore. All we got was white noise. Still, you got the idea. You looked up from your breakfast, your food untouched. Your sword, extinguished and sharp, leant against your broken chair. The morning was as black as midnight, but your eyes made up for the dawn.

"What do you mean?"

"Fire. Earthquakes. Flood. There was a man on TV who said it was our fault. That we'd caused these things. People like us. Every kiss, every touch, bringing disaster."

You frowned, thought about it for a while.

Then you looked at your palms, the ash there.

"There's a power in that," you said.

Were you joking? I wasn't sure. Trying to lift the mood, I said,

"Well, He sent a rainbow afterwards, didn't He?" I shrugged, then waved a hand at the street outside, the smashed and overturned cars. The burnt and twisted bodies. The sky. "I don't think He's sending one this time."

But you didn't find that funny.

We were fallen. Fallen in love.

And in Paris! *Quels imbéciles!* Hand in hand, we walked through the radiation, kicking through the dirt in the Musée d'Orsay. People had looted the Van Goghs, although who they planned to sell them to was beyond me. These days, money was as useful as toilet paper. No one could eat the Masters. Others had slashed the Monets, while Bartholomé's sculpture of 'The Weeping Girl' lay in pieces, a symbol within a symbol.

We lingered awhile, looking at the art. But we didn't linger long. The mutants came hissing from their holes in the murk, but your uniform served to hold them at bay. As did your sword, smouldering at your side.

We ate pineapple from tins in La Tour d'Argent, righting a table that overlooked the shell of Notre Dame. Sat beside a fallen chandelier, you told me that King Henry III had used a fork here for the very first time, forever changing the way that we eat. And here we are, I replied, dining like royals, relatively speaking, while most of the city starved.

We were silent for some time after that. When you pushed aside your tin, I reached for you over the table. You'd lost your appetite. I gave you mine.

Later, after a circuitous route that took in the Square Langevin and Saint-Étienne-du-Mont to avoid a riot outside the metro station, we ran, breathless, into the lobby of the theatre. It had started to rain, the acid hissing through the awning and smoking on tarmac, likely dispersing the gangs. Inside, the Cinéma du Panthéon stretched silent and dark, empty of survivors. Perhaps they avoided the memory of the films that had once played there, shining on the screen for a hundred years. Between rococo pillars, the screen sagged now, a flap of dead skin, dead dreams. The projector was broken, its visions stilled. This was no time for entertainment.

Up in the back row, on squeaky red seats fanged with springs, you put your wing around me. You told me the story of Rick Blaine who owned a nightclub in Morocco. He'd discovered that his old flame had come to town, albeit with her husband, a World War II resistance leader with Nazis on his tail... It was a sad tale, but romantic. Yes.

It wasn't until later that I realised what you'd been trying to tell me.

The ash must've gotten into my eyes, my alcoholic haze replaced by tears. I was drunk on you. The ruins had blurred, a new architecture. Shadows trembled between obelisk and fountain like pairs of hopeful hands. Crows had fluttered from the statues with the speed of last-minute prayers. What were the screams in the night but the cry of a new-born world? All was ash, but weren't we the phoenix, rising to remind each other that, despite everything, Paris was made for love?

Oh, Uri. Poetry again.

Imbécile.

I was blind.

"THE GREAT FLOOD. The Black Death. The Second World War..." It was our seventh night together, yours and mine. You'd flown me to the top of the Eiffel Tower, my knuckles white on the railings, my words snatched by the wind. "This."

"John," you said and pulled me close. Making sure I didn't fall. "What are you talking about?"

"*Survival,*" I said. I glared down at the Champs de Mars as the beam from the tower slashed across it, illuminating the rubble. "All that shit happened. But we're still here."

I kissed you then, ash to gold. I pulled away when I tasted salt and looked up at you with a question. My fears burned inside of me. Burned like hell. Your frown, your silence, spoke volumes.

"What is it? Tell me."

The wind smelled of death. In Invalides, they were burning corpses. Or cooking them. The streets below were a map of doom. How could I have thought otherwise? Worms writhed, vicious in the Seine. Somewhere, a beast with many eyes and horns was laughing. Couldn't I hear the echoes in the sky? Or perhaps it was your boss. I wouldn't put it past him.

Your shoulders slumped like that day on the bridge, an anchor around my heart.

"John," you told me. "I have to go back."

And our eyes rolled heavenwards, the sky black.

WE FOUGHT. OF course we did. I made you sleep on the couch in the living room and curled up with my photograph, crying half the night. But everything was night now. Then, when you didn't come, I marched in on you with the vengeance of the Lord. I didn't give a shit about your job, I said, whatever you were about for the heavenly fucking host. To hell with you, I said. You had given into temptation the moment you followed me home. You were meant to be the best of us, I said, and other things besides.

Fuck off then, I said, broken and exhausted. Fuck off back to God. Don't think of the ones left behind. Fuck *us*. Then I slammed the bedroom door.

How does one wrestle with an angel? It's as tough as dancing on the head of a pin. Past midnight, I rose. Weeping, I drew you to my bed.

Oh, I'm your whore of Babylon now.

I'm your Fall.

And you know it.

IN THE BLACK morning, you left to make a semblance of patrol, your wings dragging through the arrondissements. Perhaps you went out there to cut down demons or turn water into wine, for all I know. The tip of your sword was hissing, aglow. As for me, I sat down at my escritoire to write, a story in place of a memory. This. We won't always have Paris, will we?

No, and we won't always have memory either. Or an earth on which to walk to remember. What we have is time. Time, times and half a time, according to you. According to Revelation. Whatever.

You came home late. Had you been out standing on bridges? I wondered, but didn't dare ask.

"*Et le jour pour moi sera comme la nuit,*" I said as you shrugged off your trench coat in the hall and gave me a sorry look.

"What's that?"

"And the day for me will be as if it were night." I said. "Hugo. He was talking about how he'd never leave someone, even after death."

You sighed. The gold on your face told me you'd been crying. Like honey falling on bones. Wasted on the carcass of Paris.

"John, I have no choice." You said this with a click of your fingers to show me how quick you'd be recalled. Plucked up by your wings, powerless. A dove caught in a whirlwind.

You turned away then, fumbling with your sword in the umbrella stand.

I went into the kitchen to boil rats. Earlier, I'd gone hunting for sauerkraut in the supermarkets. Dijon mustard. Anything to mask the taste. The meal that we shared in silence had tasted of defeat.

It was the end of the day and the End of Days. But at least I was there with you.

THERE WAS NO poetry that night.

Bugs screeched outside. People screamed and ran. The moon rose in blood. The sky *et cetera.*

You fucked me senseless over the couch.

*

AN HOUR BEFORE dawn, I came to you. Mon destin. My Uriel.

No sun will rise again over the Seine. A question shone in your eyes as you saw me standing by the bed. You looked up at me, molten gold. In fear. Or in hope.

"John... what are you doing with that?"

"Divine intervention?" I said, with a twist of my lips.

It wasn't meant as a joke, but you laughed. Laughed at my desperation or perhaps the sin. The sword shook, dull in my grip. For all its provenance, it was hard to think of the weapon as good. I would bind you to me. I would nail your wings to the ground. Yes, I would defy God if God dared to take you from me.

If we burn, we'll burn together.

You shook your head like you had that day on the bridge.

"I didn't know it would be like this."

Trembling, I raised the sword. At once, the blade burst into flame. Golden in our eyes.

"Who does?" I said.

With a breath, you nodded. Then you bowed your head.

Oh, my lamb. My angel.

I lowered the blade, singeing feathers.

Then came the smell of something sweeter, filling up the room.

We are fallen.

Fallen in love.

Acknowledgements

A COLLECTION LIKE this one, covering as it does a reasonably broad publication history, requires many thanks. The author would like to thank the most relevant of them here:

POLLY SCHATTEL WHO read a first draft of Morta and told me I had a decent story. John Linwood Grant who beta-read a couple of the tales herein, was brave enough to tell me what wasn't working, and even published one of them. Sean Wallace of The Dark Magazine for taking a chance on my stories and for his inclusion of minority and marginalised voices. Jim McCleod of The Ginger Nuts of Horror for the same, and for always having my back. Steve Berman of Lethe Press, the esteemed publisher of this collection, for believing in me. Steve published my first ever gay-themed story in Icarus Magazine way back in the mists of 2011. It's fitting to put out this collection with him now. Adele Wearing and Chloë Yates of Fox

Spirit Books, for angels and pie. Other first readers, Cat Hellisen, Theresa Derwin and Essie Fox. I appreciate your input and kindness. My incomparable agent John Jarrold who's given me endless sound advice and stuck by me through thick and thin.

Last but not least, I want to thank all my family and friends, and my readers worldwide, for your tireless love and support.

The writer's road is often a lonely one. All of you make the journey worth it.

JB
Seville 2024

Publication Credits

Morta *The Book of Queer Saints, March 2022*

Husk *The Horror Collection: LGBTQIA+ Edition, May 2023*

Changeling *BFS Horizons, 2022*

Frankenstein Uncut *is exclusive to this collection.*

In Hades, He Lifted Up His Eyes *The Dark magazine, July 2022*

Of Gentle Wolves *The Dark Magazine, January 2023*

Ídolo *The Dark magazine, July 2022*

Sulta *The Dark magazine, December 2022*

Queer Norm *is exclusive to this collection.*

Facts Concerning the First Annual Arkham Parade *Occult Detective magazine, October 2023*

Vivisepulture *The Dark Magazine, April 2024*

The Cicatrix *Tales From Between, Jan 2023*

End Times in Paris *The Fox Spirit Book of Love, April 2021*

Milton Keynes UK
Ingram Content Group UK Ltd.
UKHW050802010924
447674UK00010B/91